HIGHLAND HEAT

MARY WINE

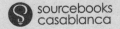

sourcebooks
casablanca

Published by Sourcebooks Casablanca, an imprint of Sourcebooks, Inc.
P.O. Box 4410, Naperville, Illinois 60567–4410
(630) 961–3900
FAX: (630) 961–2168
www.sourcebooks.com

Printed and bound in the United States of America
QW 10 9 8 7 6 5 4 3 2 1

To my comrade and confidante… the Weasel.
For all the times you've listened and been there.
For all the adventures past and yet to be…
Karen, you are the best friend anyone might ever have.

One

1439

Spring was blowing on the breeze.

Deirdre lifted her face and inhaled. Closing her eyes and smiling, she caught a hint of heather in the air.

But that caused a memory to stir from the dark corner of her mind where she had banished it. It rose up, reminding her of a spring two years ago when a man had courted her with pieces of heather and soft words of flattery.

False words.

"Ye have been angry for too long, Deirdre."

Deirdre turned her head slightly and discovered her sister Kaie standing nearby.

"And ye walk too silently; being humble doesn't mean ye need try and act as though ye are nae even here in this life."

Kaie smiled but corrected herself quickly, smoothing her expression until it was once again simply plain. "That is my point exactly, Deirdre. Ye take offense at everything around ye. I am content. That should nae be a reason for ye to snap at me."

Her sister wore the undyed robe of a nun. Her hair was covered now, but Deirdre had watched as it was cut short when Kaie took her novice vows. Her own hair was still long. She had it braided and the tail caught up so that it didn't swing behind her. The convent wouldn't hear any vows from her, not for several more years to come.

"But ye are nae happy living among us, Deirdre, and that is a sad thing, for those living in God's house should be here because they want to be."

"Well, I like it better than living with our father, and since he sent my dowry to the church, it is only fitting that I sleep beneath this roof."

Kaie drew in a stiff breath. "Ye are being too harsh. Father did his duty in arranging a match for us all. It is only fair that he would be cross to discover that ye had taken a lover."

Melor Douglas. The man she'd defied everything to hold, because she believed his words of love.

Deirdre sighed. "True, but ye are very pleased to be here and not with Roan McLeod as his wife. Father arranged that match for ye as well, and yet you defied his choice by asking Roan McLeod to release ye. There are more than a few who would call that disrespectful to our sire."

Her sister paled, and Deirdre instantly felt guilty for ruining her happiness.

"I'm sorry, Kaie. That was unkind of me to say."

Her sister drew in a deep breath. "Ye most likely think me timid, but I was drawn to this convent.

Every night when I closed my eyes, I dreamed of it, unlike ye…"

Kaie's eyes had begun to glow with passion as she spoke of her devotion, but she snapped her mouth shut when she realized what she was saying.

Deirdre scoffed at her attempt to soften the truth. "Unlike me and my choice to take Melor Douglas as my lover."

It was harsh but true, and Deirdre preferred to hear it, however blunt it might be.

"He lied to ye. Ye went to him believing ye'd be his wife."

"Ye do nae need to make excuses for me, Kaie. I made my choice, and I will nae increase my sins by adding dishonesty to them. Everyone knows, anyway. It seems all I ever hear about here, how I am unworthy of the veil ye wear so contentedly." Deirdre shrugged. "At least no one shall be able to claim I am intent on hiding my actions behind unspoken words and unanswered questions."

Her sister laughed. A soft, sad little sound that sent heat into Deirdre's cheeks, because Kaie was sweet and she didn't need to be discussing such a scarlet subject.

"Ye have ever been bold, Deirdre. I believe ye should have been born a son for all the courage ye have burning inside ye. For ye are correct, I am content, and there is no place I would rather be but here. Living a simple life. Roan McLeod was a kind soul to allow me to become a bride of Christ instead of his wife. Wedding me would have given him a strong alliance with our clan."

Kaie bent and picked up a leather bucket that was

sitting near the doorway. "I do nae know why the man gave up something that is so important in the Highlands, but I am grateful for it every day."

Her sister left, which granted Deirdre the freedom to frown. Allowing Melor Douglas to seduce her had been called many things, none of them good. It was slightly shocking to hear her sister label it "spirit."

Aye, the sort that knights must feel as they surged forward in one glorious charge and then came home missing limbs or an eye, or not returning at all. Such made for good talk around the fire at night, but the reality of living with those injuries during the day was anything but grand.

She sighed and took the tapestry she had been holding out to the simple wooden stand in the yard. She tossed it over the single bar of wood and reached for a thin branch that had been folded to make a rug beater. Clouds of dust began to tickle her nose as she swung the branch quickly back and forth.

It had been a relief to discover the convent wouldn't hear her vows.

Deirdre beat the tapestry harder as she struggled with her guilt. She wasn't ashamed of the fact that she wasn't pure anymore, but that only intensified her misgivings, because it left her wondering just what she did believe in. Kaie was correct in saying she had been angry too long.

Now that her broken heart no longer hurt and her temper wasn't as hot as a spark, she was left trying to decide what she wanted out of life. Her father wouldn't be making any further matches for her, and her dowry had been sent to the church. Her options were slim. But what kept her at the convent day after day, performing the tasks the mother superior heaped upon her in an effort to humble her, was the fact that the choice was resting in her hands.

That was something she had taken so brazenly when she rode out to meet Melor Douglas. She'd craved choosing her own man, not waiting for her father to send her to Connor Lindsey as an assurance that the two clans would always stand united. She'd thought the love in her heart worthy of the risk. She'd always been told to follow her father because he was her laird. Her marriage to Connor Lindsey would have brought a better life to every man wearing the Chattan colors, but somehow, the moment that Melor had sneaked up beside her at spring festival and whispered in her ear, she had lost the resolve to do what she knew was right. She had followed his honey-coated promises, and he'd spit on her once she'd yielded her purity to him.

It seemed rather odd to gain anything from taking a lover, and yet she had. She was the poorest of the poor, without any possessions of her own, but she had choice. A freedom she had never even thought to possess. Even her decision to continue to meet Melor Douglas had only happened because an alliance with the Douglas would have been considered strong enough to please her clan.

She stopped for a moment, the branch frozen in midair. Would she have found the will to resist her affection for Melor if he hadn't been a man her father would have been happy to see her wed? That question burned inside her. She wanted to say yes and honor her sire, but that would mean she was fickle. True love didn't consider what worth a man came with. There was only devotion to the affection of the heart.

The sound of approaching horses drew her attention. The nuns who had been down near the river that ran behind the church came hurrying up the hill. The times were uncertain with a boy wearing the crown of Scotland. The undyed robes the women wore flapped up showing their ankles. Even Kaie moved faster than her normal, floating pace that left not even dust stirring behind her.

The sisters all clustered together, pushing their way toward the sanctuary of the church. Deirdre lifted a hand to shade her eyes so she might see the colors the men were wearing. They were Highlanders, with their knee-high boots laced tight over antler buttons which ran up the outside of each boot. They rode their horses hard, but the animals were strong stock and took to the pace easily. A long sword was strapped to each man's back, with the hilt secured at the left shoulder so he might draw his weapon in a single fluid motion. The folds of their plaids bounced with the motion of the horses, but beneath the yellow, orange, and black wool, she could see their thighs tightly clutching the backs of their stallions.

They were Camerons, and she didn't need to wait for the dust to settle to know that their laird was among them. She felt the damned man's eyes on her even before she set her gaze on him. Quinton Cameron was just as huge and arrogant as she remembered him. She felt her temper stir when the man sent her a grin. The way he looked at her sent a shiver down her spine. It was indecent and, to her shame, exciting.

"I swear on all that's holy I never expected to see ye here, Deirdre Chattan."

Deirdre swung the branch viciously through the air. It made a slight whistling sound before smacking the tapestry. Quinton's stallion perked its ears, but the man reached down to pat its sweaty neck with a soothing motion, never taking his eyes off her.

Deirdre frowned. "Well, ye are the one who suggested it to my father, so enjoy gloating."

Several of the nuns gasped from where they were peeking around the large arched doorway of the church. Quinton Cameron laughed at her audacity, tipping his head back and allowing the sound to fill the morning air. Behind him, his retainers chuckled, sharing their laird's amusement, but they kept their eyes on her.

Quinton lowered his chin and considered her from beneath his dark brows. The man was a dark Highlander. His hair was true black, and his eyes the shade of coldest ice. Beyond being laird of the Cameron, the man also held the hereditary title of Earl of Liddell. Such noble peerage stations were becoming very rare in Scotland.

"Laird Cameron, what brings ye to our convent?"

Kaie stepped forward to greet the newcomers. She was training to become the mother superior, and it would be her duty to welcome all who came to the doors of the church. Her sister tucked her hands into the wide sleeves of her overrobe and faced the earl.

Quinton Cameron dismounted, out of respect for her position among the inhabitants of the holy order. The air filled with the sound of leather creaking as his men followed his actions. The church was a unifying presence among clans who sometimes fought each other. He might be one of the highest-ranking nobles in the land, but the church was set above earthly titles. Even the king knelt in church.

"Forgive me, sister, but I plan to search every inch of this abbey."

Kaie drew in a harsh breath. "Men do nae belong in this convent. It is a place for those women who have devoted their lives to God."

"It's also a place for anyone seeking sanctuary, sister. I know well ye are bound to offer charity to those who appeal to ye for it." Quinton's gaze strayed to Deirdre.

"Of course that is true, but ye do nae need to search the abbey for my sister. She stands before ye, Laird Cameron."

Deirdre felt her heart accelerate, but her logic firmly argued against there being any reason for Quinton Cameron to seek her out. His face didn't give her any clue as to his mood. He hid behind an emotionless mask, but something glittered in his eyes that irritated her. *How arrogant the man was,* she thought.

"Would ye be relieved to hear me say I've come for yer sister?" Quinton aimed his attention back toward Kaie. "Is that yer way of telling me she has yet to take the veil? Or that ye would gladly be rid of her?"

Kaie stiffened. "Unkindness has no place here, nor does judgment."

Quinton's expression hardened. "Aye, sister, I trust in yer devotion enough to know ye will nae tell me if the one I seek is here or no. Which is why I plan to send me men inside to search."

Her sister gasped, horrified by the idea of having the abbey invaded by the Cameron retainers.

Quinton's face reflected his distaste, but there was also hard determination shining in his eyes.

Kaie stepped back, as if she might prevent the invasion by blocking the door with her body. "Ye shall nae." Her words were whispered, and the men behind the earl didn't care to hear her displeasure.

The Cameron retainers surged forward, but Quinton raised one hand, and they froze instantly. Deirdre dropped the branch and stepped up beside her sister. The Cameron laird considered her with a slight spark of amusement flickering in his eyes.

"My sister told ye no. Only English scum trespass against the tradition of the church. Men never enter the convent. Do nae shame yer clan colors by acting like an invading army."

There was a soft murmur of agreement from the nuns hiding behind the doorway, but only Kaie stood with her in the yard against the men whom they could only turn away with words.

The Cameron didn't look as though they were going to depart simply because Kaie had reminded them of church tradition. Several of them glared at her for comparing them to the English.

"My apologies, Kaie Chattan, but I will be searching this structure from the belfry to the privies."

There was no hint of weakness in his tone, and he moved forward, all his men doing the same. Deirdre refused to give way, standing her ground and tipping her chin up so she could glare at him. Quinton Cameron didn't stop until his boots were touching the hem of her robes.

"I am nae impressed with ye, Laird Cameron. Tell me what ye seek, and stop insisting on going where ye know men do nae belong. I am no' a liar."

"I seek the queen, Joan Beaufort, and if she is here, I intend to find her." His expression hardened. "I will nae accept yer word on the matter."

Deirdre felt her eyes widen, but a moment later, she let out a hiss full of anger. Quinton Cameron swept her right off her feet, cradling her like a child in his arms as her father had done when she was half-grown.

"Put me down!"

He chuckled at her instead and carried her up the stairs through the open doorway and into the first chamber of the abbey.

"I warned ye, but I suppose I should nae be surprise that ye did no heed me. I noticed when I first met ye that ye are a true hellion." He lowered her to her feet. Deirdre sent a vicious shove at him, but the man didn't budge even a step.

The man smirked at her as his men swarmed around them and into the sanctuary. The nuns squealed and fled toward the yard. There were too many bodies trying to use the doorway, and Deirdre was crushed up against Quinton. He rocked slightly, but his arms came about her, protecting her from the surge of bodies.

"Take yer arms away." Deirdre didn't need to raise her voice, because she was pressed against the man from her ankles to her head.

"Well now, hellion, there isna anyplace else to put them, except between us."

He whispered against her ear, a hint of enjoyment in his tone. She bristled but couldn't push herself away from him with so many of the nuns trying to get past them. His arms wrapped all the way around her back, and she felt his hand cup her nape. She shivered, the contact jarring to her senses. It should have been. She should have felt only repulsion for his touch, but her body betrayed her as sensation rippled down her back, a sense of enjoyment that was deeply rooted in her flesh. He slid his hand up to grasp her thick braid where it was looped up beneath her simple linen hood.

"So ye have nae taken vows of any sort." The full length of her hair told him she hadn't taken any vows; if she had, her braid would have been cut to relieve her of vanity. "Now that I like knowing, hellion."

There was a touch of heat in his voice that stoked a memory she had tried hard to banish from her mind. There had been a moment a year past when they had been just this close and the arrogant man had stolen a kiss from her. Passion flickered inside her, refusing to obey her order never to rise again. She growled at the disobedience of her flesh and shoved away from Quinton.

Enough of the nuns had made it into the yard now, allowing her to step back from him, but he took the opportunity to stroke her back and sides as she moved, his hands open, the fingers sliding over her curves with unmistakable experience. There was a flicker of enjoyment in his eyes, which irritated her, because she discovered that she liked knowing he found her body pleasing.

Another betrayal from her flesh...

"What promises I make are none of yer concern, Laird Cameron. I live here, so ye'll be keeping yer hands off me."

"Is that a fact, Deirdre Chattan? Ye are nae a sister with that thick hair still long enough to cover a man's chest. Ye're a woman who is still searching for her place. Maybe ye have found that today."

She snarled beneath her breath, "Ye're a Blackguard to suggest such a thing while standing on holy ground." It was a curse, but she didn't care if he cuffed her for daring to insult his noble person. She tossed her head in the face of his displeasure. "Just because ye think me a fallen woman does nae give ye the right to touch me in plain sight of others. I took a lover because he promised me his name. I was nae a whore for hire."

"I never labeled ye such a thing, Deirdre. Ye might be surprised to learn what I think of a woman who is bold enough to follow her desires instead of cowering in front of those who tell her what to do."

There was a hint of approval in his tone, but she forced herself to ignore it. The last time she'd followed such impulses, she had disgraced herself and her clan.

"Stop using my name. We are nae familiar with each other. One stolen kiss does nae make ye anything more than a man I loathe."

"Careful, lass, I think I enjoy the sound of that challenge more than either of us should." His attention settled on the fabric covering her hair.

She gasped and then sputtered, because she didn't care for how weak sounding her response was. "Have ye no honor?"

She was insulting him now, and her attack didn't miss its mark.

He stiffened and hooked his hands into his wide belt. The thick leather circled his waist, binding the pleats of his kilt in place. Above his left shoulder, the pommel of his sword gained her attention.

"Weapons are forbidden inside the sanctuary."

He frowned. "So are cursing and lying, Deirdre Chattan."

His voice dipped low as he spoke her name, and there was a challenge lurking in his eyes that sent a quiver down the backs of her legs. She decided to focus on why the man was there so she might see him on his way that much faster.

"No one lied to ye here, Laird Cameron. Ye assume the queen is here, but ye never asked."

His knuckles began to turn white. It was an odd little hint at what the man was truly feeling. She certainly couldn't gain much by looking at his face, for he was showing her nothing but a stone-solid mask.

"I am seeking Joan Beaufort, queen of Scotland." He spoke through gritted teeth, betraying his frustration. "Is she here?"

A few of his men stood near his back. They tilted their heads so they might watch her face and gauge her true reaction to their laird's question. Deirdre scoffed at him. "Yer men are already swarming through the sanctuary. It's too late to ask now."

She could hear the muffled protests of the priests and the nuns who had been in the inner chambers of the abbey. Out in the yard, there was the stomping of the horses and the conversation of the members of the holy order as they tried to comfort each other.

Quinton snorted. "But ye did nae answer the question, which makes me suspicious of ye."

Deirdre glared at the man responsible for shattering the peace. "Ye and yer men are acting like hell's army."

He should have been insulted. Instead he chuckled. "If I were a Viking, I'd no have allowed ye out of me arms quite so quickly. A true Norseman ravishes first and takes the plunder after he has sated his primary desire."

That challenge returned to his eyes, flashing brightly as heat twisted through her belly. It was such an unexpected response that her hands moved to cover her lower body, the instinct to protect herself too strong to ignore.

"Enough out of ye." She shook her head. "I'm nae impressed, I assure ye. Only more disgusted by yer lack of respect for this holy place and the way that ye know ye should be behaving."

His lips rose into a smile that showed his teeth. "But I am impressed with ye, Deirdre Chattan. Ye are too much woman for this abbey, and I am very displeased to be so burdened with finding our queen, because it does nae leave me any time to enjoy yer fiery spirit." His smile faded as his eyes darkened, and a promise lurked deep inside them. "A true pity that is, I'm thinking."

"Well, stop yer thinking when it comes to me. It's naught but a waste of time."

He chuckled. "Aye, but a pleasant one, and I'm spending too many hours trying to keep our

Highlanders from fighting one another nae to take the opportunity to enjoy something when it stands directly in front of me."

The man had the audacity to reach for her face, but she slapped his hand before he touched her. The sound bounced off the stone walls, and he chuckled once again.

"A true shame, for I'd enjoy seeing what ye thought of me inviting ye to ride off with me, Deirdre."

"I'd curse ye, and that is a promise, yer lairdship."

He chuckled but it was a dark sound full of promise. "That makes me even sorrier that I cannae devote any time to discovering how to make ye purr for me."

Her mouth dropped open in surprise when she heard such brazen talk in the doorway of the abbey. Two of the nuns crossed themselves in the yard when they overheard him.

His men began returning. They shook their heads, which made him frown. Laird Cameron sent them back to their horses with a flick of his fingers. His attention remained on her.

"If Her Majesty should arrive, be sure to tell her she will be better off with me than William Crichton."

"I cannae imagine the queen coming here."

Quinton Cameron's expression hardened. "I can. It is the only reason I would have sent my men into an abbey. Her Majesty is first cousin to the king of England, and there are many who will extort her if she makes the mistake of becoming their prisoner."

Deirdre discovered herself shocked into silence. There was no missing the fact that Quinton Cameron had no real liking for what he had just ordered done.

But he stood firm, facing what he considered a necessary task.

She might not care for his method, but she couldn't fail to respect him for the dedication he applied to keeping the clans from feuding. If the Highlands dissolved into bloody raids, England would find it simple to invade. Joan Beaufort wasn't just queen of Scotland. When she and her husband, James I, had arrived after being ransomed from England, Scotland's nobles had sworn their allegiance to both of them. Many considered her a monarch in her own right, and the English might use that to overthrow her young son, who had been crowned James II.

Quinton Cameron was watching her, studying her reaction to his words.

"Go on with ye now that ye know the queen is nae here."

He grunted, narrowing his eyes for a moment, the fact that he wanted to remain evident in them. Deirdre lifted one hand and pointed toward the doorway.

"Do ye need a map to find yer way, my fine Earl of Liddell?"

He groaned and thrust his hand out faster than she could avoid. This time, he captured her wrist, closing his fingers around her smaller arm. She gasped, but not because his grip hurt. The man controlled his strength expertly, tugging her hand up until she felt the warm brush of his breath and a moment later the soft press of his lips against the inside of her wrist.

"Nay, lass, I know my way around a spitfire sure enough, and if ye needle me, be very sure I will no' retreat from the challenge ye offer."

Sensation rippled down her arm and into her body like lightning. The delicate skin of her inner wrist was suddenly alive with a thousand points of recognition. Passion flickered in her belly again, tighter and more intense than before. She gasped, her body unable to contain all the impulses rushing through it. Quinton didn't rush the kiss but lingered over her flesh while watching her reaction.

"Truly do I regret needing to depart so quickly, Deirdre Chattan." His thumb passed over the spot he'd kissed, sending a softer bolt of pleasure through her before he released her arm. "But I must, else I'd remain and do my best to prove I know well how to deal with the fire ye breathe."

She jerked her arm away from him with a hiss that would no doubt gain her a reprimand from the mother superior.

"A true blessing. I shall thank God tonight for taking ye from my sight."

He snorted with amusement but turned toward the yard and his men.

She followed him to the doorway and watched as he fitted one foot into the stirrup and mounted. The man rode a full-blooded stallion that didn't remain still but shifted from side to side with eagerness to be moving. He reached down and patted the animal with a sure hand, but his gaze shifted to her.

"I hope yer memory is sound, Deirdre Chattan."

His lips twitched, and her temper flared up once again. Oh, there was nothing wrong with her memory, but without a doubt, the man was not asking her if she recalled what he wanted her to tell the queen.

There was a flare of heat in his blue eyes she recalled very well from the night he'd kissed her.

"Ye are no' one who I care to remember, nor anything ye have to tell me."

He laughed at her, and so did his men. The arrogant beast shot her a look full of promise.

"Perhaps I'll return to take up yer challenge to make a more lasting impression upon ye." His stallion danced in a wide circle. When he was facing her again, his expression was serious. "Maybe ye might add that hope to yer prayers."

"I shall not," she sputtered. "Yer suggestion is most misplaced in this holy place. Are ye color-blind and cannae see I'm wearing an undyed robe?"

His gaze lowered to her clothing but centered on the swell of her breasts. "I see ye very well, and the robe does nae belong on ye, lass."

He drew in a deep breath and raised his attention back to her face.

"But duty first, eh, hellion?"

He didn't wait for a reply. Quinton Cameron turned his stallion toward the road and let the animal have its freedom. His men followed, forming two columns that raised a cloud of dust while the sound of the horses' hooves diminished into the distance.

Deirdre found herself the object of scrutiny from the nuns standing in the yard. Her face heated, but she held her chin steady.

Curse the man.

And damn her for responding to him. She turned her back on those watching her. Her heart was still beating too quickly, and she knew what it was that heated her insides. It was passion or lust; both promised her hours of worry as she tried to decide if she was beyond redemption.

How could she favor a man such as Quinton Cameron? That would gain her nothing but another lover who would use her and then discard her once he was finished with her.

She chewed on her lower lip, a sliver of guilt assaulting her.

Quinton Cameron was not a dishonest man. He'd never lied to her as Melor had done, but that bit of knowledge didn't settle her thoughts any.

He was still, without a doubt, a man she needed to avoid. He was far too dangerous for her to make the mistake of ever seeing him again—much less trust him enough to allow him to do any of the things she had seen flickering in his eyes.

❧

"Ye did what ye had to. The man provoked ye." Kaie's voice was low, but it didn't mask her distaste.

Deirdre looked up from the floor she was scrubbing; the day was almost gone now, but there were still chores for her to do. "Do nae bother to try and soothe my feelings when ye clearly disapprove of my actions."

Her sister watched as she leaned over to dip the rag she was using into the nearby leather bucket. The smell of lye rose from the water, and her hands burned from the countless nicks and scrapes she had earned with other duties. Among those seeking to humbly serve the church, she was the lowest of them all. The fact that she toiled alone was proof of that. The other nuns had sought their cots and were enjoying being off their feet, while she remained on her knees in the last hours of the day. The sunlight no longer filled the room where the holy order ate. There was now only a dim evening gloom. Even the coals in the hearth were hidden by ash to keep their ruby glow from offering any cheer. But Deirdre refused to grant them the victory of hearing her beg to be allowed to seek her own bed before she had completed every task assigned to her.

"Ye think too harshly of me, Deirdre."

Deirdre looked up at her sister as she let the rag drop to the stone floor. It made a wet *splat* and sent water onto her skirt, but she didn't care. "And you are too mild in temperament, Kaie. It's hard to believe we were born of the same parents."

Kaie smiled, but it was a gentle curving of her lips that didn't show any of her teeth. She had her hands tucked up inside the sleeves of her overrobe and looked so serene Deirdre simply shook her head.

"I envy ye yer happiness, Kaie, but I am also glad to see ye so content."

A soft sound passed her sister's lips. It was a bare whisper of a laugh and made Deirdre smile.

"And yet I envy ye the courage to have stood so confidently in Laird Cameron's path. I was bending to his earthly position of power without enough protest." Disgust edged her sister's voice.

"For all the good it did me." Deirdre began to scrub at the floor again. "No' that I regret it."

"No one thinks ye're repentant."

There was a note of regret in Kaie's voice that made

Deirdre grateful for the chore, which made it possible for her not to look at her sister. It wasn't shame making her want to avoid eye contact, but a desire not to quarrel. Kaie enjoyed the humble life.

"I'm no' proud of arguing with the man like a shrew."

She heard her sister sigh. "I believe Laird Cameron could take notice of nothing short of what ye gave him in a woman. That man needs a wife who can demand his attention."

Deirdre jerked her face up toward her sister. "Do nae begin with that, Kaie."

Her sister returned her glare with too much sweet serenity. That brought a touch of heat to Deirdre's cheeks, for it felt like she was being surly with an innocent child.

Or arguing with a mother superior. Deirdre smiled at her sibling. "Ye are raising to the challenge of yer station here, Sister. Maybe I should have pushed ye in front of Laird Cameron."

There was a rare flicker of pride in Kaie's eyes, but she shook her head. "Nae I believe ye stepped up to the man for a reason, one which will become clearer in time. I'd send some of the others to help ye, but I know ye would refuse the kindness."

"I would." Deirdre dunked the rag again. "I shall endure. I promise ye."

Kaie's expression became somber once more. "Spite has no place here; the chores should be shared by all. The novices need to be reminded of that fact." She paused, her eyes narrowing with consideration. "I also believe yer spirit has its place, Deirdre, and it isn't inside these convent walls."

Her sister didn't give her any chance to respond. Kaie turned without making a sound and walked with soft steps along the side of the room. Deirdre watched the way her sister kept near the wall, even when she entered the hallway. Kaie didn't go down the center of it. Instead she drew as little notice to herself as possible. That had always been her way, and somehow, Deirdre had never considered that Kaie belonged wearing the undyed robe that had been given to their younger sister, Brina. The third-born daughter went to the church; it was tradition, and their father had followed it.

Deirdre smiled as Kaie disappeared from sight. Well, it might have been expected that Kaie would marry, but she hadn't, and she was happy. Brina was pleased to be wed to Connor Lindsey as well, or at least Kaie claimed that was what Brina's letters said.

Deirdre heard the wind howl outside and looked down at the section of floor she had yet to wash. It would be past dark when she finished, but that did not send her looking for a candle to light. She continued to work, moving fast enough to keep warm while the wind rattled the wooden shutters covering the windows. Her eyes adjusted to the fading light, and soon she could see the faint red glow of the coals in the hearth in spite of the layer of ash covering them.

She suddenly lifted her head, a sound rising above the wind gaining her attention. Her fingers tightened on the rag, making water stream out of it to soak her robe.

The sound came again, this time closer, and the huge wooden doors, which were closed against the night, vibrated as someone pounded on them.

Fear shot down her back, but she stood up, unwilling to cower on the floor with a washrag in her hands. Deirdre shook off the whispers of a hundred remembered tales of raiders and Vikings that she had heard around the winter fire during her childhood.

Hell's army had not been seen in many years. Many of the Highlanders were descendants of the Norsemen who had settled down instead of raiding their entire lives. Besides, raiders wouldn't be knocking.

She went to the window nearest the door and unlatched the shutter. She opened it and looked out to see who was standing in front of the doors.

"Sanctuary, we seek sanctuary."

The words were whispered, from one of four forms standing near the door. But the voice was undoubtedly male.

"This is the convent," Deirdre informed them. In the dark, it was impossible to see any details about who they were. The moon hid behind dark clouds that promised rain before morning.

The group shifted, turning toward one while they whispered. They leaned in to conceal their words while the wind whipped at the hems of their long cloaks. Deirdre felt suspicion ripple its way through her thoughts as the group argued among themselves for several long moments before there was a short grunt from the man who had requested sanctuary. He turned back toward her.

"I request shelter for the ladies."

Deirdre set her teeth into her lower lip, but she could not refuse a request of sanctuary. It was a strict order of the pope, and living beneath the roof of the abbey meant she must be obedient to that dictate.

Deirdre pushed up the heavy bar that held the door secure, and stood it beside the doors. A single lantern burned outside, its flame protected by tin that had numerous tiny holes punched into it to allow the light to illuminate the door for pilgrims who needed the church's mercy.

"We will return at dawn, Yer Ma—"

The man shut his mouth, but it was too late. Deirdre recalled instantly Laird Cameron's reason for searching the abbey.

It would appear that the queen had arrived.

Three people entered, flipping their hoods back to reveal that they were women. The men who had escorted them turned and disappeared into the shadows beyond the light of the lantern.

"We are grateful for your hospitality."

Joan Beaufort was English, and her words carried an unmistakable tone from her native country. There was also a regal edge to the way she swept inside the abbey and stopped when there was nothing but darkness to greet her.

"Are there not candles in this abbey?" she asked quietly, almost as if she didn't care for the night like a child who had yet to grow past her fear of the shadows.

Deirdre closed the door and lifted the bar up and into the slots that would keep it secure. She turned to find the queen of Scotland watching her. Although Deirdre had never met the woman, her name was well-known, for prayers were offered every day for the king and his mother. Quinton Cameron's visit also confirmed that the fair-faced woman was in fact the cousin of the king of England and the mother of the king of Scotland. It was slightly amazing to see her standing with only two handmaidens.

Joan looked about. "There must be candles."

"We are very careful when using anything, for nothing belongs to the inhabitants of this order, Yer Majesty."

Deirdre began to lower herself, an action she did without thought, because she had been taught to offer deference to her parents and other nobles from the time she could walk.

"Do not." Joan Beaufort hissed. "How did you know me? Have you come to court? That is odd, when you were promised to the church."

The queen obviously wasn't accustomed to allowing others to speak until she was finished with her thought. She finally stopped and looked toward Deirdre to answer her questions.

"I was nae promised to the church, Yer Ma—madam." The queen made a motion with her hand.

"But you are here." Joan pointed to her undyed robes, the garments of piety that nuns wore to shun earthly vanity.

Deirdre felt her temper rise as she recalled the reason she was at the abbey. Her anger was still too hot, just as Kaie had told her it was. But she refused to lie about what she had done. She had gone to Melor Douglas willingly and eagerly.

"My father sent me here for disgracing him by taking a lover. I have taken no vows, and the order will hear none from me."

The queen's ladies shook their heads, one of them clicking her tongue in reprimand. Deirdre held her chin steady.

"Enough." Joan raised her hand to silence her escort. "Do not be so dim-witted. This might be exactly what I seek."

The two women with the queen looked at her with confusion showing on their faces. Deirdre felt her own forehead creasing too as she walked toward the table where a single candle stood in a wooden holder. She grabbed a handful of her skirts and swept them aside as she knelt next to the hearth. The coals were still hot enough to bring life to the wick, and the flame cast a warm glow around her as she rose and placed it back in its holder.

Deirdre jerked when she discovered the queen so close to her. The woman studied her with the help of the candlelight.

"You favor me in many ways," Joan announced suddenly. Her two ladies stepped closer and scrutinized Deirdre in response. One of them began to smile.

"Ye are correct, my lady." The one who had spoken reached out and pushed the edge of Deirdre's head covering back so they might see her hair.

"Excuse me, Yer—madam, but what are ye about?" Deirdre yanked her head veil forward and then frowned when she realized how quick she was to hide something she had sworn not to feel shame over. It was only hair, and she wasn't a bride of Christ, so there was no reason she should jump to defend her modesty. With a soft snort, she shoved the head covering completely over the top of her head until it drooped down about her neck.

"You are not repentant." The queen wasn't asking her a question; she was making a firm statement.

"I am sorry the man I trusted with my heart was only lying to me to strike at my betrothed, but that is the only thing I regret. He promised to wed me or I would never have gone to him."

Deirdre expected her bluntness to shock the queen. Instead, Joan Beaufort slowly smiled. She reached out and fingered a lock of Deirdre's hair. "Many a woman has loved a man who was unworthy of her tender affections." She paused for a moment. "We have the same shade of blonde hair too—how fortunate."

The last two words were spoken in a soft tone of awe, or maybe it was satisfaction. Deirdre felt a shiver shoot down her back, and it woke a memory of the way Melor had sounded when he informed her of the fact that he wasn't going to wed her as he'd promised.

"What are ye seeking beyond shelter, Yer Maje—" Deirdre simply shut her mouth on the second part of the word. The queen frowned but looked about the room before answering.

"I need your assistance." She said. "What is your name?"

"Deirdre Chattan. My father is Laird Chattan."

The queen's ladies' faces brightened. One of them clasped her hands together. "An excellent bit of luck. If ye're the daughter of a laird, even a Highlander, ye will have some sort of education in finer manners."

"I'm proud to be the daughter of a Highlander." Deirdre didn't care if her tone was too sharp for the noble station of the women standing in front of her. Those who attended court liked to think of themselves as more civilized than the Highlanders, but she would have none of it.

The queen waved her hand to dispel the tension in the air. "Of course you are, I'd not be interested in asking anything of any daughter who didn't hold her head high when she spoke of her kin."

There was a note of compassion in Joan's voice that softened Deirdre's displeasure. "I am quite confused… ladies. The assistance ye seek here is offered to any who knock on the door."

The queen stepped closer. "But I seek something quite different than anything a bride of Christ might offer me." She reached forward and took Deirdre's hand, clasping it between her own, which were chilled from the night air. She aimed eyes full of apprehension toward her. "There are many seeking me—men intent on imprisoning me for their own gain."

"Laird Cameron was here today, and he had his men search the abbey from top to bottom."

All three women drew in horrified gasps. The queen's grip tightened until it was painful. Deirdre pulled her hand free.

Joan looked stunned that she had moved without permission. She shook it off quickly.

"Forgive me, but as I said, there are many seeking me who would see me set behind stone walls and denied my freedom."

"Ye are the…" Deirdre stopped and searched for another word to use. Joan did not allow her time to think.

"A fact which makes men crave locking me away for the power it shall give them." The queen looked furious, her fair features darkening with her temper. "I want to be happy, Deirdre Chattan. If you chose a lover and risked your future to embrace him, you must understand how I feel. I want to wed again, and I've run away, but there are too many seeking me. We have been hiding for days to avoid being captured."

Deirdre felt shock run down her spine. The queen's marrying again would indeed be cause for alarm among the Douglas clan as well as a few others. She had shared her husband's crown, and any further children she birthed would be considered by England to have a claim to the Scottish throne. Her son, James II, was the only son she had given her late husband, and he was a boy too young to wed.

"Archibald Douglas would see me withering away while he controls my son, and Alexander Livingston is no better. That man kept me locked up for months."

The queen began pacing, agitation fueling her rapid steps.

"But is there a man who can safeguard ye?" Deirdre asked. "There is little point in running if ye do nae have a place to go."

Joan turned toward her and smiled. It was radiant one, which brightened her features, exposing how very beautiful she was.

"Oh yes, there is such a man. I've permission from the pope to wed him. I desire so much to be with him. It seems so very long since my James was murdered." She held out her hands. "I implore you, Deirdre Chattan. Help me meet with my bridegroom."

Temptation nipped at her. Deirdre tried to ponder the wisdom of following her impulses, but there was no

controlling the urge to answer the plea she witnessed
shimmering in the queen's eyes. For a moment, Joan
was simply another woman who wanted to be loved.

That was a yearning Deirdre suffered the harsh
burn of every night she lay in a narrow bed which was
devoid of any human touch. She understood what it
was like to be forced to be alone, because Melor had
stolen any future happiness from her and condemned
her to a cold future with his need to strike out at
Connor Lindsey through her.

Yes, she understood the pain of being used because
of who she was connected to.

"How would I help ye do that?"

Joan's smile became one of satisfaction and cunning.
"By riding off at first light dressed as me. Those
hunting me might be distracted and follow you." The
queen sighed. "I am asking much, I know. But you
tell me of the reason why you are here so plainly that
I suspect you of having the courage to test yourself
against the odds. To take your fortune into your own
hands in spite of all those who warn you to keep your
eyes lowered and stay in the place they tell you is
yours. I've committed sins, but I have loved, and it
was worth it."

Joan stopped and drew in a deep breath. "If you are
content here, forgive me for asking, but I am desperate
to join the man I want to wed."

Deirdre's thoughts raced faster than a river in
spring. Excitement surged through her at just the idea
of feeling a horse beneath her while she let the animal
take her across the hills fast enough to feel the wind
burning her cheeks.

But there would be no returning to the abbey. Falling from grace once might be forgiven with enough penitence. Any further deviations from the path of righteousness might see her barred from the holy house out of fear she'd poison the others with her wicked ways.

Joan stepped forward, reaching out to clasp her hand once again. This time the queen stroked the back of it with slow, soothing motions.

"I would not forget your service to me. Help me reach the man I shall wed, and you will never long for a place to call your own. I swear it."

Joan's hand was smooth compared to hers. Deirdre felt every rough patch of skin as the queen's fingers gently moved over the top of her hand. Every cut and sore spot made itself known, while her back suddenly complained bitterly about how many hours she had been bent over in her quest to endure what was being demanded of her.

But that wasn't the true reason she began to nod with agreement. It was the memory of Melor Douglas, the man she had fallen in love with, sneering at her. He'd shown her first what it was like to be looked upon as worthless. Her pride had carried her away from him and his demand that she be his whore because she had already given him her purity.

She'd loved him, in a foolish manner, but it had been affection that sent her into his arms and the promise that he would seek her father's permission to wed her. She'd been stupid to give him her virginity before she saw him shake her father's hand, but there was still part of her that wasn't sorry she had found the courage to embrace the man she had chosen. Joan was correct. Deirdre was bold enough to face the unknown, if the reason was something she could believe in.

"I will help ye."

There was solid conviction edging each word, because she might own nothing, but she had her pride. The narrow cot waiting in the dark offered nothing but an icy future full of others condemning her for her choices. She suddenly realized she resented the fact that Kaie had been allowed to embrace her love for God, while she was being berated for love. Kaie had defied tradition and the match their laird father arranged for her as well, yet Kaie had respect. She'd take her chances with the opportunity at hand. After all, she was a Highlander.

Deirdre nodded again. "Indeed I shall assist ye. I hope ye keep yer word, for it will cost me my place here, and my father has already given the church my dowry."

The queen beamed at her. "You shall not regret it. If you are caught, no one will keep you, for you are not me. I have not told you who I plan to wed, so there shall be no need for them to keep you long."

"How will ye keep yer word to me, if I do nae know where to seek ye?" It was a bold question, one that slightly shocked the queen. Obviously, the members of her court took her word without any questions. But she was fleeing from that position, and she wouldn't have any influence at court if she married without Archibald Douglas's consent. The man was the lieutenant general and ran the country while James

II was still a boy. Joan Beaufort might be the king's mother, but she was also English, and there were many in Scotland who didn't want her influencing her son. There were even more who considered the young king past the age of female coddling, at nine years old. Deirdre felt herself sympathizing with the woman, because she knew what it felt like to be told she was worthless in the eyes of the men who surrounded her. It was a sting that burned even on the coldest nights.

"Yes, that is a good thing to ask." The queen considered it for a long moment. "Once I have wed, the news will spread quickly, and you shall be welcome at my husband's castle. I give you my word. You may seek me out, and you will have your reward in coin or as a position among my ladies."

It was a good offer, to serve such a high noble would bring an alliance to the Chattan, one that would help erase the shame she had cast on her father's name. It wouldn't wipe it completely away, but Deirdre discovered her thoughts returning to what she had pondered during the daylight hours.

Choice.

It sat shimmering in front of her. All she had to do was grip her courage and step forward.

"It's an agreement." Deirdre succeeded in not muttering "Yer Majesty" after her words. She felt rather awkward not giving the woman the respect due her station, for those manners had been instilled in her early. Society needed its rules, or there would be savagery such as the Vikings had brought with their raids a couple of centuries past.

The ladies serving as the queen's escort clasped

their hands with excitement, their eyes shimmering in the light of the candle. They clustered about their mistress, drawing her away from Deirdre as they began to whisper.

Deirdre walked over to the bucket and looked down at the small patch of floor she had not washed. The rag was still sitting on the stone, and she smiled at it, relief flooding her in a wave so large that she felt as though her knees might give way. She suddenly realized how heavy her burden had been for the past year. It felt as though a yoke was being lifted away.

Kaie had been correct. She had been angry too long. There was suddenly a future full of possibilities. The only tarnish was that she would have to trust the queen to keep her word and not forget her. That set her to worrying once more, for she had not trusted anyone since Melor had revealed his true intentions. Her instincts told her to refuse to place her faith in any person, for any reason, but the cold water sitting so quietly in the bucket for her to return to sickened her more.

She was not lazy, but she was weary of being shunned. Her life at the abbey promised her nothing but more of the same until the day she breathed her last. There was uncertainty in trusting the queen, but she was a woman seeking the man she loved, and that was something Deirdre understood. The queen was giving up much to have her choice of what her future might be.

Deirdre wanted that choice too. It burned inside her belly, refusing to be quieted even as Deirdre thought of her sister Kaie. She doubted her sibling would be pleased to discover her going with the queen. Deirdre suddenly stiffened as she considered the possibility of failure. If the queen was captured and returned to court, there would be no reward for her. Only more shame when she was forced to seek shelter from the abbey once again or turn whore to feed herself. A lump tried to clog her throat, but she forced it down. She refused to turn coward. Even if the queen's plan failed, Deirdre decided that she wanted to try, not lie in her bed fearing the unknown.

"We shall have to leave now, else the sisters will stop me from going with ye."

The queen turned to look at her, lifting one hand to silence her ladies. Deirdre stepped forward and watched their eyes narrow slightly as she invaded their circle.

Deirdre kept her chin level, returning all their stares with a steady confidence that earned her a grudging acceptance.

"There is also the fact that ye do no' want the sisters to know ye are here at all. I told ye that Laird Cameron was here looking for ye."

The queen hissed, "That one is the least of my worries, at least I do not think he wishes to imprison me."

"But ye are nae sure?" Deirdre asked, disliking the feeling that invaded her belly. Part of her didn't care to think of Quinton as a man who would use a woman to gain the power he sought. She honestly shouldn't have a care for the man one way or the other, but the feeling persisted.

"I trust no laird in Scotland, and one who is a noble even less. Quinton Cameron is known to have different opinions than Archibald Douglas. They argue often, but men have a habit of sticking together when it benefits them." Joan was speaking as she thought, not pausing to consider her words at all. "He is an earl, and that might make him stand beside Archibald in wanting to make sure I have no more children."

It was a possibility that could not be overlooked.

"Well then, I suggest we leave now, before anyone awakens. Once ye are discovered here, anyone who comes searching for ye will know where ye were last," Deirdre said. "Besides, it will be much simpler to leave this abbey under the cover of darkness than by first light."

Joan appeared unsure. She looked toward the doors and shivered. "I do not care for the night."

One of her ladies reached out to comfort her. Deirdre watched the way the attendants gently tried to soothe their lady. Attending the woman would take a measure of patience, for she had never been one to hold back her words, even when they were not what anyone wanted to hear. But the memory of Quinton Cameron ordering his men into the abbey against tradition and church policy stiffened her resolve.

"If ye truly wish to wed again, ye'll have to be more cunning than those who seek to capture ye," Deirdre instructed her firmly. "Fortune will favor the bold."

The queen suddenly straightened her sagging back, lifting her chin high. "I believe I shall hope that you choose to serve me, Deirdre Chattan, for I sense you have the will to tell me the truth, even when you know I do not wish to hear it." Her attendants looked hurt, and she sent them both smiles of reassurance before turning back toward Deirdre. "I believe you will complement my ladies by bringing something new. Sternness is needed in times such as this. We shall depart as you suggest."

Deirdre felt her throat tighten, but she refused to falter. She turned and walked toward the wall where several long cloaks hung from wooden pegs. Her hand shook slightly as she reached for one, and she wasn't sure if the reason was fear or excitement. The fabric felt rough between her fingers, but she smiled as she considered the fact that she would not be sealed behind the closed doors and shutters of the abbey all night long.

It seemed like each night had lasted twice as long, now that she was contemplating riding away into the darkness. Many would call her wicked, and maybe she was. The way her body had leaped to life beneath the touch of Quinton Cameron wasn't pious. That was a solid truth.

She swung the cloak about so the heavy garment would swirl up and around her body. A simple length of fabric crossed over from the right to the left side of it and was held there with a button made from a slice of antler horn. The wool was rough and worn, but sturdy enough to cut the chill of the Scottish Highlands.

Deirdre turned her attention away from the row of cloaks hanging so silently in the dark. They all looked alike, each one the same as the one next to it. Just like the women who wore them. Deirdre admired their dedication, but she admitted she did not long to serve humbly for the rest of her years. She yearned for something she could not name. The only thing she was certain of was that she would never be happy inside the abbey walls the way Kaie was. Perhaps she would have learned to find contentment in time and gratitude to have shelter from the snow, but she would never commune with the church the way her sister did.

It was that knowledge that sent her back across the floor, along with the hard truth that there was happiness in life, if you managed to find it. She intended to try.

"Aren't you going to fetch your things, Deirdre?" One of the ladies asked the question.

Deirdre lifted the bar again and sat it beside the door before answering. The lump had re-formed in her throat, and she had to swallow it before she might speak.

"No one here owns anything." She turned to look at the queen. "I offer ye my service in exchange for yer keeping yer word. I come with nothing but my wits and courage. Even the clothing upon me is the property of the church. If ye wish to change yer mind, now is the time to tell me."

"I have not changed my mind. If you will wear my clothing and ride across the road in plain sight to trick my pursuers, then we have an agreement that I shall honor without fail."

The night was black beyond the doorway, but Deirdre found it as welcoming as spring.

Two

THE QUEEN AND HER LADIES WERE OBVIOUSLY NOT accustomed to being outdoors past sunset. In spite of the thick clouds overhead dropping tiny raindrops on them, Deirdre could tell what direction to go by looking at the landforms. But her companions hung back, reluctant to stray far from the solid stone walls of the abbey. Deirdre had to stop and look back at them. The three stood beneath the arched doorway, their eyes wide and reflecting the meager light. They crowded close about the queen, and it was Joan who finally stepped forward. Deirdre heard the woman pull in a stiff breath before snapping her fingers to get her ladies moving.

Deirdre lifted one finger to her lips to caution Joan against making any noise. The queen stiffened and nodded before she reached down and grabbed a handful of her skirts so she might raise her hem.

Deirdre had no such problem with the length of her robes. They were hemmed far enough above her shoes to allow for her chores. The queen was dressed in ones that hid her shoes, and there was even a train trailing behind her. It would be simple to see she was a noblewoman, even in the dark when there wasn't enough light to see the rich fabric or the tiny pearls sewn to the trimming at the neckline.

"We must find my escort."

Deirdre nodded without breaking pace. The queen reached out and gripped her arm.

"How do you know where to find my men?" she asked.

Deirdre turned to face her so her words might carry the least amount. "They would have sought cover, and the forest is the best in this area." Lifting one hand, Deirdre pointed toward a thicket.

"Oh…yes…of course."

"We must make haste," Deirdre informed her hesitating companions.

"Why? It's black as sin out here."

Deirdre shook her head. "Highlanders have no fear of the night. I assure ye, if the Camerons are anywhere near, they will see us standing here in the open. With horses, they will run us down like rabbits."

A shiver went down her back as she considered being caught by Quinton with darkness wrapped around her. There was no doubt in her mind that the man might abandon every bit of civilized behavior when it meant gaining what he desired.

Another ripple of sensation traveled down her body as she considered what it was the man desired. His eyes had been full of passion. She'd listened to poems that spoke of that sort of thing, and never truly believed a person might see such a thing in another, but she had. But that was where her comparison between sweet, rhyming couplets and Quinton Cameron ended.

The man was no gallant knight, full of honor and chivalry. He was a Highlander, solid and sturdy. He'd do whatever it took to achieve his goal, and the man was very much at home in the wilds of upper Scotland. In fact, he thrived in the remote places that the English feared and even the Roman legion had failed to conquer.

Deirdre cast her gaze about, peering into the darker shadows as she tried to decide if there was anyone hiding in them.

"Hurry," she whispered, but there was no masking the urgency in her tone.

"Yes... we shall."

The queen tripped when she took her first step, because she forgot to lift her hem. She stumbled and snapped a stick lying on the ground. The *pop* of the wood made Deirdre flinch, for it sounded too loud compared to the quiet of the night. Her ears were straining to hear even the most distant rumble of horses. Her own breathing sounded harsh, while her heart was thumping too hard.

Deirdre drew in a slow breath to steady herself. She led the others forward, then sighed when they reached the first trees. It felt as good as entering the kitchen after being outside during the dead of winter. The dark branches with their newly grown leaves were as welcoming as a mother's arms. She pushed her way deeper into their comforting shelter, still listening to every sound in dread.

The faintest whispers touched her ears. Deirdre

froze and bent her knees to lower herself to the forest floor. The night wind slapped the leaves against one another, but it also carried the unmistakable sound of human conversation.

The queen held her tongue for once, and Deirdre turned to discover the woman sealing her lips with one of her hands pressed tightly over her mouth. Her eyes were wide with fear as she hunched down behind her.

It was a wonder the woman had not been captured. She had determination, but little skill when it came to crossing the land. Deirdre eased forward, watching the ground to keep from placing her feet on fallen branches that would be brittle. They moved closer, and the sounds continued, becoming clearer.

"There are my men." Joan stood up straight. "I know their voices well."

Deirdre reached up and pulled the queen back down with a sharp tug. "Yer grace, those seeking ye would nae bother yer men if ye were no' among them but instead sit back and wait to see if ye appeared."

"Oh God. You are correct." Joan stifled a whimper with her hand. "I am ignorant of how men hunt other men."

Deirdre was not trained in the art of warfare either, but she had listened to a great deal of boasting by the fireside. She doubted such conversation was common at court, though.

"Do nae fear until we have a reason to. The Camerons rode out quickly when their search of the abbey failed to discover ye hiding there," Deirdre instructed her. "If we frighten ourselves into whimpering like children, it is certain we shall be captured."

"Wise words, Deirdre Chattan." Joan leaned close so her words did not drift. "Are you sure your father didn't think you a son? You seem to have the knowledge of a Highlander."

"I was raised as a woman. I assure ye, madam." Deirdre smiled as she considered the nights in the great hall of Chattan Castle with her father's retainers all talking over their mugs of ale. "Men talk while the ale flows, and they seem to forget we women are the ones serving their tables."

The queen snorted. "It is the same at court. Those arrogant lords all think to keep us in our place by insisting we serve their fine suppers, but they never stop to consider what is falling from their lips while we shuffle so meekly behind their tables. I wonder why they believe we are struck with deafness whenever it will suit their purpose. More likely, they simply consider us too timid to take action when needed."

Each word dripped scorn. Deirdre held her thoughts and kept her lips sealed, but she couldn't help noticing that the queen was far angrier than she. Perhaps there was hope in that bit of knowledge. Or at least there might be hope in knowing they were both intent on doing something to change the facts that upset them so much.

But the world often wasn't fair, and reality didn't care who was content with their lot. Their actions might be admired during fireside tales, but during the bright light of day, there would no doubt be harsh consequences.

"I was raised a proper daughter, but I'd think there is a difference in the manner in which women are reared in the Highlands."

The queen let out a soft, silvery laugh. "Aye, Deirdre Chattan, there is. One I am grateful for, I assure you." Joan snorted as she discovered herself caught by a branch. Deirdre reached out and gently swept it aside. "You were taught to survive against the harsh land, just as I learned to navigate the hostile environment of court."

Deirdre held those words close to her heart. She was risking a great deal to help the queen, but she had made her choice. They moved closer, but the queen and her ladies did not have any skill when it came to masking their steps. The men stopped talking, their eyes scanning the trees around them. There was no fire, evidence that they were indeed trying to avoid capture.

One of them drew his sword.

"It is I, Sir Richard."

The knight peered in the direction of the queen's voice. She moved forward, but Deirdre hung back. She didn't trust the night. It could conceal those waiting to capture the queen so easily.

"My lady, you should be safe behind the door of the abbey."

The knight offered his queen a courtesy while the others gained their feet and followed his example.

"But worry not, Sir Richard. Going to the abbey has gained us the advantage."

"How so, my lady?" The man fitted his sword back into the scabbard that hung from his hip. The Highlanders wore their swords across their backs, and the difference made Deirdre hesitate.

"I've discovered someone who will help us escape those who seek me."

The queen turned toward her. Deirdre drew in a stiff breath to banish the reluctance holding her back. A tiny voice in the back of her head warned her to turn and return to the abbey, but her pride refused to let her abandon her course. She stepped forward, and the knights considered her through narrowed eyes. Bathed in darkness, the moment felt slightly surreal, as though she might be only dreaming of escaping from the dawn that would rouse her to another day of serving at the abbey.

That stiffened her resolve.

"I suggest we trade clothing now, before anyone sees us."

The queen's men stepped in front of her, surprising her with how abruptly they abandoned their polished manners. One of the knights actually hooked his hand around her forearm and sent her stumbling in order to stand between them.

"This woman is a Highlander."

"I know it well." Joan insisted, "She is exactly what we need, for her knowledge of this land will help us succeed in avoiding those who seek me."

The queen tried to cross in front of her guard, but they refused to let her. Sir Richard extended one of his arms straight out to keep the queen where he felt she was best protected. Joan didn't care for his insistence. Deirdre lifted her chin and sent a hard look back at the queen's escort. She'd made her choice, and no one was going to stop her from achieving a place that would honor her father.

"I bid her join us." The queen informed him.

The knight frowned but lowered his arm.

"You cannot see it, but she favors me. Our hair is the same shade, and our features similar. She has agreed to be a decoy so we may make our way while those looking for us follow her."

The men all lost their brooding expressions. Several nodded, even Sir Richard. "That's exactly what we need, madam. A brilliant idea."

The queen smiled. "You see? God is favoring us. We shall succeed, I am sure of it."

"Not if we do nae stop talking," Deirdre informed them all. She closed the distance between them and lowered her voice. "I assure ye my Highlander kin will have no trouble discovering where we are if we continue to speak. We need to exchange clothing, and yer ladies should discard their fine overrobes too."

"Aye. That is true. The Highlanders know their land well, and those courtly robes are out of place here," Sir Richard agreed. He raised a hand and pointed at one of the other knights. He pointed toward the forest, and the man seemed instantly to know what to do. He turned to the queen and laid one finger against his lips. Joan didn't look pleased, but she did remain silent.

The wind was still rustling the new spring leaves. Somewhere an owl cried out as it hunted. Deirdre listened for that cry again, for many of the Highland clans used birdcalls to communicate in the dark. Steps came softly through the trees, and she stepped back, but Sir Richard shook his head.

Men came through the trees, but their swords hung from their hips, confirming they were English. She was shocked, because she had never once thought to be grateful to see the English instead of her own countrymen.

Men continued to appear until there were a good thirty of them. Sir Richard raised his hand and made several signals that sent the men back into the forest. He gestured her forward as the queen turned and followed her escort. The knights cleared the branches from Joan Beaufort's path as they crept through the dark. Deirdre suppressed the urge to laugh, because she had never encountered a woman who needed such pampering.

Deirdre heard the horses before she saw them in the darkness. The English knight was wise to have the animals resting away from his men. Horses made noise, after all, for the creatures didn't understand the struggles their masters engaged in.

The queen turned and gestured Deirdre forward. Her two ladies were already pulling on the straps of some sort of bundle secured to the back of one horse. The animal was being used to carry only bundles, and that brought a frown to her lips. Such baggage would slow them down, as well as announce the fact that they were most likely noble. The Highlanders traveled light and often by night. That fact accounted for their ability to surprise their enemies. It was a skill boys learned young and men had perfected by the time they were old enough to be called Highlanders.

The ladies shook out clothing. There wasn't enough light to see the color, but when Deirdre reached out to touch the overrobe, she sucked in her breath with surprise. The fabric was as soft as a baby's head. It was plush too, telling her that it was velvet.

There had only been a few pieces of such finery at Chattan Castle, but she had enjoyed sneaking a few chances to finger the expensive cloth when no one was about to smack her hand.

The lady tossed the gown over a nearby rock, making Deirdre gasp to see such a costly item treated so causally.

"It's an old one our mistress doesn't care very much for."

The woman whispered her words as she began to pull the headdress off Deirdre's head. Both ladies knew their duties well, for they disrobed her without any hesitation, with smooth and even motions. The knights remained on the opposite side of the horses, but Deirdre still wrapped her arms around her bare body. The night air raised her nipples into hard points, and she shivered, standing in only her stockings and boots.

But one attendant knelt and began to work the leather lace that was woven between the antler-horn buttons loose so the sides of her boots separated.

An image of Quinton Cameron sweeping down on them sent a flood of urgency through her. She didn't trust for one moment that the man was satisfied with his search of the abbey.

A memory of the look in his eyes made her knees quiver.

She bit her own lip in frustration. It was ridiculous to respond to only a memory. He was a man seeking his own rewards, and that was all. She had sampled what men did with women once they had sated their desires. It would be wise to recall just how painful it had been to have her affections ground beneath the boot heel of the man she'd risked everything to have.

The queen's attendants began to dress her as quickly as they had disrobed her. Stockings were gently rolled so she had only to point her toe and slip her foot into them. They were smooth and soft, not even a hint of rough wool. The women eased her feet into dainty slippers tied with ribbons. Deirdre frowned at them. Satin slippers would see her toes freezing in the Highlands. They also lacked any sort of good sole. She could feel every rock and stick through their thin fabric.

The clouds drifted above them, granting them just enough moonlight to see by.

An underrobe was lifted up for her to slip her hands and arms into. It slithered down her body as smooth as water. It was longer than she was accustomed to, the hem trailing behind her. The velvet overrobe was next. Deirdre enjoyed its weight, because it promised her relief from the chill as soon as her body warmed the fabric. But it was cut low in the front, with a square neckline. The two women began to lace it closed up the back. Her eyes widened as she felt the garment forming to her figure. She had never worn anything so revealing, and she felt her breasts swelling up to fill the neckline as the back of the gown was secured across her shoulder blades.

"Perfection." The queen walked in front of her, studying her while the women pulled the plait from her hair. "No one shall guess you are not me."

"She should wear your head signet. Many know it as your favorite." One of the attendants spoke.

"Another good idea." The queen didn't reach up

to remove the slim ring of gold that encircled her forehead. The attendant moved toward her mistress and lifted the costly item off her head.

Deirdre stepped back and winced when a stone jabbed into her unprotected arch. "That is too precious a thing for me to be responsible for."

The queen waved her hand in the air, dismissing her protest. "No one shall believe you are me if you do not have gold." She pulled a ring off one finger. "And no one shall believe I am a bride of Christ if I do not appear humble."

The signet crown was gently pressed down over her head, the metal still warm from the queen's skin. The woman behind her pulled the front sections of her hair back and tied them with a ribbon. The final touch was a silk veil that fluttered in the night breeze. The clothing was far finer than anything Deirdre had ever worn, but it was also completely impractical. Deirdre discovered she was afraid to move in it, for fear she might damage such costly fabrics. The queen held out the two rings she had removed, and her ladies carried them to Deirdre.

"You must be at ease. I care not if I ever see that robe again, so worry not about it."

The queen's attendants began to disrobe their mistress and re-dress her in the undyed robe Deirdre had worn. The queen wrinkled her nose but remained silent until even her hair was concealed beneath the thick nun's veil.

"I am grateful our feet are close in size." She tested the boots with a few steps, and her lips lifted into a pleased smile. "I can see why you wear these. Although ugly, they are quite comfortable."

Deirdre looked at her boots with envy. Her toes were rapidly losing every bit of heat as she struggled to find a spot to stand on that did not have some rock or lump of dirt to hurt her. In the Highlands, that would be a chore indeed.

"We should take you away now." Sir Richard appeared, gesturing to the queen. "I have several volunteers who will stay and act as her escort."

The queen nodded. She stepped forward and grasped Deirdre's hand, squeezing it tightly. "I shall keep my word and pray you make it to me so I may reward you. Do not be frightened."

"I'm born of Highlander stock, madam; there is naught here I fear. It is my home."

The queen's grip tightened a fraction more. "Excellent."

She stepped away, Sir Richard urging her away until the night shadows swallowed them. Deirdre listened to the sound of their footsteps until they faded as well. Only a few of the horses were left; the one the attendants had taken the clothing from remained near her. Deirdre reached out and ran a sure hand along the side of the creature. There was comfort in feeling the heat of the animal. In spite of her brave words, she discovered loneliness assaulting her.

There was the true root of the reason she had taken her place at the abbey instead of remaining under her father's roof. It was in every person's nature to seek the company of other living souls. Very few could resist that urge for long. Remaining on Chattan land would have seen her falling from grace again. Oh, it might have taken years; in fact, she was certain of that, for she had more than her share of pride.

Yet she was still weak enough to recall exactly how Quinton's lips felt against her wrist. She had enjoyed it. Now, when there was no one about to judge her, and darkness to hide in, she had to face the truth of her own nature. She did not like being alone. She suddenly understood why women lived as mistresses; they were unable to ignore their need for companionship even if fate had been cruel enough to see them loving a man who was already wed.

There was a crunch of dry wood, left behind as the snow melted, and new plants had yet to cover the ground with soft leaves that would mask the sounds of men moving through the hills. Every Highlander knew to wait until spring was full in bloom before attempting to raid. The queen's escort was obviously English.

"We'll wait until dawn breaks."

The man held out something shapeless. She reached for it and smiled when her fingers felt the unmistakable roughness of wool. The fine garments she wore didn't hold back the chill, and the coldest part of the night was yet to come. Deirdre wrapped the cloak about her and raised the hood. The English knight didn't linger near her. He rejoined the small group of men who had been chosen to be sacrificed for their queen.

Deirdre felt their frustration as she tried to ignore a growing sense of impending disaster. She held the edges of the cloak tight and forced herself to sit down near a smooth boulder that might offer her a place to lean her head. She pulled her legs up against her chest and sighed. At least her body heat was no longer seeping away into the night. The wool might be rough and scratchy, but it was warm. Her toes began to thaw now that she had her feet drawn close to her body. She leaned her head against the stone and tried to force her thoughts to stop spinning so fast.

But that left only Quinton Cameron's face behind. For some reason, she recalled his face with vivid detail, the square jaw and hard features, which lacked excessive fat because the man kept pace with his men.

Deirdre stiffened, annoyed with the direction of her thoughts.

Her eyes opened, and she watched the shadows again. She didn't know much about Quinton Cameron, but she was sure the man was every inch a Highlander. There was a boldness in him that a man might only earn. More than one arrogant English lord had tried his hand at demanding respect from the Highland clans. They failed because they sent their servants to do their hunting.

Quinton Cameron had walked into the abbey first, doing what he ordered his men to do without hanging back. She discovered herself respecting the man even as she felt her temper sizzle once more.

With a snort, she forced herself to seek out what little sleep might be hers before the day arrived. She would need every bit of strength to accomplish the task she'd set herself. Deirdre banished the memory of Quinton Cameron from her mind. For the moment, there were far more important matters she needed to be concerned with.

But she frowned, because the man invaded her sleep once her mind was no longer obedient to her will.

Curse and rot her nature.

"Rise. It is dawn."

Deirdre felt a boot tip nudge her, and she opened her eyes to see one of the English soldiers was frowning down at her.

"We've a duty to attend to."

His voice was edged with solid determination. It sent a shiver down her back, because it sounded like a man who had already accepted he would be cut down in the service of his master. She rose and felt her cramped muscles protest.

But the long hours of labor at the abbey had made her strong, and the ache dissipated with a few steps. The horizon was pink, with golden rays beginning to stretch out over the landscape.

"You need to cast off the cloak so the fine clothing Her Majesty gave you can be seen."

The soldier reached for the thick wool keeping her warm, but Deirdre shifted away from him. "Then we must find something else to keep me warm, for no one shall believe that the queen would be riding while shivering from the morning chill."

The man let his hand drop while he frowned. "Aye, you have a point there." He pointed to the horse the queen's attendants had taken the clothing from during the night. "See what you can find among the things she left. I'm no lady's maid, and I don't know one of their fancy garments from another. A pair of robes and shoes is all a woman needs, to my way of thinking."

"And a cloak when traveling in the Highlands," Deirdre insisted.

The soldier shrugged. "Aye, but we need you to be seen in that fine velvet so those we pass will talk about you. That cloak is too common looking for our purpose."

Deirdre reached up and fingered the gold resting on her forehead. "This will gain plenty of attention."

She was still surprised to feel the smooth surface of the gold resting against her skin. Her father had a gold ring that had been worn by her grandfather as a symbol of the laird of the Chattan clan. Her mother had left a chest containing several gold chains she had brought with her as her dowry, but Deirdre had never worn them, only sneaked into the chamber where the chest was stored and gently touched the precious metal. Her father had promised once that she'd take one of those chains with her when she wed.

She frowned and cast the wool cloak off her shoulders. She wasn't wed, and the reason was that men were untrustworthy. The soldier reached down and grabbed the cloak, taking it away with him without another word. A soft groan rose from her as she turned to begin looking through the bundles tied to the horse. Men certainly did enjoy having the women around them doing what they wanted. She honestly shouldn't be so surprised by that, for the world was run by men, yet still it chafed at times.

For the moment, the chill of the early morning was more pressing than her desire to argue against what any man wanted her to do. She began to unlace bundles, marveling at the rich fabrics contained inside. But there was no way to tell what anything was without shaking everything out to see what type of garment it was. Soon she had several more robes made of costly velvet lying over the rock she had leaned against. The sun shone off the rich colors of the threads and illuminated the trim attached to their necklines.

At last, she unrolled a surcoat made of wool so fine, she had to look closely at it to confirm that it was truly wool. The threads were thin, and Deirdre shook her head as she thought of how difficult it must have been to spin such delicate strands. The garment was lined too, and she eagerly shrugged into it.

She hesitated when she reached to close the front of it and discovered gold buttons sewn to one edge. Each one had a design on the top.

Fit for a queen…

Deirdre forced her fingers to push the buttons through their holes. She'd agreed to the deception, and that meant wearing the clothing of a highborn lady. At least the surcoat began to warm her, and she turned to rolling the garments she'd placed over the boulder. Once they were tied onto the animal again, she looked toward the soldiers to discover them watching her.

She felt her stomach tighten with dread. Every one of them looked as though he was ready to walk to his own execution. She forced down the lump that appeared in her throat. But that didn't stop her from feeling like the fine clothing she wore was burning her. She wanted to cast it off and had to quell the urge by recalling why she was wearing it.

The future. She wanted more from life, and she would have to earn it.

Deirdre lifted her chin. "Shall we go?"

❧

Time felt frozen.

In spite of the way the sun rose and warmed her face, Deirdre would have sworn every minute was as long as an hour while the soldiers took her up the rocky roads that led to the Highlands. She could see the heather beginning to bloom and smell it, because the Englishmen kept their pace slow. By afternoon, she was ready to flinch from the sound of the horses' hooves hitting the ground. Every one of her senses felt strained, and her neck ached from how much she was jerking her face around to look for attackers.

Joan Beaufort had earned her sympathy for living under such horrible stress.

"There looks to be a village ahead. We'll see if they have an inn."

Deirdre jerked her face around again, because the solders had ignored her for the entire day. They'd spoken to one another, but never to her. This man looked tired, as though he was as exhausted as she felt, but there was a spark of kindness in his eyes that she found very welcome.

"They should have something to offer for supper," he said before closing his mouth with a shrug.

"That would be very nice." Deirdre searched her mind to recall how the queen had spoken. She lowered her voice and tried to wash the Scottish brogue from her pronunciation, but feared she failed.

"Aye, that's a good trick to practice," he remarked. "I suppose this ruse won't work very well if anyone hears that accent of yours. Best leave the conversation to us." He waved his hand in the air. "Ladies don't generally talk to their escorts anyway. Just smile and nod or shake your head."

"If you believe that is best." Deirdre felt confidence building as she remembered to say "you" instead of "ye." The word felt slightly awkward, but the man grinned.

"You're a clever one, I can see why our lady choose you."

Satisfaction edged his voice now. He offered her an approving look before nudging his horse forward so he was once more riding close to one of his companions. Four of the men were in front of her, and four behind. It felt like the sun was shining brighter on her, illuminating her to anyone who looked up as they passed. There were houses along the road now, and the scent of cooking food drifted to her nose. Deirdre heard her belly rumble, low and long. The tension of the day had made it possible for her to ignore her hunger, but now that she could smell bread baking, it was impossible to miss how empty her belly was.

A sharp whistle broke through her attention. The soldier at the front of their party was pointing at a weathered sign hanging in front of a large building. There were long rails set outside it to tie horses to, but the sign advertised stable-boarding services as well as rooms for rent.

Her escort stopped, smiles appearing on the faces of the men. Deirdre sighed, the tension that had plagued her most of the day doubling as the patrons of the establishment peered at her intently. It was an effort to hold her chin steady, as if she were accustomed to wearing gold and velvet upon the road.

Only Englishwomen did such a thing, and that was

a fact. No Scottish noble rode the Highland roads in his court clothing. One of the soldiers offered his hand to her. Deirdre realized she'd been lost in thought and was still sitting on top of her mare. Her cheeks colored, but she was grateful for the lapse of attention, because it made her look more like the queen. Joan would have waited for one of her escort to help her down.

But it seemed so wasteful of the strength Deirdre had in her own body. She placed her hand in the one offered and slid from the back of the mare. She reached up to pat the animal on the neck, without thinking, and the appreciative gesture gained her a frown from the soldier who had assisted her.

Deirdre continued to stroke the neck of the mare. She might have agreed to wear the queen's clothing, but she would not be so arrogant as to deny a horse that had carried her all day a kind touch.

"This way, Majes—madam."

The soldiers stumbled over the word "*madam*," his tone loud enough to drift to those watching them enter the inn. Deirdre stepped up and through the doorway while whispers rose around her. They died away when she appeared, the patrons staring at her over their wooden bowls of stew and broken rounds of bread.

The soldiers directed her to a large table, and two men who sat too near were sent to another table with a harsh look from the captain. A serving girl quickly appeared to sweep a cleaning rag across the surface of the chair before Deirdre sat on it.

"Ye must be cold and hungry. I'll fetch ye up a serving of me mother's supper. It's the tastiest in the area."

Deirdre opened her mouth but closed it when the captain interrupted her.

"That will be good. Thank you." His words were clipped and the girl hurried away. He sent a hard look toward Deirdre, clearly attempting to remind her to remain silent. The man nodded to her, but there was no mistaking the glint in his eye.

Deirdre stared straight back at him, refusing to lower her chin. She was posing as a queen, after all, and she doubted Joan Beaufort would allow a member of her escort to put her in her place. The soldier frowned but ducked his head after a moment.

"Straight off the fire, mistress."

The serving girl returned with a tray that contained a steaming bowl. Her face was flushed from how fast she was moving, but her eyes glittered with anticipation of earning some additional coin for her troubles.

Deirdre lowered her eyelashes to veil the shame that entered her eyes. For the first time, she was ashamed of the fact that she was deceiving her own countrymen in the effort to gain what she wanted.

The stew smelled delicious, though, and when it was placed in front of her, she couldn't think of anything except tasting it. She burned her tongue because it was too hot, but that didn't keep her from smiling.

"I told ye it was tasty. The bread is warm too, and I brought ye some sweet-cream butter me sister churned from this morning's milk."

Deirdre looked up, but the captain answered for her.

"Our mistress is well pleased with your offerings. We would have your best room for the night."

He flipped a silver coin onto the tabletop that made

the serving girl smile wide enough to show off her teeth. She scooped the silver off the table almost before the sound of it hitting the wooden surface faded.

"I'll get me sister to seeing to the room." She was gone in a moment, on her way back to the kitchen, where an older woman with fabric wrapped tightly around her hair to keep it out of the fire looked back toward her with excitement. The girl held up the coin, and the woman took it, nodding before she snapped her fingers at someone else in the kitchen.

"That was a great deal of silver."

The captain leaned toward her to keep their words from drifting to the others eating nearby.

"We needs inspire talk, madam. Let them think we have so much money that we never bother to count it."

"As if there is such a person alive."

He shrugged. "You'll discover there is, if we achieve our goal."

Deirdre heard hope in his words, but he turned his back on her, leaving her to eat alone. The moment she was finished, the serving girl appeared to lead her abovestairs. The room the girl took her to was small but clean. It was certainly larger than the cot she had slept on for the last few months at the abbey.

The captain followed her in, sending the girl away with another silver coin.

"Should we stay here?"

The man grunted. "I believe so. It will get the locals talking about you and leave the queen unnoticed." He scanned the room. "My men and I will be below, but you need to stay here, or no one will think you are anyone important."

He left while Deirdre was considering his words. She scoffed at the closed door, but that gave her little comfort. Her pride stung, but worse than that, she knew she had no right to be offended, because she wasn't anyone of importance.

It shouldn't bother her, and still it did. She sat down on the bed and felt fatigue wrap around her.

Well, there was no reason to waste a good bed. She lay down and closed her eyes, silently praying her fortune might be brighter tomorrow.

❧

Fate wasn't so kind.

Her dreams were filled with dark suspicions. She twisted and opened her eyes, feeling unrested. The room was dark, and the seam where the shutters closed over the window was still black too. But her heart was beating faster than it should have been, and her fingers were curled into the bedding like talons. Her mind was trying to decide why she was so ill at ease, and a moment later she heard the sound of steps on the stairs.

They were soft footfalls, but she sat up, rigid with the knowledge that whoever had been searching for the queen was coming.

Maybe she was panicking, but that didn't stop her from finding the little slipper shoes where she had left them on the floor. A creak of wood announced that whoever was climbing the steps was closer now. Deirdre felt her heart accelerating, and it became impossible to remain sitting on the bed. She looked around the room, her attention settling on the window. For the first time, she was grateful for the delicate shoes, because they made no noise as she crossed over to the window. She found the latch in the darkness and pushed one side open.

The door to her room began to open, sending panic rushing through her. Deirdre didn't stop to think about what the queen would have done. She shoved the other shutter out of her way and swung one leg over the opening. Moonlight streamed in, illuminating the kilts worn by the men coming through the doorway.

"Stop right there."

Deirdre didn't listen. She sent her body over the edge of the window, controlling her drop to the ground with a hard grip on the windowsill. Her robe fluttered free around her legs, and the crisp night air chilled her, but she didn't hang there for long. A head appeared above her, and warm hands covered hers.

"Are ye daft, woman?"

Maybe she was, but Deirdre let go, and her fingers slid easily out from beneath the ones that attempted to hold her. She hit the ground, and pain surged through her legs. Her knees failed to hold her, and she crumbled into a ball, rolling over several times. She gasped, dragging huge breaths into her lungs while shiny spots swirled past her eyes.

"Get down there after her, lads!"

Deirdre shook off the pain and scrambled to her feet, but the overlong robes tangled beneath her feet. She stumbled and fell to her knees again. Pain slashed through her once again; this time a moan escaped her lips because she couldn't stop it.

Such stupid clothing…

She struggled to kick it aside but was suddenly lifted off her knees and set on her feet by two men.

"Here now. Enough of this, lady."

A lantern was shoved close to her face, the yellow light from the flame sending a tiny pain through her eyes as her night vision died. She could only see things within the circle of light cast by the lantern, but she shivered when she looked about her.

"Is she the right one?"

Highlanders surrounded her. There was no mistaking their height or wide shoulders. Each of them had a sword strapped to his back with the pommel rising above his left shoulder so they might pull the weapon with their right hand.

"She's wearing gold and velvet."

"But is she Joan Beaufort?"

The man in front of her considered her from his greater height. His hands were propped on his hips as he stared at the signet crown circling her forehead.

"It's the truth I never expected a noblewoman to go out a window, but I never thought to be tracking any Englishwoman through the Highlands either."

The men surrounding her chuckled. Deirdre stumbled back a step, only to turn around, because they ringed her completely. There was no sign of her English escort either.

"Here now. There is no need to frighten the woman."

The one who spoke reached out and turned her back to face him with a firm grip on her bicep. Deirdre gasped and jerked her arm away from his touch.

"Forgive me, ma'am. I meant no disrespect toward

yer ladyship, but me laird is looking to meet ye, and I'm charged with the duty of taking ye to him."

Deirdre forced herself to take a deep breath before answering him. She ordered her thoughts to stop racing and focus on the task of concealing who she truly was. She lifted one hand and covered her lips with it to muffle her voice even more. "And who sent you after me?"

"The Earl of Liddell."

The proprietor of the inn suddenly appeared on the steps of his business. "Why are ye Camerons causing trouble with me paying customers?"

The man carried a torch that lit the area far more effectively. A crazy jolt of hope tore through her, but it was quashed by the number of Cameron retainers the torch showed her. There were three dozen of them at least, standing back from the circle surrounding her.

"We're about the earl's doings." The retainer in front of her dug in his pouch and produced two silver coins. He tossed them to the innkeeper.

"And he sends his appreciation for yer understanding." The coins landed at the proprietor's feet. The woman who had been in the kitchen appeared beside him in nothing but her underrobe. She bent down to pick up the money. She tossed the coins a few times before nodding with satisfaction over their weight. She looked toward Deirdre, concern wrinkling the skin around her eyes, but she scanned the number of Highlanders in front of her and shook her head before closing her fist around the silver.

"The Camerons are always welcome here." She turned around and went back into the inn. Her husband looked at Deirdre, but a moment later he followed his wife, taking the torch with him.

Desolation bit into her. For the first time in her life, she understood how it felt to be scorned simply because you had been born in another country. It was a harsh truth Deirdre realized she'd not had enough pity for.

"I'm Coalan, ma'am, one of Quinton Cameron's captains, and ye have me word ye'll come to no harm while I escort ye to him." His voice lowered, hardening with intent. "But ye will be going with me, so no more of yer escape attempts."

Coalan reached out and hooked his hand around her bicep again. This time the grip was hard, and even when she shrugged, she did not gain her freedom. He pulled her along with him toward horses standing nearby.

"This must be her mare. I've never seen gold used on a saddle before."

Coalan grunted. "Aye, I've never had enough to use it as a decoration meself."

His hands closed around her waist, and he lifted her up with only a tiny grunt. Deirdre landed on the saddle sideways and had to fight to throw her leg over the side of the mare before the slippery-smooth velvet saw her landing in a heap at Coalan's feet.

"Are no' ye going to tie her hands, Captain?"

Coalan chuckled as he mounted a larger horse and looked across at her. "Tell me, lady. Are ye going to behave, or shall I take the advice of Dirk there and bind yer hands to keep ye from running off into the night?"

His arrogant grin informed her he didn't think she

could give him any worry even with her hands free. Her temper simmered, and she lifted her chin and clamped her lips shut, refusing to answer him. She was grateful it was still night, or the brute would have seen her temper glittering in her eyes.

Coalan scoffed at her. "I've a mind to see Drumdeer before sunset, lads. Let's take Laird Cameron what he wants."

The name Drumdeer sent fear through her. The castle was well-known, even if she'd never laid eyes upon it. It was built along a ridge, which was where it got its name of drum, which meant *ridge* in Gaelic. There were plenty of stories of how strong the castle was, and more than one army had learned that lesson through defeat. Once inside, she wouldn't be leaving until Quinton Cameron said she might.

Coalan reached across and took the reins from her fingers with a quick snap. "Do nae be giving me any cause to regret my choice to leave ye free, lady, for I tell ye I can be a mean bastard if ye come between me and what my laird expects of me. That's a promise. I swear it."

The mare followed Coalan's stallion, and the Highlander took to the night with every bit of skill Deirdre expected of any man she might call by that name. The English feared the Highlanders with good cause. Not every Scot was a Highlander, but Coalan was one. It was in the way he faced the night with confidence. The man wasn't shivering as he guided them into the forest. There was no hint of unease many would have felt while challenging the shadows the old wives claimed were haunted with specters or demons.

That was a Highlander for you. Deirdre felt it in her blood as well. She'd taken to the night to meet her lover with no more than a single prayer said to ensure her safe travel.

She ducked her head low to prevent a branch from hitting her. The smell of the horse touched her nose, as did the scent of the earth being churned up by the hooves of the animals in front of them. Her hearing was keen, detecting every small sound while they made their way.

In spite of it being a year ago, she recalled how she had challenged the night for what she wanted. Many called her too bold for her gender, but she was her father's daughter. Fate had been cruel in making her female, for she felt every urge the Cameron retainers did. Deirdre clasped the mare between her thighs without any hesitation. She refused to believe it would make her sterile, and even if such were true, she would not perch herself on the side of the animal. That was a dangerous way to ride and robbed a girl of the ability to hold tight to the horse she rode. Every Cameron retainer was at ease in the saddle, and she refused to behave any differently.

Yet she was a woman among them.

And they believed she was English too.

Deirdre smiled and fought the urge to laugh. It amused her to discover herself once more in the position of being shunned by those she was so close to. After enduring it at the abbey, she was well accustomed to the feeling. She noticed several cutting glances from the other Cameron retainers as the night went on, but it wasn't until dawn that she truly confirmed her suspicions about her place among them. With light washing over them, their distrust could be seen very clearly.

Coalan finally raised his hand, calling a halt to their progress. Deirdre slid from the back of her mare gratefully. There had been no horses at the abbey, and she was sore now, because riding was something that toughened the body. Her back ached, and so did her tender parts.

Something she would delight in blaming Quinton Cameron for, and that was a promise.

She stomped her feet against the ground to restore circulation in her toes. But the little slipper shoes were too thin, and she jabbed a sharp stone into her foot through her own actions. A small yelp escaped her lips as she hopped about on the other foot and snarled with frustration. The queen might know how to survive at court, but if Deirdre hadn't changed clothing with her, it was very possible the woman would have been dead by now.

"Ye should have waited for me to assist ye down." Coalan didn't sound very sincere.

"I will see to my mistress," the English captain interrupted Coalan, earning scowls from the Cameron retainers nearby. He didn't allow their deadly looks to stop him from joining her.

That took courage, and Deirdre wasn't blind to it. The English captain stood firmly in front of her, refusing to shrink in the face of Coalan's glare. The Cameron retainer might order that the man be run through, but that didn't send the Englishman back to cower with his men.

"Aye, that's most likely a better idea even if it did come from the mouth of an English soldier." Coalan raked her with a harsh glare. "Seems right ye should look after yer own women. I admit I do nae understand any female who would take to the Highlands wearing that bit of finery."

Coalan's voice was thick with scorn, and the English knight growled, "I've been in your country for most of my life, and your king is half-English." He stepped forward, stopping only inches from Coalan. They were well matched, for the Englishman was every bit as large as Coalan, but the Cameron retainers all pressed in, making it clear Coalan wouldn't be the only man the English knight had to fight.

Coalan snorted. "Ye have courage, man. I'll grant ye that. 'Tis surprising to find such in an Englishman, but as ye have said, ye've been here in Scotland long enough to learn something from us, it seems."

The Cameron retainers laughed and began to turn back to taking care of their horses. Coalan shrugged and pulled a leather pouch from the back of his saddle.

"I'm nae sure if they teach ye at court what a man makes do with when he's on the road, but that's what we have to offer. What did yer mother name ye?"

"Simon."

Coalan grunted. "Good thing to know, since ye're intent on challenging me. I want to make sure I can tell the priest yer proper name when I confess I ran ye through."

"Simon Paul Smithson." The Englishman spoke each word loud enough for every Cameron retainer to hear. "My father earned his bread by the sweat of his brow, and I assure you I know very well how to make do on the road. That isn't unique to Scotland. Many an English boy has been raised to serve the noble his father sent him to."

Simon turned and extended his hand toward where the other English soldiers sat. They no longer had their swords, the scabbards hanging limply from their belts. Deirdre lifted the front of her underrobe and joined them. Her jaw ached from holding her tongue, but she took a place beside the English escort she had agreed to accompany.

She felt completely misplaced, like a fresh strawberry in the dead of winter. No matter how delightful it might smell, you'd still hesitate to bite into it, because you simply knew it did not belong.

"Well done…" Simon whispered as he leaned close to her. "Let me speak for you, or that charming brogue of yours will give our game away."

Simon opened the pouch and handed her one of the oatcakes that was inside. She took it without comment, but that drew a frown from the English knight.

"I'm sorry there isn't better fare, mistress."

There was a firm warning in his tone to recall her place in their charade. Deirdre lifted the oatcake and wrinkled her nose before nibbling on one corner. Two of the Cameron retainers chuckled before turning their attention to their own meals. Simon passed the pouch to another of his men. Their demeanor appeared gloomy, but if any of the Cameron had taken a closer look, they might have noticed the victory flickering in their prisoners' eyes.

Deirdre felt guilt collide with her reasons for doing

what she was. She was a Chattan, her father laird of a Highland clan, and that meant that the Cameron were kin. Deceiving them chafed, but she filled her mouth with a bigger bite of the oatcake to keep any emotion-ally fueled confessions from spilling over her lips. She was doing what she had to in order to carve out a place for herself in the male-dominated world.

They lingered only for a short time. The horses were allowed to drink from a nearby stream, but Coalan had them all riding again before an hour had gone by. Deirdre had one precious moment of privacy to see to her personal needs, but she resisted the urge to run from behind a large boulder. In full daylight, the Camerons would run her down with ease. Running on foot while her pursuers had horses was unwise at best. She'd wait for darkness.

But she would run.

That thought kept her company throughout the day. She dreaded making it to Quinton's castle. Drumdeer was large and solid. Once behind those gates, she'd be at its laird's mercy.

She shivered as her memory offered up what Quinton could choose to do with her if she was imprisoned inside his home.

Ye might enjoy it…

She ground her teeth with frustration as a voice taunted her with that notion. She didn't need her flesh turning traitor again. Once was plenty, and that was a solid truth. She refused to listen to her body when it came to men, even if it was only one man drawing her attention. That was one too many.

Besides, Quinton would delight in taking her

to his bed, but she was a fool if she believed she would stay there very long. The man would take his pleasure, and the only thing she'd have from the experience would be whatever delight she might gain from the moment.

His kisses delighted you…

Oh, curse and rot it all! She had liked his kisses, and that further annoyed her. She had thought Melor Douglas killed every weakness she might have for the opposite gender, but obviously not. Deirdre lifted her head and noticed the setting sun. She would have to make sure she did not find herself near enough to temptation for Quinton to take advantage of her.

If the Cameron retainers lost her, they'd resume their search, and that would satisfy her promise to the queen. Joan Beaufort need never know Deirdre had run from Quinton Cameron for any other reason.

Besides, there was a bit of satisfaction in being able to take advantage of the lax nature of the Cameron retainers. They were too arrogant by far and too judgmental of women in general.

Coalan didn't stop them until past sunset. The horizon was still slightly bright from the day, but with only the faintest of glows. Deirdre found herself anxiously awaiting the blackest hours of the night. Or at least darker ones. She doubted the Highlanders would rest the entire night through; their rest was for the horses, not the men who wore the Cameron colors so proudly. They lay down near their horses, only a few losing the draw to stand guard for the night. The last of the oatcakes were handed out, but Deirdre wasn't interested in eating. She forced herself to consume the food given to her, because she would need the strength.

Her mind was too full for sleep, but she closed her eyes and listened as the camp became quiet. The horses shifted from time to time, and the wind picked up, but the breathing of the men became low and even. She forced herself to recite long verses from the Bible, quoting word for word to make sure enough time had passed.

She opened her eyes and searched the area around her. Simon slept closest to her, diligent even though she wasn't his true mistress. She admired the man in spite of his English blood.

Deirdre frowned, shame heating her cheeks as she continued to scan the shapes of the sleeping men. She was the one being judgmental now. Where a man was born did not prove his strength when it came to upholding honor. Melor Douglas was proof of that. The man was Scottish and born of the Douglas clan, but she would never call him a Highlander. He was a liar and a cheat, no matter how fine he boasted his blood was.

She remembered to pull the excessive length of her underrobe up before trying to move. She crawled until she was behind a rock and then crouched behind it for several long moments as she listened to the men. Her heart rate began to accelerate, forcing her to seal her lips to contain her rapid breathing. There was no sound from the camp, so she began to move deeper into the forest, working her way slowly away from the Cameron retainers.

The sound of the horses diminished in the distance,

and she could no longer see them through the tress. Her legs ached because of the low position she forced herself to maintain, but she continued several more paces before standing up. Her heart was racing, but hope flowed through her veins as she lifted her hems high and began to run.

A startled cry left her lips when she was jerked from her tracks by a hard yank on the back of her surcoat. She stumbled back, off balance, and collided with the solid body of a man.

"Now, I warned ye no' to make me sorry I did nae tie ye up."

Three

COALAN WAS ANGRY WITH HER, BUT DEIRDRE FELT HER temper burn far hotter. She turned and swung her closed fist at his head. She aimed for the side of his face, hoping to hit his temple and knock him senseless.

He moved, but not far enough, and her fist collided with his cheek. A dull flesh-on-flesh sound made her flinch, but she forced herself to send her other hand toward his opposite temple. Desperation lent her strength, and this time she hit her target.

"Christ Almighty!"

He staggered and collapsed to his knees while shaking his head. Deirdre grabbed the fabric of her clothing and turned toward the thickest part of the forest. She made it only two strides before Coalan hit her. The man lunged at her and tackled her to the ground with his entire body. The rocks scratched her unprotected face, and she cried out as something sliced into her thigh through the soft fabric of her garments.

"Do nae be thinking that whining will sway me thinking now."

Coalan hauled her up but kept a hard hand on one

wrist. She felt him loop something around it before he grabbed her opposite hand and lashed it as well.

"Ye're going to me laird, and I told ye that ye'd best settle yer thoughts to doing that, or I'd turn mean."

Her thigh burned, stealing any reply she would normally have made. Coalan pushed her back toward the camp, and several of his men watched from where they had stood up.

"Mount up, lads. I've a mind to be finished with this hellion." He finished pulling her toward her mare and tossed her up onto the animal's back before his men finished grumbling. Even in the darkness, she felt their glares on her.

But the injury to her leg pulsed with pain so brightly, clasping the horse took all her attention. She clutched at its bridle, leaning over the neck of the beast. The first few steps sent sparkling dots dancing before her eyes. She gulped deep breaths and forced them down to keep herself from sliding into oblivion. Succeeding at that allowed her to endure every moment of agony the wound on her leg inflicted.

The Cameron retainers all filed behind her. Coalan made their pace brisk, and dawn showed them the Drumdeer's towers. Her Cameron escort all sent up a cheer, their happiness making her wince. It also drew curses from the English who had been selected by their mistress to remain with her. Deirdre discovered herself feeling better as she considered the soldiers. Her fate promised to be brighter than theirs. She should have felt guilty, for those men being pulled along in the midst of the Cameron retainers would no doubt be heading to the dungeon of Drumdeer.

Ye might as well…

She couldn't help but shudder as that idea rose from her mind. It was actually more like her inner fears, but she shied away from admitting she was afraid.

Doing so would surely see her fate being something she did not like. The only way to claim victory in a game that included Quinton Cameron as a player was to be bold.

"Ye need no' look so worried, lady. The earl is a fair man, but ye should know that since ye have met him at court."

There was an edge of suspicion in Coalan's voice. Deirdre raised her chin and ordered herself to remain silent.

She couldn't expect the queen to give her a position if she did not earn it. Such was life. So she only shot a hard look toward the Cameron captain and denied him any answer that might betray the fact she was as Scottish as he.

"I suppose ye can be talking to him about whatever complaints ye have about me and me men, but he ordered me to bring ye back, and I'll no' be apologizing for following me laird's instructions."

A few of the other retainers were listening in, and they cast her hard looks. It was clear they expected her to whine to their laird about her treatment.

For God's sake, she wasn't so delicate. But her leg was throbbing once more. She looked down, wondering why it still pained her. A hard grunt drew her attention back to Coalan. The man was facing forward once more, but his expression was tight. Guilt began to twist its sharp point into her because she was causing him such unrest. The man fully expected her to whimper the moment she was near another noble.

It was for certain Coalan wouldn't be very happy when his laird unmasked her.

She looked once more at the huge castle where Quinton made his home. It was built on an outcropping of rocks that rose up like a frozen wave. Towers overlooked the land below, and even from a distance, she could see that those towers were at least four stories high.

Her mouth went dry, and she counted the number of towers twice because her mind didn't want to believe how many there were. But the second time she counted eight of them, exactly like the first time. There were thick walls between them, and as they rode closer, the very tops of roofs peeked out from inside those walls. That meant the castle was wide enough for building between the walls. It was the sort of fortification that would never fall. All around it, the land was being turned for planting. The sound of rushing water touched her ears as they passed rivers swollen with spring melt-off. Women looked up from where they washed clothing, their eyes widening when they noticed the gold signet resting on her forehead.

They rode through the main village, the people making way for the laird's retainers. Children pointed at her, and the blacksmith stopped his endless pounding when Coalan tugged her mare past his shop.

But Deirdre was absorbed with watching the way the walls seemed to grow higher and thicker with every step the mare took. Fear raced through her, and

there was no way to master it completely. She forced
herself to recall what the queen had told her. That
Quinton wouldn't want her, because she wasn't in fact
Joan Beaufort.

Truthfully, Deirdre had never been so pleased to
know someone wouldn't want her.

A steep road was the only way into the castle. It
was well packed with dirt, but her mare still hesitated.
Coalan turned and gently tugged on the reins to coax
the animal through the huge gate waiting with its iron
bars raised to admit them into the fortification. He
frowned when he looked at her.

"Ye should have listened, lady." He shook his
head. "Now I'll have to be explaining why yer face is
marked. The laird will no' be liking it."

Coalan turned his back while still muttering beneath
his breath. Deirdre failed to suppress a smile at the
ridiculous nature of the moment.

She wasn't marked.

She lifted her hands and brushed her face, there
were only a few scrapes to testify she'd been shoved
into the ground. It was nothing at all. Unless she was
some English queen too tender for the Highlands. She
choked back a laugh as she considered Joan Beaufort
making her home with her new husband. It was for
certain the queen would like Deirdre's boots even
more once winter set in, no matter how ugly she
decided they were.

The inner yard was wide and filled with buildings.
What shocked Deirdre was the attention to aesthetics.
There were colored glass windows in the church, and
several large bells hung in its steeple. Built down the

center of the yard were wells. That surprised her, but it also sent a shiver down her back, because so many wells meant the castle was well supplied. The inhabitants might outlast any army besieging it.

The scent of flowers touched her nose, and she looked up to see long vines trailing down from the walls. Plants grew along the inside of the walls, like some castle she'd heard about in the Far East. A closer look at the plants revealed they were all fruit or vegetable bearing. With a continuous water supply, those plants would further help the castle outlast attackers. From the outside, no one would know they were growing food.

"Laird Cameron will be wanting to see ye straightaway. He'll be breaking his fast in the main hall."

Coalan led her mare to the far end of the castle. Men leaned over the wall to look at her, and women froze in their tracks as their mouths dropped open in surprise. More than one person lowered themselves as she passed, and guilt colored her cheeks. The queen had been correct; the clothing was convincing all that she was Joan Beaufort.

Quinton Cameron would know differently, though.

Her belly tightened, and her mood sobered. The confidence the queen had in Quinton releasing her wasn't keeping her from dreading the coming confrontation with the man. She cast another look around the castle yard and shivered because she was truly trapped inside it. Without the laird's permission to leave, she'd find getting past the gate difficult indeed.

"Here now. No need to look so concerned. The earl is a fair man."

Coalan's voice startled her. She'd been absorbed in her own thoughts and failed to notice the man dismounting. He reached up and grasped her waist before she finished focusing her attention back on the present.

There was concern etched into Coalan's face, and Deirdre pushed his hands away from her the moment she touched the ground, because she couldn't afford to weaken. The look in his eyes made it too simple to allow her own fear to grow, so she lifted her chin and shot him a harsh glare.

He stepped back with his hands in the air. He pressed his lips into a hard line. "And right happy I am to be delivering ye to him."

He reached out and clasped her bound hands. With a tug, he began to pull her up the stairs, but the length of her robes made her stumble since she couldn't use her hands to catch them up.

"I need my hands." Anger made her words come out too quickly to control her Scottish accent. Coalan frowned, suspicion brightening his eyes. Deirdre grabbed a hand full of silk velvet and climbed the stairs in front of him to escape from the scrutiny. She heard him snort before following her.

The hall had double doors that were open to allow the spring weather inside the stone room. The Camerons were not suffering a lack of profit for the hall was set with long tables that had plenty of food on them. The scent of bread, fresh from the oven, teased her nose. Her belly rumbled in response, but the sight of Quinton Cameron sitting at the high table distracted her from her hunger. His table was set up on a platform, and there was a carpet beneath it. Silver plateware sat on that table, and the Earl of Liddell drank from a silver goblet.

Quinton was deep in conversation with several of his captains, the pheasant feathers in their knit caps a clear symbol of their rank in a noblemen's house. But those eating at the lower tables began to whisper, and the noise spread quickly up the entire length of the hall until he looked up to investigate what the cause was.

Deirdre held her chin high, determined to stand steady. There was one thing she was sure of—Quinton Cameron would not see her shivering with dread.

Even if her belly was knotted with it.

Quinton Cameron placed his cup on the table in front of him. The boy assigned to the task of looking after his laird's drinking vessel had to climb partway onto the table to retrieve it, because Quinton was so focused on her. He planted his large hands on the surface of the table and stood up.

A shiver went down her back, but she stood firmly in place, refusing to allow the growing silence to make her buckle. The Cameron retainers grew pensive as they leaned forward to see what their laird had to say.

"Coalan, did she tell ye she is Joan Beaufort?"

Coalan turned his head toward her for a moment. Confusion appeared on his face while he considered his answer. Heat surfaced in her cheeks, but Deirdre did not lower her eyelashes.

"Coalan," Quinton growled from the high table. "Did she tell ye she is the queen?"

The Highlander turned to face his laird. "No, she did nae say it, but ye've only to look at her to see her clothing befits a queen."

"So it does," Quinton agreed, but his voice was hard.

"We found her with an English escort as well and a saddle fitted with gold tassels."

Deirdre felt every person in the hall assessing her. They stared at the rich velvet with its intricate trim sewn so carefully around the square neckline and sleeves. The pearls gleamed with the help of the morning light, and she saw several young girls eyeing the gems with envy. The gold signet band resting so lightly against her forehead drew the most attention.

"Bring her."

Deirdre flinched, because Quinton Cameron spoke with a solid authority that made it plain he ruled the clan that surrounded her. His retainers instantly responded to his order, reaching out to sweep her forward.

She brushed off their hands with a harsh hiss that earned her dark frowns. "I can walk very well."

In her agitation, her Scottish brogue began to reappear. Coalan looked suspicious, opening his mouth to ask her a question she didn't want to answer. Reaching down, she grabbed the front of the overgown and lifted it enough so she could follow Quinton. The man had disappeared through an arched doorway behind the high table.

His men followed closely, but they didn't touch her again. The arch led to a private solar, which was clearly the domain of the Earl of Liddell. Deirdre froze upon getting a look at the large chairs and weapons rack sitting in the room. The retainers behind her ran into her, sending her stumbling the last few paces.

"Leave us."

Deirdre raised her eyes from the floor to discover Quinton staring at her.

"And close the door, lads."

The skin on the inside of her wrist suddenly tingled. It was a horrible response to the man, and she lowered her eyelids to conceal it.

The door closed with a loud sound that sent her eyelids back up.

Quinton chuckled. "I was correct. Ye look quite fetching out of that nun's robe." His gaze traveled down her length, tracing the curves the court-fashioned robes outlined. Heat burned her cheeks instantly, and his eyes settled on the bright color for a long moment.

"I did nae tell yer men I was the queen."

He sat down in a huge chair with a high back that was carved with the shield of the noble title he bore. Even sitting down, the man's head was even with her own. It was unsettling, no matter how hard she tried to ignore it.

"I believe ye, but that does nae absolve ye of the sin of dishonesty. Ye allowed them to assume ye were the queen." He pointed at her. "And it's clear ye have seen Joan Beaufort, for ye are wearing her clothing."

He suddenly laughed. "But I find the idea of her wearing a bride of Christ's robe rather entertaining. It's for sure she has never worn something so humble before during her pampered life."

Deirdre smiled, able to appreciate the humor of the

situation. It was a mistake to let her guard down, for Quinton abandoned his lazy position the moment her lips curled.

"Ye're a fool to attach yerself to this mess, Deirdre Chattan. A bloody fool who does nae understand just how lucky ye are it was my men who found ye." He closed the distance between them and grasped her bound wrists. The morning light flashed off the polished blade of a dagger as he skillfully slid it beneath the leather binding her. A swift jerk cut through the loops, freeing her. He cupped her chin, forcing her to stare into his furious gaze.

"The Douglas would have slit yer throat in the hopes ye were the queen and killing ye would have ended any threat of her producing any more blue-blooded children."

She gasped, horror flooding her. "Stop it. Ye are just trying to reduce me to a woman who will cling to ye helplessly. Well, I will nae. I made the choice to help Joan Beaufort, and I'll no' be listening to ye about the wisdom of it."

"Well, ye sure as hell should, woman. Do ye honestly think the Douglas would nae have left ye to rot in a ditch?" His gaze lowered to the swells of her breasts, which were visible above the square neckline of the overrobe. "Mind ye, that would have been after they raped ye."

She shoved at his wide chest. "Get yer hands off me, brute! I do nae care if ye are an earl. Ye do nae have the right to handle me like some child who has displeased ye." She gained her freedom but stumbled over the train of the overrobe. She recovered quickly, turning in a swirl of velvet to face the man glaring at her. He was growling, and it touched something inside her that unleashed a need to stand up to him. She snarled in return.

Quinton's face registered surprise, but only for a moment before his eyes narrowed and his lips thinned in a purely sensual way. She felt a prickle of warning move through her, but it was also exciting. Part of her wanted to run, simply because she could see in his eyes his desire to chase her.

She was insane to think such a thing…

"How should I handle ye, Deirdre?" His voice was soft and menacing. "That robe is cut to flatter every part of ye so a man might admire yer curves." One of his dark eyebrows rose as he took a step toward her and then another one.

"It's lying smoothly over yer hips, showing me that my hands would fit perfectly around them."

"Stop it." She retreated, unable to stand firm when his eyes were glittering with promise.

"Ye should nae wear something so provocative, if ye do nae want the attention it was designed to capture." His gaze dropped to the neckline. "Yer breasts look plump, and I'm very interested in discovering how they feel against me palms."

Deirdre crossed her arms over her chest. It was a protective instinct, one she performed without considering how it might undermine her determination to face him boldly. "Ye're being crude just to injure my feelings. That's a coldhearted thing indeed. Is no' yer power enough for ye? Or do ye enjoy grinding yer heels on the backs of those who do nae have retainers to force ye to treat them decently?"

Fury tightened his features. "Ye dare a great deal with yer insults, Deirdre. Ye'd best be aware that Douglas would nae tolerate such from any woman, even the queen."

"Which is why she wanted to flee from him." Deirdre felt her sense of balance returning as the topic shifted away from what he thought of her figure. "Surely ye can agree it is better she is no longer near the lieutenant general to needle him with her lack of humility."

"Aye, I can." He eyed her from behind a guarded expression. "Do nae make the same mistake me men did, lass."

His voice was rich with warning, but she was too curious to not ask him what he meant.

"And what might that be?"

His eyes flashed with satisfaction. "To assume that because I agree with ye that it's better for the queen to be away from Archibald Douglas means I consider it right for ye to be involved in this mess."

Deirdre felt her eyes narrow. "Well then, I wish ye joy of yer discontentment with my action. Ye are nae the first man to feel such, but ye are nae my father, and I have no husband."

Quinton lifted a single finger between them. "Ah, very true. Which leaves the position of being yer lover open for me." His eyes flashed a warning at her once more. "Now does it nae?"

"It does nae." She informed him in a tone that made her grateful for the closed door. She didn't need any witnesses to carry tales to the priests. Quinton was an earl as well as laird of the Cameron. She'd end up on her knees for a solid week if the church heard her disrespectful voice.

That bit of knowledge only made her more determined to face the brute down. His position had spoiled him too much.

He laughed at her, the sound bouncing off the stone walls of the solar chamber. "Ye tempt me, Deirdre." He shook his head but unfolded his arms and spread them wide. "Ye cannae expect to play such a dangerous game without tasting a few bitter consequences."

The brute was trying to intimidate her. He loomed over her with his arms outstretched. It would have been simple for him to pounce, but she propped her hands on her hips and stood her ground. He couldn't chase her if she did not turn and run.

"If ye're saying that yer attempting to charm me into allowing ye to be my lover would be bitter, I agree. It would be distasteful indeed."

He chuckled, his teeth flashing through his lips. "Is that a fact, Deirdre?"

"A solid one in my opinion, Laird Cameron." She spit out his title in defiance of the way he was using her name so familiarly. Deirdre tossed her hair back over her shoulder and felt the silk veil flutter about her ears. "So I will be on my way."

Quinton masked his feelings once again behind a stony expression, but there was a flicker of determination in his eyes, which slashed at her confidence. Warning rippled down her spine once more in spite of her determination to remain unmoved by him. He was a powerful man, and no amount of confidence would help her overlook it.

"Will ye now?"

"I shall indeed leave yer land, sir, for there is naught here for me."

He turned his back on her, walking back toward the chair. The man didn't hurry, leaving her with the opportunity to do exactly as she had claimed she would.

Part of her was disappointed.

That knowledge stoked her temper, and she turned around to face the closed doors.

"I doubt Coalan will be allowing ye to leave."

Deirdre spun around so quickly that the velvet robes lifted to show her ankles. Quinton Cameron took the opportunity to notice, and a smug grin appeared on his lips, infuriating her.

"Since I am no' the queen, there is little point in yer men keeping me here."

Quinton grasped the arms of his chair and leaned forward, all traces of amusement gone from his expression. "Ah, but I'd have to be telling me men ye are in fact no' the queen."

He sat back and considered her. "I ken ye do nae know the ways of court, Deirdre Chattan, which is in yer favor. It's a place full of plots, ones that often claim the lives of innocents such as yerself. I've no doubt Joan pleaded her case well to ye. Ye're a kind lass to be helping out someone ye thought sincere."

Deirdre moved back toward the man. "She wants to wed again. I'd think since ye are a man, ye'd agree that is her place."

He slowly shook his head. "She's considered a co-ruler with the late king by too many countries."

"A king who is dead, and his son crowned, to the approval of all those same countries."

"But James II is her only son, and he's too young to wed," Quinton said quietly. His voice was low and deadly, drawing her forward a few more steps to make sure she didn't miss his next words.

"If something befalls that boy, there will be civil war. If his mother births sons for James Stewart, the black knight of Lorn, there will be many who say they should inherit."

A chill went down her back. "That does nae give anyone the right to lock her away or keep me here. The queen has permission from the pope to wed."

"Of course she does. The woman shares family connections with half the crowns of Europe." Quinton rose and stepped toward her. She was too fascinated by the look in his eyes to back away from him. Part of her wanted to know his reasons, more than she wanted to be cautious by retreating.

Quinton stopped in front of her and looked down from his greater height.

"The queen knows very well how to play the game of maintaining power. She was raised to be a queen, and this new marriage will ensure she reclaims a powerful position. There are powerful men intent on controlling her son. She was the captive guest of one of them at Stirling until a few weeks ago."

Deirdre gasped, shocked by the revelation. "She said naught of that."

Quinton grinned. "Of course she would nae, for ye are no' unintelligent." He studied her for a moment. "And ye favor her in too many ways. It was a stroke of luck that she encountered ye. I can see why she took advantage of the opportunity."

Deirdre didn't care for the way his words made her feel. "Ye men may be concerned about matters of politics with good cause, but it does nae change the fact that the queen is a woman who wants to live her life while she has the chance. I helped her because—"

"Because ye know what it's like to be used by men for the furtherment of their causes."

She snorted and moved away from him. "Ye do nae ken so very much about me, Laird Cameron."

When she looked back at him, he was watching her from the same spot, but there was a twinkle of something in his eyes again that warned her the man was making ready to be entertained by her once more.

"Well now, since ye'll be staying here in my home, lass, we'll be having the chance to learn more about one another," he announced with solid certainty.

"I will nae be staying."

His lips rose and parted in a smug expression of arrogance. His gaze traveled down her length once again, stopping at the hem of her overrobe with its trim pulled in several places from the rugged terrain of the Highlands.

"Well now. Those little slippers are suited to walking on Persian carpets, and no' much else."

Her feet agreed, renewing their complaints over how many sharp stones she had felt jabbing into her unprotected arches recently. Quinton raised his gaze to her face, and her throat contracted when she looked into his eyes. Determination blazed there.

"That velvet will nae keep ye warm in the spring

rains. I believe the queen is more comfortable in yer undyed nun's robe. Ye'll freeze if ye try and cross me land."

"I'll take my chances."

He lifted one finger between them again. "To do so, ye'll have to escape me men, and I ordered them after ye. I believe ye'll find they do what I say, because my orders are most often given for the benefit of every Cameron."

"Ye sent them after the queen, and I am nae who ye seek."

He waved his finger between them. "Ah, but ye allowed them to assume ye were the queen."

"A mistake easily revealed for what it was."

"Aye." He nodded agreement. "But me men are Highlanders, lass. They will nae be happy to hear ye duped them. In fact, I suspect they just might wait to hear from me on the matter of whether or no' ye are the one I wanted them to bring to me." His grin faded. "I doubt they will allow ye to depart until they have my word that ye may depart."

Shock held her in its grip. Words felt too large to force up her throat while she stared at the pleased expression on his face. She opened her mouth twice before managing to form her thoughts into words.

"Ye... ye must tell yer men I am no' who ye seek."

He turned his back on her. Deirdre watched as he returned to his chair and settled himself without a care for the way he was tormenting her.

"Ye must, Quinton."

"Ah... I enjoy hearing my name on yer lips." His expression became smug once more. "It's the truth I am looking forward to having ye here so we might get to know each other better."

"I will no' remain here." She shook her head and returned her hands to her hips.

"I cannae wait to see how ye plan to outwit me men, lass. Ye began this game, and I believe they will be happy to continue it so they might score a few points of their own. Highlanders do like to win."

"I'm from Highland stock myself, sir."

His eyes narrowed, and his attention slipped down her body once more. "Aye, lass, I've noticed that, more often than I should. There are no women like the ones who live in the Highlands. Ye have more than yer share of boldness, and I find it captivating enough to tell ye I shall nae make it simple for ye to ride out of here into the hands of men who might slit yer creamy throat."

"Ye do nae have the right to keep me here."

He stood up and came toward her. Deirdre didn't retreat, but it wasn't because her pride demanded she stand and confront him.

It was worse than that. She felt desperation clawing at her as the walls of Drumdeer seemed to be collapsing inward.

"I will nae clear the way for ye to leave, Deirdre. That is my final word on the matter."

He stroked the back of his hand across one side of her face. It was such a simple touch, and yet its tenderness stole her breath. So pleasing, in every way. Somehow, she'd forgotten how good it felt to be touched.

She gasped and made to step away from his touch.

"Quinton—"

He leaned down and sealed her protest beneath his lips. He cupped her nape, pulling gently so her face rose and his kiss might become bolder. She jerked, shaking her head to break the connection, but he moved as fast as a leather whip, twisting along with her as his other hand slipped over the curve of her hip and settled on the flat of her lower back to hold her in place.

She moaned, a tiny sound of panic, because she expected his kiss to turn savage. He soothed her nape with a slow stroke, but he did not release her. His mouth moved against hers, pressing her to open her jaw until she yielded. He deepened the kiss but didn't thrust his tongue inside her mouth as she expected. Instead he teased her lips with his own, tasting her mouth like he might a fine glass of French wine.

She began drowning in sensation. Her senses were too full of him for her thoughts to penetrate. She raised her hands to push him away, but her fingers became too aware of how hard his body was beneath his clothing.

How could a man feel so good to only her fingertips?

Her heart was racing, and along with it, her lungs labored to pull more air into her chest. The scent of his skin flooded her senses, threatening to send another moan past their joined lips, because she enjoyed his scent.

She mustn't…

Deirdre struggled against the overwhelming surge of enjoyment, pushing against his chest while she ducked her head to separate their lips. The tender skin of her mouth was too alive with desire for her to retain any grip on rational thoughts. She struggled out of instinct and the need to maintain herself. If she failed, she'd melt into his embrace without a care for where she might land when he finished taking his pleasure from her flesh.

"I will nae be yer slut!" Her voice was frantic, as were her attempts to twist from his grip. He snarled something beneath his breath before she felt his grip slacken. She took instant advantage, stumbling across the floor as she flung herself away from him as fast as she could.

"I swear it, Quinton. So tell yer men to let me leave, because I will nae warm yer bed."

His eyes were bright with desire. "Ye enjoyed my kiss. So do nae act as though warming my bed would displease ye so greatly, woman."

It was true.

Deirdre drew herself up, forcing her mind to resume rational thought. She refused to think about how much her lips wanted to return to having his upon them. She shook her head to dispel the sensations of yearning that were pulsing through her.

Quinton growled at her, "Ye kissed me back, Deirdre Chattan, so do nae be crying that ye didna."

"Only one more reason why I am intent on leaving. The queen has promised me a place in her service, and I will take it because there will be no men to try their hand at using me."

He laughed at her. His ice blue eyes sparkling with amusement. "Ye've a thing or two to learn about court, lass. There will be plenty of men trying their hand at seducing ye with the hope ye will mutter important facts while they are muddling yer wits with their cocks."

He was being blunt on purpose. But she saw his harsh words as more of a challenge, one she had no intention of failing.

"Ye see? There is the reason why I am intent on departing. Men think of women as nothing but things to be used. Yer coarse words prove it." She glared at him. "Ye will take yer pleasure exactly as Melor Douglas did, and scorn me when ye are finished."

Quinton frowned, his amusement vanishing. He considered her from narrowed eyes.

"I do nae care for being compared to Melor Douglas."

He was furious too. Deirdre heard it in his voice and witnessed it on his face.

"Then tell yer men I am nae the one ye wanted brought to ye, for I will nae ever think of any man differently than I do Melor Douglas. Best I am gone from here, and soon."

The chamber was silent, but Deirdre would have sworn she could hear him grinding his teeth with frustration. She felt the tension across the space between them, or maybe it was her own unhappiness that made it seem like each second lasted forever. He suddenly moved, startling her because she was so absorbed with the emotions swirling around inside her. He walked past her and reached for one of the double doors his men had closed to give them privacy.

Deirdre had to force a lump down her throat, because victory was bitter indeed.

"Thank ye." The pair of words was torn from her desperation.

He turned his head and looked at her over his shoulder. "Yer tone almost makes me regret I will nae allow ye to leave." He pulled the door open. "But no' quite."

The moment his laird appeared, Coalan lifted his head up from where he was eating. The man was on his feet, along with the other captains who had been sitting with Quinton when she arrived.

"Ye've done well, Coalan. I'm pleased. Greatly so."

Deirdre was stunned into silence. The Camerons sitting at the long trestle tables filling the hall all stared at her. But what horrified her more was the way they nodded. Approval of their laird's actions spread through them like fire did in a summer field. The women serving the tables stopped to mutter to one another while they looked at her. Children pointed at her, and their mothers leaned down to explain who she was.

But she wasn't the queen.

Quinton Cameron strode down the center aisle and out into the yard without another look at her. His captains followed him, and the retainers left their benches too. The hall soon became filled with the sound of dishes being cleared and women chatting now that the rush of seeing the morning meal set down was over.

"Would ye sit and eat, lady?"

Deirdre jerked around to discover a woman no older than herself standing behind her. She smiled in welcome and lowered herself.

"I do nae deserve such deference."

The girl frowned but straightened. "Well, ye certainly look as though ye do."

Deirdre lifted her hands and looked down at the velvet she wore. "I was given these robes to wear; they belong to the queen."

"Well then, I admit I envy ye the opportunity to feel such things against yer skin." The girl grinned as though they were friends and shared such little conversations regularly. "I am Maura; Coalan is me brother. Come and eat. Coalan ate like a starving wolf, so I can guess ye are famished as well."

"I am." Deirdre sent one last look toward the open doors but forced herself to be practical. She would not get far on an empty belly. Maura set off and returned with a tray containing a bowl with steam rising from it. She set it on the table nearest where Deirdre stood and left a cup of fresh morning milk as well.

"There's plenty, so eat yer fill."

Deirdre's belly rumbled, and Maura laughed before she turned to clear the table where she had set Deirdre's meal. The Cameron girl left behind a broken round of bread and a small wooden bowl of butter. For how early in spring it was, it was a fine morning meal. The Camerons had clearly not suffered from a poor harvest the year before. The cereal had chunks of autumn apples, and she smiled in spite of her frustration over where she was eating.

It was still sweet and warm, and only a shrew would have frowned with such a meal set before her.

Whispers still touched her ears as the women working in the hall cast curious looks at her. Deirdre forced herself to eat slowly, because she didn't need Maura running to tell her brother that Deirdre looked to be in a hurry.

Even if she was.

If Quinton didn't order his men to keep her inside the castle gates, she doubted they would notice her leaving. Drumdeer was a busy place, and spring a time for hurrying as the fields were turned for planting. She finished her meal and looked at the uneaten bread with longing, but left it on the table. There were too many watching her for her to risk taking it, even if she knew it would be a welcome comfort on the road.

With or without the bread, she was going. The yard was a bustle of activity. Wagons were being unloaded, and the sound of men shouting to one another echoed between the stone walls. Water was being pulled from the wells, and many of the buckets were dumped into long wooden troughs that flowed toward the kitchens.

People made way for her, and she frowned because the queen's clothing made a spectacle of her. In the morning light, the silk velvet looked like it was glowing. The stables were along the far end of the castle, and a young lad ran up to her the moment she appeared in the doorway.

"What do ye seek, lady?"

Deirdre swallowed her distaste for the noble title. "My mare, if ye would be so kind."

The boy looked confused. "Ye sound like a Scot."

"Do nae be running yer mouth with the lady, lad," an older man barked at the boy, who reached up to tug on the corner of his knit bonnet. "I'll be back with yer mare quick."

In fact, three lads wearing the Cameron yellow, orange, and black plaid brought her mare forward. They had it saddled in a flash because they all dropped what they were doing to attend to her request.

Guilt chewed on her once more. She didn't care for others thinking she was above them. But she took the reins when they were offered, because she wanted to be away more than she wished to be completely honest with them.

"Mount up, lads."

Coalan's voice was deep and brassy. "Yer mistress appears to be ready to take her morning ride."

Deirdre turned to discover the Highlander smirking at her, while six retainers went to different stalls to saddle their stallions.

"What are ye doing?" she asked.

One of the man's eyebrows rose. "It's strange how ye seem to have found yer voice now."

Deirdre bristled. "Ye never asked me whose daughter I was."

She heard his knuckles pop as he gripped his belt too tightly. "No, I didna, and 'tis a fact I am still no' asking ye."

"I am Robert Chattan's daughter," she informed him.

The retainers returned and looked at her with confusion on their faces. Coalan shrugged.

"Well now. I didna hear my laird saying anything about yer name making any difference on whether or no' ye were the one he asked me to bring to him." There was a glint of heat in his eyes and stubbornness. The man was set on giving her grief, and that was a fact.

Deirdre set one hand on her hip and faced him. She wasn't the queen, and she would not be intimidated by his bruised temper. Her own brothers were Highlanders, after all.

"Ye know I am nae the woman he sent ye after. So be gone. I am no' the woman yer laird sought. I am no' even a noble who might be of some use to him because someone would pay a ransom for me. For certain ye have more important things to attend to than a common Highlander girl."

There was a flash of surprise in his eyes and then a slight curving of his lips that showed he was impressed with her ability to stand up to his growling.

"Well now. I don't know how it is on Chattan land, but we Cameron do nae think what our laird sets us to doing is less important than anything else. Do we, lads?"

There were several mutters of agreement from the men making ready to ride with her. A few of them were smirking, obviously thinking it very fitting that she wasn't gaining what she wished.

"Yer laird sent ye after Joan Beaufort. I am no' her. Perhaps ye should go and find her if ye are so concerned with pleasing yer laird."

The damned man refused to do anything but grin at her rising frustration. His companions all followed his example and stood firmly in place to accompany her.

"Enough of this nonsense. I will be on my way."

"And we shall give ye good escort," Coalan announced. A stable lad brought him his stallion while the brute smiled at her.

Deirdre glared at Coalan and the amusement he was

failing to hide. "I do nae require escort, as I just told ye I am no one of importance at all. Yer laird would nae be wanting one of his captains wasting time on one such as me."

She lifted her foot and fit it into the stirrup. She gasped when Coalan lifted her up and sat her on the back of the mare.

"I do nae need assistance."

Coalan mounted, and his stallion danced sideways as it took his weight. He leaned down to rub the animal's neck to soothe it.

"Well now, lady. I'm bound to serve my laird."

"It is no different on Chattan land," she insisted. "That has naught to do with this ridiculous notion that I require an escort."

Coalan cocked his head to the side. "She sounds like a noble lady to me, lads."

They chuckled and nodded, irritating her beyond belief.

"I do nae want ye riding with me," she stated loud enough to have the grooms looking around their stalls at her.

"Then ye will nae be riding... lady," Coalan announced. "That's yer choice sure enough, because me laird told me he was pleased with the woman I brought him. So ye will nae be riding out of the gate without me and my men. That's a promise."

Firm and hard, his voice left no doubt in her mind. Deirdre looked at the faces of the other retainers and felt a noose tightening around her neck. She ground her teeth, but there would be no riding out of the gate while these men were determined to hound her.

She slid off the mare and walked from the stable while chewing on the words she wanted to fling at them.

Coalan was not her true target. It was Quinton Cameron, and she had something to say to the arrogant man for sure.

But she was afraid to do so.

That was a shame that darkened her cheeks as she walked with no true destination. She hated admitting she was afraid of anything, but being alone with Quinton terrified her. The man unleashed a weakness inside her that she couldn't seem to control. Maybe she was right to fear him and his effect on her. Wasn't that the way of life? You conformed and obeyed because you feared the consequences.

Indeed, she feared the way she melted beneath the man's touch. It was a deep shame, one she detested, but she had to be honest and admit it to herself. If she weren't, she'd be in his bed before the week passed.

Never again…

The words she promised herself rose from the memory of the pain Melor had inflicted upon her. She refused to feel so strongly about any man, even if it was only lust. Quinton wouldn't have that power over her; she would make sure he didn't have the opportunity to touch her.

She stopped and looked about. Her steps had carried her far from the stables, but a look over her shoulder showed her Coalan pointing at her from the walkways at the top of the curtain wall. The men standing on duty there lifted their hands to shield their eyes so they might see her more clearly.

That tight feeling about her throat returned.

But at least it distracted her from her fear. She'd rather be irritated than afraid.

"Were ye looking for the bathhouse, lady?"

Deirdre turned to see a woman looking at her from the bottom of a stairway.

"It is down here."

The woman extended her hand toward a doorway set behind her. The stairs were made of stone, and as she descended them, they grew colder because the sunlight had yet to warm them. The thin slippers allowing her to feel the deepening chill. The sound of water grew stronger when she reached the bottom and stood in the doorway.

"Armelle, the lady has come to bathe."

"My name is Deirdre Chattan, and I am no lady."

The girl looked unsure and turned her attention to the older woman standing near the large hearth that took up one of the walls. A ring with keys on it hung from her apron, declaring her a woman of importance. Those keys would unlock the more valuable items used in the bathhouse, and she would be held responsible if anything went missing. She had her hair wrapped in strips of cloth to keep every last strand out of her face. There were wrinkles around her eyes marking her years, but her gaze was keen and sharp.

"Well, ye look like a lady to me," Armelle announced. Her words had instant effect on the women who worked beneath her command. They moved off toward one of the corners and pulled a large cloth off something. Armelle nodded approvingly at them as they lifted a large tub and carried it into the middle of the room. The woman who had greeted her pulled the door closed for privacy.

"I can well imagine ye would be longing for a bath after being on the road."

The other maids were already filling the tub with water. A wooden spillway ran along one side of the room, and Deirdre realized that water must be running down to it from the trough she'd seen in the yard. A rope hung from the wall, and one of the girls gave it a sharp tug. A moment later, water began to flow from an open slot in the wall.

"We've plenty of water here."

Deirdre couldn't contain the smile that raised her lips. "I will be grateful for a good washing, but I can see to the chore myself." She bent down to pick up a bucket, only to have Armelle step into her path.

"Ye'll ruin all that fine silk. My girls will fill yer tub and see to the chores, lady."

"Please do no' call me by such a noble title. I told ye, I'm a Chattan."

Armelle nodded. "I heard ye full well. Ye be the daughter of a laird and a friend of the queen, else ye would nae be wearing her finery." The older woman flicked her fingers, and Deirdre felt the delicate touch of two of the girls as they began to lift the silk veil off her head.

"But I am no' a lady."

Armelle clicked her tongue, the subtle reprimand making Deirdre close her mouth in deference to the woman's longer years. Even a noble lady respected a woman who had lived as long as Armelle had, for there was something the older woman was doing correctly. Anyone younger would be wise to listen when in her presence.

"The laird said he was pleased to have ye brought to him, greatly so." Armelle gestured to the girls once more, and they began to unlace the back of the over-robe. "My laird does nae say things he no' means."

The older woman turned and dipped her hand into the tub to test the water temperature. The girl tending the fire watched her, waiting for the bath mistress to indicate if she wanted more hot water from one of the large copper kettles hanging over the fire on iron hooks.

A soft snap of Armelle's fingers sent the girl reaching for a hook that she used to pull one of those pots out of the hearth. She lifted the pot with the hook and walked toward the waiting tub.

"We've fine rosemary soap to make yer hair smell sweet."

The hot water hissed as it poured over the edge of the pot. The women behind her lifted the overgown up and over her head.

"What is amiss with yer leg?"

Armelle proved her worth as the mistress of the bathhouse when she noticed the dark stain marring the underrobe. Deirdre had believed the woman to be watching the bathtub, but she had her attention fixed on her right thigh.

"Well… I do no' recall…"

Her memory offered up a hazy recollection of the pain that had assaulted her after Coalan had thrown her to the ground. She'd dismissed it as nothing more than bruising, but the stain went all the way to the floor, proving she had bled quite a bit.

Armelle reached for the overrobe, running her fingers down the side of it until she found a slice. When the garment was hanging down the length of the body, the plush fabric disguised it.

"Someone cut ye with a blade."

It wasn't a question, but a firm statement. The women took her underrobe from her, and the girl at the fire gasped. The wound was ugly and larger than Deirdre would ever have thought.

"That should have been stitched," Armelle declared as she leaned closer to inspect it. "But it is too late now. Ye'll have a mark from it."

"I'm nae vain."

Deirdre lifted her good leg over the rim of the tub and sat down in the water before she truly tested the temperature. Standing nude in front of the other women was wearing on her nerves. But she surged back up out of the water when it touched the wound on her thigh. Pain slashed through her, and her knees buckled, sending her back into the water.

She gasped again, unable to stop tears from flooding her eyes. The pain was excruciating. It robbed her of any thoughts except enduring the agony.

"Breathe, lady. It will help ye work through the pain."

She did as Armelle directed, unable to think of anything herself. The first breath felt like a lump being forced down her throat, but the second was easier. The pain did begin to subside as she felt someone remove the gold signet from her forehead. But she gasped again as she felt the women begin to wash her.

"I do nae need assistance."

A snap from Armelle's fingers drew an irritated

look from Deirdre. The older woman sent her a stern look.

"If ye are Laird Chattan's daughter, ye'll mind me, for ye would have been taught to respect yer elders."

And if she had been a lady, she would expect such service, even during her bath. Deirdre ground her teeth but remained silent while the women washed her. They used sea sponges and the rosemary soap Armelle brought from a locked chest. More water was brought to rinse her hair, and the soap was worked through the wet strands before being washed away.

All the while the wound on her leg ached. The hot water irritated it, but Deirdre took a square of linen and rubbed at it to clean it.

Armelle left while the girls finished her hair, and they had her wrapped in a length of linen before the bath mistress returned. She was followed by another older woman and a younger girl carrying a small box.

"Sit down and allow Tully to care for that wound."

Tully waited until Deirdre had sat down before moving the linen aside. She drew in a stiff breath before gesturing her box closer.

"That's a right nasty slice. How did it happen?"

Tully was digging through the contents of her box while she asked, but she lifted her head when Deirdre failed to answer. Coalan might be an arrogant brute, but she was not going to turn into a whining noble lady and name him as the culprit. She would take the wound as her earnings for not making a better escape attempt. She was born of Highland stock, after all; she could take a slice as well as any woman in the bathhouse.

"It does nae matter, 'tis no so bad."

Tully scoffed at her. "Well, I'll say this. Ye are nae a weakling, else ye'd be happy to name the man who did that to ye."

She pulled out a small bundle of cloth and removed the tie. It smelled musty, but she sprinkled it over the wound, and Deirdre felt it begin to sting. Tully took another length of fabric and wound it around her thigh to cover the wound.

"Sleep bare and leave the binding off so the air can help keep it from festering."

There was a giggle from one of the maids, which drew a stern look from Tully. "Mind yer judgmental thinking, girl. When it comes to wounds, ye'll do as I say or risk a fever. Better sleeping in the skin God gave ye than burning when infection sets in. 'Twould be a shame to cut that hair off her head."

The room became silent in response. Tully inspected the binding one final time.

"And stay off that mare of yers until it's sealed."

"But—"

"A fortnight at least," Tully insisted. "Heed me, lady, or I'll be talking to the laird, for I'll be the one he calls to tend ye when yer skin begins to flush."

"I'll mind ye," Deirdre said quickly. "I'm sure yer laird has important matters to spend his time on. I am no' a lady and do nae expect others to look after me."

She stood up to prove her point. "But I thank ye for tending to the wound. I've no desire to suffer the fever."

It was a true thing to fear. Infection killed. Deirdre swallowed her distaste over sleeping nude; she'd worry about that when the sun set.

The women came to dress her, but they were holding more of the queen's silk and velvet robes. Armelle truly was a keen mistress of her position, for she must have sent the girls off to find the clothing while Deirdre was being washed.

"Please, is no' there anything else for me to wear? I do nae own those costly garments."

"The queen gave them to ye, so that makes it right ye should wear them," Armelle declared with a firm nod.

"But they have no place here."

The bath mistress grinned and gestured her staff forward. "We've a fine woman's solar that is outfitted well for a lady. The laird bid yer escort to take ye there once ye are ready."

"My escort?"

A soft underrobe fluttered down her body. Deirdre was glad to be covered again, but she glared at Armelle. The older woman stood firmly in the face of her displeasure.

"Aye. I left them outside and warned them no' to step foot in this bathhouse. It is nae a place for men."

The bath mistress walked over to the stained underrobe. "This will need soaking and mending. We've some silk thread in the solar that will serve nicely."

"Is nae the solar for the laird's wife and sisters?"

"Aye," Armelle answered. "But his only sister is away serving the lady of Portsmith, and the laird has no wife." A gleam entered her eyes that set Deirdre's temper alight once more.

"Well, I am nae intended to wed the man, so there is no need to take me to the solar. That's the place for his betrothed."

Armelle shrugged. "Well now, the laird has nae got one of those either, no' since the last one he contracted ran away the night her father told her of the match." Armelle scanned her up and down before giving a satisfied nod. "Ye look like ye belong in the solar. All that fine clothing is nae fit for the yard; that is for certain."

"Armelle, ye are a competent mistress here. Surely ye can find me some robes that are more suitable to whose daughter I am."

The woman's face became a mask of deep consideration for a long moment. "I'll wait to hear from the laird if he's wanting me to do that."

The bath mistress gestured toward the doors, and Deirdre felt a rush of air as they were opened.

"It was a pleasure serving ye, lady."

Armelle lowered herself, and every girl working in the bathhouse followed her example. Deirdre turned around and walked toward the door in spite of the fact that one of Coalan's men stood there.

It would seem she was going to the solar.

Four

"THE SOLAR IS IN THE EAGLE TOWER."

Coalan was still too amused by her plight for her comfort, but Deirdre followed him because she simply didn't have any better idea.

"It's the tallest one, and ye'll have a fine view of the land beyond the castle walls."

"All that much better to torment me with seeing what I cannae touch... is that it, Coalan?"

The Highlander shrugged. "All that much better to surround ye with strength and protection. That's what women enjoy."

"No' this woman. I would have ye turn yer back and let me be."

"I would no' do such a thing since me laird has nae told me that ye are no' the woman he wanted brought to him. Turning me back would dishonor the feathers in me bonnet and no mistake about that."

Coalan lost his teasing demeanor. Deirdre stiffened, because she knew the look; it was one she'd learned to respect throughout her childhood. She'd offended the man's sense of honor, and he was a Highlander.

She was neatly caught in her own web of deception, without a doubt.

She sighed. "Show me to the solar."

The man looked disappointed instead. He stood with his fingers curled around the wide leather belt that held his plaid around his waist. "I thought ye claimed to be of Highlander stock."

"I am, and do nae be thinking I'm crying defeat, man. I just cannae think of anything else to say at this moment, and I was raised to respect men like ye who consider honoring their laird more important than what they think. So lead on, or get yerself off someplace else so I can get on with doing what I need to be about. I understand honor because I have me own, and yer laird is standing in the way of my doing what I should."

He snorted, but his lips lifted slightly. "I believe ye are Chattan's daughter; no English princess would have such a solid spine or grasp of the Highland way. It's possible the laird has the right thinking in keeping ye."

It was a compliment she wasn't happy to receive, because she didn't want to hear any of Quinton's retainers saying it was good idea for her to remain inside the castle. Her ideas of escape were strangling on the approval she witnessed in Coalan's eyes.

So she turned and began walking. She heard a sound from the man behind her but didn't look back to see what expression was on his face.

"This way, lady. It's in the eagle tower."

Deirdre fought back the urge to flinch. Eagles nested higher than any other bird of prey. The fact that the solar was placed in a tower with such a name promised her yet another obstacle to overcome before she was free.

She wanted to snarl with frustration. But at least that was better than feeling defeated as she began to cross the yard. She could feel the gazes of the curious again. The eagle tower was on the far side of the castle, the one facing the steepest drop off.

Of course it was. Such was the most protected corner of the fortification. It rose into the air, with the aid of arches and buttresses to reinforce its structure. But it wasn't merely built with strength in mind. There were decorative touches added above the doorways, stonework with leaves and vines curling around the thick blocks designed to withstand siege weapons such as trebuchets. Inside, the air was still cool from the night, confirming the stone was thick.

The stairs were narrow and wound in a spiral up the sides of the tower. The floor above them hid how many there were. Her leg began to burn before she made it to the first floor. But she continued to climb, suddenly having more pity for the queen. Being imprisoned inside a castle was a grim fate.

Well, there was some good that had come of her actions. Deirdre forced herself to dwell on the fact that Joan Beaufort was no longer locked up. She would believe that the queen was happily with her intended groom, because she didn't think she could bear knowing all their effort had been for naught.

"It's a fine solar. The laird had it furnished when he was negotiating for his bride."

"Then it's for sure I have no place stepping foot into it."

Coalan's voice trailed off, and he frowned. "Maybe that was nae the best way to explain…"

"It was well enough, and I am correct. The solar is for yer laird's bride, no' me."

The Cameron retainer extended his arm and pushed in the door in front of them. He didn't make any move to enter, as the area was considered a woman's domain.

"Well, lady, there is no place else suited to yer clothing or that can be secured as well."

She turned large eyes toward him. "Ye mean to set yer men to guarding me?"

He inclined his head, and she looked past him to see two of the Cameron retainers climbing the stairs behind them. Her throat tightened, but her temper ignited.

"This is taking injured pride too far."

He stared her straight in the eye as his men reached the landing behind him. "Serving me laird is something I will nae compromise on. He said he was pleased with ye being here, so ye shall be here when he goes looking for ye."

Damned Highlander.

She wasn't sure if she was cursing Coalan or Quinton, but it applied to both, in her opinion. Deirdre stepped into her prison. She never heard the door close, because her mind was busy trying to understand what her eyes showed her.

The entire floor was furnished with every possible luxury a woman might desire.

Or she should say… noble lady. The solar would have pleased even Joan Beaufort.

There were true Persian carpets laid out carefully

on the floor. They were woven with bright colors
and intricate patterns. For the first time, her feet felt
good, with the carpets cushioning each step. Someone
had opened the shutters, and fresh spring air filled the
room. It took more than thirty paces to cross it.

There were benches set beneath the windows, with
plump pillows added to their hard tops. The pillows
didn't soften the view from the windows. To any
other, the sweeping scene of newly turned fields and
green hills would have been bliss. She found it horrible,
because it was everything she could not touch.

With a sigh, she returned to looking around the
solar. It was outfitted for a bride. A small tapestry
loom stood near one window, a large box of colored
thread standing ready for a noblewoman to begin
weaving intricate pictures with it to be displayed in
the main hall.

She passed by it and stopped at another table. This
one was wider and longer. Stacked neatly beside it
were bundles. Reaching out, she fingered one coarse
sackcloth covering. Beneath it was fine fabric, the
shade of the summer sky. There were numerous
bundles, some thicker than others, and a box with
its lid lifted to reveal sewing tools. She couldn't resist
touching one fingertip to the shiny surface of the scis-
sors. They were made of silver and looked razor sharp.

She moved past the sewing area and stopped in front
of two musical instruments. There was a five-stringed
lyre set into a stand that had obviously been made for
it. The bow hung nearby, ready for an accomplished
bride to begin showing off the skills she had been
studying in order to please her noble husband.

Such was the way of the nobility. Deirdre moved to stand in front of the harp, watching the way the sunlight shone off the strings. Quinton had spared no expense in making sure the solar befitted his bride. There were six Scottish princesses who would need husbands, and it was possible he was negotiating for one of them.

Deirdre frowned once more.

Why did she feel disappointed?

She had no right to be melancholy simply because she could see the proof of the fact that Quinton wanted a blue-blooded wife. The man was an earl, and his family had not earned such a position by marrying for affection.

But he'd kissed her so passionately...

She was a fool to dwell on such things.

She snorted at herself and turned her back on the musical instruments. Indeed, she was acting the fool. She'd had good cause to push the man away. He wanted bed sport from her, sure enough, but that would be all. The best she might hope for was she'd ripen with his bastard, and it would be a boy whom Quinton would recognize. She'd gain some small alliance from him and a place to live.

It wasn't the worse fate that might befall her.

She chewed on her lip and went to the open window once more. Her future was with the queen. Even if Quinton's kiss made her long to discover what it was like to lie with the man, she had no right to bring a child into the world who would forever be branded with her sin. Bastard was a harsh title to bear.

As difficult as being a fallen woman.

She sighed and muttered a prayer of gratitude for her safe journey. Quinton's words rose up from where she had pushed them away while arguing with him. But the man was correct. There were men who would have slit her throat if they had captured her first. The wound on her leg served as a blunt reminder of just how simple it might be to have her flesh cut.

So she would be grateful, but she would also stare at the fine things in the solar and remind herself what yielding to Quinton's kiss would gain her—nothing but sharing her shame with an innocent child. She refused to do such a thing. She might be a fallen woman, but the stain was hers to bear.

❧

Quinton looked up. Coalan didn't flinch beneath the glare he sent toward the man, which restored his humor, but only slightly so.

"Are ye here to argue against the duty I set ye on?"

His man bristled. Quinton pushed himself back from the desk where he was sitting.

"Forgive me, Coalan. Being forced to deal with this endless pile of documents sours my disposition."

Coalan nodded but there was still a hint of discontentment glittering in his eyes. The man was one of his most trusted captains, and he didn't take his dedication to duty being questioned lightly. But he shrugged after a moment.

"Are ye sure it isna the lady needling ye, Laird? I hear they can have that effect on men."

Quinton grunted. "Aye, ye're right about that." He

pressed his hands flat on the top of his desk. "Where is our lovely lady?"

"In the solar, is that no' where those tapestry slipper shoes belong?"

"Aye, it is." Quinton straightened up, fighting the urge to turn and look across the yard at the eagle tower. It wouldn't do to have his men see him acting like a beardless lad who couldn't keep his eyes off a fair lass.

"So why are ye here, Coalan?"

"The lady asked for simpler clothing."

Quinton grinned. "Did she now? What would that accomplish, except to make it a fair bit easier for her to walk out of our gates?"

His man returned his grin, a knowing gleam entering his eyes. Quinton straightened.

"Thank ye for bringing the matter to me. The lady will continue to be robed in clothing that suits her station. I certainly would nae be wanting to offend the queen by doing any less."

"Nae we would nae want to something like that," Coalan agreed. "I put a couple of lads outside the door."

His captain was waiting to see what Quinton thought of his action. For a moment, he contemplated why he liked hearing that Deirdre Chattan was being prevented from leaving his castle.

But he only got as far as admitting that he did enjoy knowing for sure she was secure and protected, something that wouldn't last long if she was given the opportunity to try to join Joan Beaufort. Deirdre was stubborn and determined, and as much as those qualities annoyed him, they also drew him to her.

He wanted to investigate why.

"Well done. Give her every courtesy, but do nae make the mistake of thinking her fragile. That female is clever and born of Highland stock."

"As ye say, Laird."

With a tug on the corner of his knit bonnet, Coalan turned in a swirl of Cameron plaid and left. Quinton barely heard the man's steps on the stairs, which made him smile with satisfaction.

Coalan was a Highlander, sure enough. Unlike the Douglas, there wasn't a man wearing the feathers of a captain at Drumdeer who wasn't the best with a sword, bow, or tracking. Quinton smirked, and unlike the lieutenant general, he had no intention of turning to fat because everyone around the man coddled his ego. Archibald Douglas might have charge of the young King James II, but he would be wise to watch his back, for there were plenty who coveted his position.

Quinton turned and crossed to an open window. He looked at the eagle tower but couldn't see Deirdre. He smiled anyway, the knowledge that she was in the solar pleasing him.

"Well now, Mistress Chattan. We'll see which of us outwits the other first. 'Tis a battle I'm looking forward to, and that's a promise."

❧

The nuns had done her more of a favor in their efforts to overload her with work than Deirdre realized. Having too much to do was far better than having nothing to keep her from thinking about things she was better off not considering.

Like Quinton Cameron.

She walked around the lady's solar, still unable to touch any of the fine things in it. But she feared she might go mad before the sun was even straight above her, so she walked to the other side of the solar where books were carefully stored against a section of wall that had no windows. There were not even arrow slits that rain might seep in through to damage the costly paper pages. There were volumes on falconry and sonnets, but what drew her attention most were the two books on scripture. She pulled one gently from its place and opened it to the first page.

It was engrossing, but also dangerous. The church didn't care for any books that argued about matters of faith. She couldn't help but grin as she returned to reading it. Quinton Cameron was a devil, and no mistake. He'd placed those books there with his own hands, unless she missed her guess. It was a small taste of the fact that he was not a man easily frightened by the warnings of others. He was bold and wanted his bride to know what to expect from him.

His kiss had given her a taste of that as well…

She snorted and returned to reading while the day passed. It was surreal in a way, for she had never been allowed to be lazy in her father's home.

But her belly quivered as she anticipated spending the night beneath a roof Quinton owned. She found herself listening to every sound the tower made, wondering if it was him appearing to press his desire.

She was foolish to believe she might draw the man's attention away from more important matters.

But that did not make it any less true.

❦

"Lady?"

Deirdre jumped, startled to hear another voice. The pages crinkled as she closed her hand too tightly around the book she was reading. The young girl who waited near the doorway hurried forward to take it away before it was damaged further. She smoothed the pages before gently closing the book and placing it back on the shelf with a small sound of relief.

"Oh… forgive me, lady… I was sent to fetch ye to supper."

"I am no' a lady. My name is Deirdre Chattan."

The girl nodded. "Aye, I heard such already."

Of course she had; the bathhouse girls had no doubt been pestered for the better part of the day for details on everything Deirdre had said and done that morning. Her cheeks colored as she considered that her body had no doubt been discussed as well. Every castle had one thing in common—their inhabitants enjoyed gossip.

The girl smiled brightly. "The laird bid me bring ye to the high table. He's holding the blessing for yer arrival."

Deirdre felt her temper stir. "The laird sent ye for me? How kind. I did nae know the men guarding that door would allow me outside."

"Oh, they will, and they will stay with ye if ye choose to go about the castle. Ye are no' a prisoner."

Deirdre bristled, her opinion of the situation very different. Suspecting Coalan and his men were watching her wasn't as bad as having it confirmed. The girl lowered herself and extended one arm toward the open door.

Oh… the laird was waiting for her, was he?

"I am too fatigued to appear at the high table. Please extend my apologies to yer laird."

"Ye are?" the girl asked without thinking. She covered her mouth with her hand when she realized she had spoken her thoughts.

"Well… of course… reading takes skill… no wonder ye're tired…"

Deirdre paced back and forth while the girl tried to agree with her. It was clear the Cameron maid didn't think reading would tire anyone. Deirdre itched to march into the hall and tell Quinton Cameron what he might do with his insistence that she be treated like a lady.

But the man was laird at Drumdeer.

That was something she'd do well to remember when her temper was hot. Confronting him in public would no doubt earn her the scorn of his people along with the judgment of the church. As a noble, she'd be expected to respect the fact that God had placed him above her. She might find herself doing time in the stocks for disrespecting him.

"Would ye show me to where I'll be sleeping and maybe fetch me a bit of something to eat?" Deirdre forced her tone to be sweet. "I'd be in yer debt."

"Aye… I'd be happy to serve ye… the others are speculating who ye will choose to be yer lady's maid. I'm Amber, and I've been serving here at the castle since I was seven. Me mother still serves in the kitchens along with me sister."

Amber chattered on as she turned and headed out the door. Deirdre forced herself to keep her eyes on the girl's back so that the two retainers standing on either side of the door wouldn't see her glaring at them.

Quinton Cameron was responsible for their presence. Besides, she'd never escape the castle if they thought she had the spirit to try it.

Well... she did. That was something she was going to tighten her fist about and pull it close enough to feel the heat from it. She would join the queen and take the position offered her. It would be something she'd earned, which made it very precious.

Amber took her down the stairs to the bottom of the eagle tower and through a hallway to the next tower.

"It's up here—a fine chamber. I've had the chance to turn the sheets a few times, so I got a look at it. The laird had it furnished well, and it's facing the river that comes over the hills before it goes under the rocks Drumdeer is perched on."

That explained the plentiful water supply. Deirdre picked up the front of her robes and climbed behind Amber. The girl was excited, and her pace was brisk. The wound on Deirdre's leg began to burn as she pushed herself to keep up.

"There... ye can hear the sound of the water now."

The sound of rushing water came in through the arrow slits. Amber climbed to the third floor before opening a door.

"Here it is... I mean to say... welcome, Lady Deirdre."

The chamber smelled of beeswax candles. Stepping inside, Deirdre saw three long tapers sitting on a long table with their wicks lit. Amber followed her and reached for the lacing at the back of the overrobe. In a few moments, she had the tighter overgown unlaced

and removed. Deirdre sighed, because the underrobe
was much more comfortable in spite of how flimsy
the fabric was.

"I'll go and fetch ye some supper."

Amber turned in a swirl of her wool robes and the
length of Cameron plaid that was draped down her
back as an arisaid. Every member of a Highland clan
wore their colors. It was a way to discourage trouble,
because when you trifled with one, you were taking
the chance the rest of their clan might retaliate.

Of course, that fact had led to more than one feud,
each clan repaying every raid in a chain that became so
long, it was hard to recall why it had begun.

The water sound was stronger in the chamber, but
Deirdre suddenly realized she was alone. She looked
toward the door but stopped when she discovered
herself facing one of the men who had been outside
the solar doorway. He reached up and tugged on the
corner of his hat before closing the door.

Deirdre snarled. She didn't think she had ever been
so frustrated or so full of energy at the end of a day.

She turned around slowly, the idea of investigating
another chamber that Quinton had prepared for his
bride disgusting her.

But she couldn't maintain her displeasure. Everything
in the chamber was designed to please. She'd have to
be spoiled not to notice the thick bedding that waited
on the bed to keep her toes from being chilled during
the night. The edges of creamy sheets peeked out, and
she could tell they had been pressed.

The bed was also surrounded with curtains that
would make for a fine place to spend winter evenings.

Across from the bed was a fireplace that didn't have a fire in it, due to the spring weather. The sound of the river was quite soothing, and she crossed the middle of the chamber to one of the windows, which had its shutters closed. Lifting the small bar that kept it closed, she opened it and smiled. The moonlight shimmered off the water and the rocks surrounding it. The sight was magical, the river wide and rushing fast enough with spring runoff to turn frothy with millions of tiny bubbles. She laughed, low and softly, at the magic of the scene. She couldn't imagine a sight more perfect.

"Ye are a Highland lass, sure enough."

She jumped and whirled about to face Quinton. She had to blink, because it felt as though she'd imagined his voice, but the man who stood in the doorway was too real to ignore.

"No one loves the Highlands like a lass born here does." He moved into the chamber, as bold as could be. "I can see the enjoyment shimmering in yer eyes."

Deirdre propped one hand onto her hip. "What ye see in me eyes is annoyance with the way ye walk in here like I'm yer mistress and being alone together in a bedchamber is commonplace for us."

His lips split in an arrogant smile. "I never called the attraction between us common, Deirdre Chattan. I know it for the rare treasure it is."

He was very serious, the tone of his voice deep and even. She looked away to hide the pleasure that flared up inside her. She was disgusted by just how much she enjoyed hearing him praise her ability to attract his attention. His title alone would have every mother in Scotland pushing their daughters forward in the hope he'd take a

fancy to them. She'd happily have the man give some
attention to her reputation instead and seek out another.

But turning her gaze away from him was a mistake.
He was no soft nobleman. He cupped her chin, having
crossed the distance between them while her attention
wasn't on him; his warm fingers closed gently around
her jaw to turn her back to face him. Sensation snaked
down her spine, and she jerked away from him,
earning a soft chuckle.

"Besides, I am nae so sure being alone with ye is no'
more of a danger for me."

She stepped to the side, the wall behind her back
making her nervous. The man might be teasing her,
but there was a promise lurking in his eyes, which
unleashed another ripple of awareness that moved
down her body and awakened yearnings she had spent
most of the day telling herself to forget.

"Being in here with me blackens my name, and ye
know it, Laird Cameron."

His smile faded. "If ye wanted to be formal, ye
should have followed young Amber to the hall,
Deirdre." He spoke her name in a deeper tone of
voice that bordered on husky. "But I admit I prefer
sharing supper with ye in a more private setting."

She didn't miss the warning he was giving her,
or that he was showing her his power without the
slightest hint of remorse. But she realized she would
have been disappointed if he'd taken her dismissal of
him and left her in peace. It was the truth she enjoyed
his boldness, but that only sent a shaft of nervousness
through her, because it was dangerous for her to like
anything about him.

It might very well be disastrous for the future she had planned and had risked so much for. It was doubtful the queen would have a maid with scandal clinging to her skirts.

"I am nae breaking bread with ye," she informed him.

He crossed his arms over his chest. The pose made his upper arms bulge. He was only wearing a shirt and his kilt. She stared for a long moment at his uncovered hair, as shiny as a raven's wing.

"And why no'?"

The door suddenly opened, and Amber appeared with a bright smile on her lips. She carried a large platter covered with a silver dome into the room. Behind her came three other girls, all carrying things they took to the table. They set two places, and one girl poured ale from a pitcher into two goblets before she and her companions all lowered themselves and fled. But the door didn't close fast enough to stop Deirdre from hearing the giggles the girls released once they had made it to the stairs.

"Oh... ye see? They all think I'm yer slut." She threw her hands into the air and turned her back on Quinton.

But she whirled back around when he tipped his head back and laughed. Her temper sizzled, and she crossed the distance between them without thinking about it. The only thought in her head was the impulse to thrash him.

"Toad! Slime-covered, muck-caked leech..."

Her first blow landed on his shoulder, popping loudly, but he ducked, and her next slap went over his head. With nothing solid for her hand to land on, she lost her balance and tumbled forward. Quinton bent his knee, and she fell right over his shoulder.

"Now there's my hellion."

A smothered sound of rage bounced off the stone walls as he surged upward with her hanging over his shoulder like a sack of barley. One arm clamped across her thighs. Pain spiked through her in a white-hot jolt that sent her straightening up as stiff as a tree trunk.

"Put me down, Quinton!"

He did so, tossing her onto the bed with a frown darkening his face. She rolled from side to side, unable to do anything else because the pain was so intense. Sparkling lights danced before her eyes, and she couldn't seem to force enough breath into her lungs. Her entire body was as tight as a bowstring. She reached for the wound, unconsciously covering it in an urge to protect herself.

"What ails ye, lass?"

Deirdre drew in a deep breath as the pain settled into a throb that was bearable. Quinton didn't wait for her to answer him. He knelt beside her, and she felt the brush of his hand against her bare skin as he swept her clothing up in one swift motion.

"*Quinton—*" Deirdre sat up, but he pushed her back down with one hand flattened against her belly. Shock raced through her as she tried to decide how she'd managed to end up in bed with the man's hand on her bare thigh.

"Get yer hand off my thigh." she insisted and struggled back up, propping her elbows against the bed to make it harder for him to push her down. "And lower my robes this instant."

She froze when she meet his gaze. His eyes were icy

now, and she shivered but still reached for the fabric bunched up near the top of her thigh.

"Who cut ye?" Each word was razor sharp. He pressed his hand down on top of her robes, stilling her efforts to cover her leg. He used his free hand to tug at the wrapping Tully had bound the wound with. Once it was free, he tossed it aside and studied the damage.

"This is fresh." He wasn't asking a question, and Deirdre discovered herself ill at ease with the anger she heard in his voice. It wasn't directed at her but that bothered her, because it hinted at the man caring about her for more than just easing his lust.

"Ye shouldna be baring my leg like this."

He growled, the sound menacing, but she refused to be intimidated by it and struggled against the hand he was using to hold her down. With a snort, he stood. She shoved her robes back into place but couldn't hide the wince that resulted when she sat up and the muscle in her leg was forced to help her rise.

"Who did that, Deirdre? Ye'll answer me."

"Or what?" She stood and walked past him, needing to put the bed behind her while he was in the chamber with her. "Ye are nae my laird—"

"Or yer father… or yer lover, but we can certainly change that one if that is what it takes to gain a bit of cooperation from ye."

His arm came around her, pulling her toward his body. She gasped and turned to fend him off, only to have her action aid him in trapping her against his body. Her head only reached the top of his shoulders, and she suddenly felt the difference in their strength.

Her body quivered, but he didn't press a savage kiss against her lips as she had expected.

It was worse than that.

Quinton cupped the back of her head, raising her face so their eyes met. For one moment, she felt like a bolt of lightning shot into her eyes from his. He leaned down and pressed a soft kiss against her temple, the skin feeling more sensitive than she had ever noticed it being before.

"Ye smell good." His lips landed on her cheeks next, directly on the spot that flushed hot in response to his first kiss. "And ye taste delicious."

"Stop this nonsense."

He lifted his head, and she stared into his eyes once more, but this time, they had turned dark blue, passion narrowing them. She stiffened, her body responding to that look without any conscious decision. It was pure response, her flesh yielding to the touch of the man holding her.

It felt delicious…

"We mustn't, Quinton." Her words were a softly spoken plea, torn from the last shred of rational thought she possessed.

He leaned down, his breath brushing against the delicate skin of her neck before she felt the press of his lips. She found herself anxiously waiting for the touch of lips. Her heartbeat accelerated as she stopped attempting to push him away. Instead she spread her fingers wide over the hard expanse of his chest, delighting in the feeling of his body.

"Are nae ye tired of shunning every touch because men in sackcloth robes tell ye to?" He placed twin kisses behind her ear before capturing her earlobe between his lips. She gasped, pleasure flowing down her body. "What happened to the lass who went after what she wanted?"

She laughed at him, and his arms slackened. She moved away from him, turning to face him with her hands propped on her hips. "Ye understand me well enough. I agreed to this charade because I want a place that is my own, and the queen promised me one in exchange for helping her."

He grunted. "I believe ye, but that was nae the topic I was discussing with ye." He curled one finger at her. "Come back here, Deirdre, and admit ye want me to be yer lover because my touch makes ye burn and ye recognize I would give ye as much as ye give me."

"I do nae doubt ye'd be a good lover." She gasped when she realized what she'd said aloud. "Oh... do nae start smirking at me like I shined yer ego with that comment. It meant nothing."

He chuckled anyway and closed the space between them with one long step. "I disagree; it meant something to me."

She moved away. "Well... enjoy it, then, for it is all ye shall have. Men are no' the only ones with honor, ye know. Securing myself a place with the queen will make my father proud." Her gaze returned to him once more, and passion tormented her with ideas of how good it would feel to go back to his embrace. "If I take another lover, even a titled one, that will only shame my sire more." She forced herself to look away from him, and her gaze touched the meal that was laid out on the table.

"I am hungry," she announced.

Quinton muttered an obscenity in Gaelic. "Aye, ye are, but no' for food."

She sent a hot look toward him before sweeping her silk velvet robe aside and sitting down. "Yes, for food. It's little wonder yer contracted bride ran off, if ye were this crude when talking with her."

One of his dark eyebrows rose. "Ye think ye know something about that because ye heard the tale?" He pulled his sword off his back, untying it at his waist so that even the scabbard was removed. She shivered in response, because that action meant it would be much easier for him to make use of the bed.

Oh stop it!

She had to gain control of her thoughts, or she might as well walk herself over to the bed and be done with it.

"The truth is she was a calculating bitch, raised by her mother to find the highest bidder for her favors like any whore."

His voice had turned harsh, and she stared at him and the pain that flickered briefly in his eyes.

"I contracted her, but the moment a higher-ranking man rode into court, her mother sent young Mary Ross off to charm him."

"Is that why ye are still unwed?" she asked before considering the personal nature of her question. "Because ye do nae trust women?"

"I've been kept busy trying to keep the Highlanders from fighting with each other so we do nae find ourselves invaded by the English."

Quinton sat down and moved a freshly ironed cloth

aside to reveal a round of bread. He picked up the bread and tore it in half with ease.

"I could have pressed her father to honor my contract with Mary, but I have no desire to be watching me back for daggers every time me kin is near."

"Most nobles wouldn't care much about the feelings involved."

He extended his arm, offering her half the bread. "Is that how ye see me, lass? A man who has a heart so hard, I cannae understand love?"

She took the bread, finding the moment strangely intimate. "Ye seem to be set against allowing the queen to wed the man she wishes."

He sent another linen fluttering toward the floor with a flick of his fingers and uncovered a small dish of butter.

"Ye are making assumptions, Deirdre. Just because I sent me men after the queen does nae mean I am no' in favor of her wedding." He used a knife to spread some of the butter on his portion of the bread, but his eyes remained on her, and there was a hard promise lurking in them. "Save yer accusations for crimes ye know for certain I've committed."

"Such as the fact that I am here, sir, and unable to depart by yer command?"

He opened his mouth and bit off a chunk of bread. He watched her while he chewed, making her wait for his response. It was a tiny torment, because she discovered she wanted to know what his reaction was going to be.

"So ye are, Deirdre, but if I were a blackhearted knave, I never would have allowed ye to lower yer robes." He propped one elbow on the tabletop. "Unless ye want to accuse me of lacking the ability of being able to stroke yer passions."

"Stop it."

He leaned closer. "Stop what, madam? Did ye think the place the queen offered ye would be so easy to earn? Joan Beaufort is a queen. She gives nothing away."

"I am no' lazy, and will earn my place, sir. Now ye are the one thinking ye know me, when it is clear ye underestimate my determination to be something my father can be proud of. That duty has naught to do with the sordid suggestions ye are attempting to discuss." She reached for the butter with her own knife. "Ye are attempting to trick me into challenging ye so ye have an excuse to handle me."

His hand shot out in a motion as fast as a flash of lightning. He captured her wrist, and she lost her grip on the knife. It fell into the butter without a sound.

"Be sure I will handle ye when I want to, Deirdre. I do nae need an excuse to stroke yer creamy skin. I'll take credit for me own actions, never doubt that. But I can understand yer desire to escape a place where ye are considered naught but a disgraced woman."

His eyes filled with approval, and she discovered she enjoyed seeing it more than she had anticipated.

"I understand ye better than ye think, because ye and I are a great deal alike."

He lifted her wrist, rotating it so that the delicate skin of her inner wrist was exposed. He brushed his thumb over it, sending a torrent of sensation up her arm. Goose bumps rose in response, but what sent a chill down her spine was the promise glittering in his eyes. It was hot and solid, and she drew in a shaky breath because she began to doubt her ability to refuse him.

"Nor do ye seek my permission either."

His thumb traveled over her inner wrist once again, more firmly this time, and she felt the touch deeper. Her belly tightened, excitement rising in spite of her attempts to drown it with reason.

"I'd have yer permission and more." From any other, she would have been able to accuse the man of being presumptuous.

But she wouldn't make that mistake with Quinton.

No, he was dangerous. Dangerous because he unleashed a weakness inside her that she couldn't control. Failing to admit that to herself would only give him the advantage. She looked at the plate in front of her, trying to bring Melor's smirking face to mind. For the first time, her memory failed to offer up her last sight of the man she'd defied her father to have.

"Do nae do that, Deirdre Chattan." Quinton released her hand with a sound of disgust that drew her attention back to his face. He pointed at her. "Ye have more confidence than a girl who needs to stare at a tabletop because she's afraid of her own nature."

"It is nae a matter of confidence, but one of morality." She spit the word out and then realized she'd tumbled neatly into his snare. His lips twitched before he stood up in another quick motion that sent the chair behind him crashing into the floor.

"Nae, it is a matter of passion."

He looped an arm around her and pulled her out of

her chair. A soft sound passed her lips, but she honestly wasn't sure if it wasn't born from her rising excitement or her temper. Both seemed to be combining inside her to intensity how aware of him she was. Her heart was racing, and her senses keener than ever before. She reached for him this time, enjoying the way he secured her against him. His body was harder than hers, and she made another sound of enjoyment as her breasts compressed against his chest.

She liked everything about the man too much for her own good.

His mouth claimed hers in that savage kiss he had denied her earlier. It seemed like she had been waiting for it ever since, and she opened her mouth to allow him to thrust his tongue inside. He held her neck securely as his mouth moved over hers in a kiss that stole her breath.

But she kissed him back, her hands holding on to his shoulders while she turned her head slightly to allow their mouths to fuse more completely. His tongue speared deeply into her mouth, and she let hers tangle with it. A groan shook his chest, and she rubbed her hands down, stroking over the hard muscles that only a thin shirt separated her from.

He picked her up and moved her to a bare section of table. The candleholder shook and fell over, and the flames died in a quick sizzle. Darkness closed in on them, heightening her awareness of him even further. She couldn't seem to kiss him hard enough, couldn't manage to touch all the places on his body she had admired with her eyes.

She wasn't the only one who felt such a frenzy.

Quinton cursed beneath his breath before he pushed her thighs apart and used his hands to pull her hips toward the bulge of his member.

"Ye drive me insane with the need to have ye, Deirdre." He ground his hips forward, and she felt his hard flesh against her spread sex. Need tore through her, so hot that it threatened to overwhelm her. She gripped the front of his shirt so tightly that she heard it tearing at the shoulder seams.

"*Then have me.*"

There was no thinking, only responding. Her body wanted to twist and writhe against his, but most of all, her passage wanted the hard flesh pressing against her driven deep inside it to ease the emptiness tormenting her.

"I intend to, lass… I swear I'd kill to have ye at this moment."

His hands left her hips, and he tossed her skirts in a sharp jerk. They settled around her on the tabletop as he smoothed his hand up the inside of her thigh.

"But I'm going to make sure ye're as hot to have me as I am to be had." His voice had lowered, so much so that it was only a rasp in the dark chamber. The roar of the river interfered with her understanding, but all thought ceased the moment his fingers touched the curls guarding her sex. Her clitoris pulsed with anticipation, eager and needy. Her hips pressed forward, and he didn't disappoint her.

"Ye see, lass, ye are nae afraid of yer own passion, and that makes ye the most attractive woman I've ever met." His fingers delved between the folds of her sex, until he was teasing the sensitive bud that lay between them. "I've dreamed of ye since I stole that embrace at the abbey."

Deirdre couldn't think of a reply, she failed to think at all. Her body was a twisting length of rope, knotting tighter and tighter with every rub of his fingers. Her breath became raspy, and a tiny moan surfaced from the need tormenting her so acutely.

"I've wanted to wring that sound out of ye."

Her eyes opened as her pride surfaced from beneath the flood of pleasure his touch filled her with.

"Well, I—"

His arm wrapped around her hips to hold her in place when she tried to scoot back so she might regain her wits.

"I will pleasure ye, Deirdre," he snarled softly as he pressed harder against her clitoris. She lost the battle to ignore the need roaring through her. It rose into a wave and broke with a shaft of pleasure that made her cry because she simply could not contain it inside herself. She shook with it, her hips straining toward his hand, but a moment later bitterness clawed at her.

Her passage was still too empty. She groaned, the sound rising out of her unsatisfied need.

"It wasna enough… was it, hellion?" He withdrew his fingers and cradled the back of her neck so her face was angled toward his own. "Ye crave it all… do nae ye? Partway will never satisfy ye, admit it."

"No, it was nae enough. Ye arrogant man. Why do ye think I told ye I did nae want ye for my lover?" She shoved at his chest but only gained a chuckle from him.

It wasn't a nice sound. It was low and almost savage.

"Ye do crave me as yer lover. Ye want me because I will nae finger ye and think ye are content."

She felt him shift his kilt aside and then the hard head of his member was pressing against the entrance to her body.

He grasped the sides of her hips, and she shook with excitement. "Ye want me to fill ye, and I am happy to be of service."

His words were blunt, but they also promised to feed the hunger tearing at her insides. The darkness surrounding them seemed to grant permission for her body to seek what it wanted. She reached for him, her hips lifted as his hands pulled her forward, and his hard flesh split hers.

She gasped, because the entry burned. Not as badly as the first time, but it stung as he thrust forward.

"Ye're tight."

His voice was full of victory and male pride.

"That does nae mean I was saving myself for ye." It seemed ridiculous to be angry with him, considering their position, but she felt her lip curl up as she snarled at him.

Quinton laughed, low and deeply, as he withdrew. She growled at him as her body demanded more of his member. Desperation was raging through her, and her fingers curled into claws, her fingernails sinking into his shoulders.

"Yes, ye were, hellion." He thrust back into her, his hard flesh gaining more ground this time. A sound of satisfaction passed her lips even as her passage protested being stretched around his girth.

"Ye would nae spread yer thighs for any man who does nae impress ye."

He whispered his words against her ear as he began to drive his length in and out of her. His tone was raspy and edged with what had to be wickedness, because she felt like she was caught in his spell. Her body strained toward his, her hips eager to take the next thrust. She craved it insanely, every muscle she had tightening in her effort to match his pace.

"Ye need to be taken, Deirdre, and I swear to ye, I am the man bold enough to give ye what ye crave." The table creaked as he drove his member harder and faster into her. His lips brushed over her ear and down to the tender skin behind it.

A moment later he bit her. She bit him in return, but the small bite heightened her enjoyment, rippling down her body while the pleasure of his hard cock being worked against her clitoris spread upward. It was too much and yet not enough. The first climax he'd wrung from her had only taken the edge off her hunger. Now her body wanted a deeper release. She lifted her hips, trying to take all his flesh while her thighs clasped around his hips and her head fell all the way back. There was no reason to keep her eyes open or to worry that her heart might burst because of how violently it was pounding.

All that mattered was keeping pace with her lover. She needed to be closer to him, and her thighs ached with the strength she used to bind him to her.

"That's it, hellion… demand what ye want of me."

His breath was rasping through his teeth, but she couldn't pay attention to such details. Her body was beginning to erupt in a climax that was far greater than any she had ever experienced. It tore through her, she arched her back to take his member as deep as possible while she used her legs to clamp him against her. He snarled and pounded her, thrusting while pleasure lashed her in waves so intense that she cried out.

Her lover didn't lack for pleasure either. He tightened his grip around her hips as he drove his length deep and groaned savagely against her neck. She felt his seed hit her womb, the hot spurt unleashing a second tremor of enjoyment, which was deeply rooted inside her belly.

Her lungs burned, caught between breaths, and she sucked in a huge amount of air as she collapsed backward. Her hands tried to support her but slipped on the polished surface of the table.

Quinton held her, raising his arms from her hips in a flash to catch her before she fell backward.

"Sweet Christ, that was intense," he muttered before lifting her off the table and cradling her against his chest. "But too fast. Too bloody quick for how many nights I've dreamed of having ye in my bed."

He crossed the chamber, the lack of light never giving him a moment's pause. He lowered her legs, and she felt her knees quiver as she was forced to take her own weight.

"But I always imagined ye nude."

Deirdre frowned. "And how did ye do that? Ye have never seen me without me robes." She was being surly, and he caught her head, tangling his fingers in the strands of her hair. He pulled them slightly, but once again the tiny pain only managed to accent the moment and her awareness of him.

It was a truth she enjoyed feeling his strength; the fact that he controlled it excited her. Only a mere whisper of pain went through her scalp, but it sent sensation rippling across her skin.

"I enjoyed contemplating all the possibilities."

He pressed a hard kiss against her mouth, the hand in her hair holding her prisoner while his mouth played over hers, teasing the delicate skin before pressing her to open her mouth for a deeper kiss. In spite of the fact that satisfaction was still glowing warmly inside her belly, his kiss was intoxicating. Or maybe it was the scent of his skin or the grip in her hair... Deirdre didn't know. She only knew she wanted to kiss him back, and the consequences could wait until later to contemplate.

He broke their kiss and released her. She heard a soft sound of disappointment rise from her chest as he severed their connection.

"Do nae fret. It would take an army at me gates to take me away from ye this night."

"Ye assume I want ye to stay."

He framed her face between his warm hands, gently brushing his thumb over her lower lip. A breath got caught in her throat and emerged as a raspy sigh.

"The way ye tremble says ye want me to remain." His words were soft and tender. He placed a simple kiss against her lips before lifting his hands away from her face. The night air was chilly by comparison, and she shivered.

But a moment later he tore her sheer underrobe in half.

"Are ye mad?" She jumped away from him, but he

maintained his grip on the two sides of the robe, and she ended up aiding him in baring her.

"That robe is no' mine."

He chuckled and tossed the twin pieces aside. "Joan Beaufort should have her servants pack more appropriate garments for where she is traveling. The Highlands can be a harsh place for such delicate items."

The single shutter she had left open allowed enough moonlight in to cast him in silver. He looked more at ease in the night than he had sitting in the fine room where he attended to his duty as a noble peer. He pulled the end of his belt and caught the wool of his kilt before it hit the floor.

"But I admit seeing yer rose-tipped nipples through that silk was enough to make me drool."

"Ye could see..." Her voice trailed off as she heard him laughing. He pulled his shirt off and tossed it over the chair his kilt rested on.

"The candles served their purpose quite well, illuminating ye like an angel."

"Stop it. Yer words are too bold. Angels are heavenly creatures, above earthly sins."

He patted the surface of the bed. "Agreed. I'll call ye a siren, for I find myself more interested in earthly pleasures."

She stepped back, and the meager light allowed him to see her frown. "Ye've had that." Her voice dipped with disappointment because she'd known full well his interest in her was fueled by lust, and yet she had failed to resist him. She'd suffer for it once he was sated and gone, while the gossips enjoyed telling the tale.

"And ye think my only interest was to fuck ye on a tabletop? Is that it, Deirdre?"

She stiffened. "Ye need no' insult me, but I suppose I should nae be surprised to hear it, for men often spit on the women they've used to ease their lust."

He watched her for a moment, a long moment that felt like an eternity. She swore she could feel his gaze cutting into her, but what it truly did was mesmerize her, for he moved while she was frozen in place, wrapping his arms around her and binding her to his body.

"Do nae compare me to that bastard Melor Douglas who used ye to strike against Connor Lindsey. I did nae whisper promises in yer ear to get ye to allow me to part yer thighs."

She strained against his hold but accomplished nothing but a renewed shaft of pain from her wound. "I am nae a whore to want promises of what ye will give me for my favors. I learned that lesson from Melor, sure enough."

He cupped the back of her head to hold her face steady while he loomed over her. Completely nude, she felt his warm skin against every inch of her body, and sensation began to course through her.

"Nay, hellion, ye couldnae ignore the passion that has sparked between us since the moment I set eyes on ye in yer father's home. Ye spit in me eye then, just to see if I would take the challenge. That is who ye are, and ye will no' ever be content unless ye accept it."

He lowered his face until she could feel the brush of his breath against her still-wet lower lip. "It filled me with need, Deirdre. I have no' wanted a woman as fiercely as I did ye in that moment when ye refused to let me name and title make ye meek. No quick fuck is going to satisfy either of us."

He swept her off her feet and deposited her in the bed. The bed ropes groaned as she was dropped onto the surface. He didn't follow her immediately but sat down on a small stool to remove his boots.

But he never took his eyes off her. She felt his gaze slipping over the mounds of her nude breasts and lingering on the hard points of her nipples. He looked at her like he was contemplating the best way to consume her, and God help her, she felt excitement burning brightly inside her once more. He was correct; she wasn't truly satisfied.

"My nature is a curse," she muttered.

The bed rocked when he entered it. He crawled onto it like a large animal stalking his prey.

"Ye're a hellion, and I find it irresistible."

She shivered, enjoying the compliment even if there were many who wouldn't have considered his words kind.

She did, because they were honestly spoken. Quinton Cameron was a Highlander, and pretty words were something he'd only ever learned to be polite. He pressed her back against the plump pillows, sliding his hands over her bare skin slowly. It was bold and sensual, taking her back into the sweet intoxication that had seen her clinging to him.

"I cannae wait for yer leg to heal so ye can ride me, and I'll be free to watch these teats bounce." He cupped her breasts, drawing a hiss from her as sensation spiked through her. Her body seemed to respond faster to him now that it had experienced the pleasure he might give her.

"Who says I'll be sharing yer bed ever again?" She reached up and grasped a handful of his dark hair. He groaned as she pulled the strands hard and sat up so their faces were only inches apart. "Do nae be so presumptuous with someone ye call a hellion. I'll be on my way to take the place I have earned by freezing in those silk robes."

He brushed the hard points of her nipples with his thumbs. "That leaves me the option of impressing ye so that ye'll be wanting more of me company." He cupped her breasts completely, sending little ripples of enjoyment through her. "I'm agreeable to that course of action."

Deirdre kissed him. Maintaining her hold on his hair, she pressed her mouth against his, mimicking the way he'd used his lips to drive her so insane. She wanted to meet him halfway in the middle of their passion, not be bent beneath the power of his boldness. He was a man who preferred action and she discovered she did too.

He pressed her back down when he met her kiss, his mouth demanding she open hers for the thrust of his tongue. He released her breasts to cover her, using his greater size and weight to pin her beneath him but he propped his elbows on either side of her head to support enough of his weight to save her from being smothered.

"We'll take it slower this time lass… so ye will nae think me a complete brute."

His member was hard again and he sent it deep into

her once more. This time his thrusts were smooth and even. Need built inside her but he refused to rush the pace even when she became eager for more of what they had shared earlier.

"Nae, lass… there are rewards for those with patience."

He was mocking her, teasing her, and she growled at him. He laughed at her, earning a well-deserved slap, which she delivered to his shoulder. The sound popped in the quiet room.

"Oh well… I suppose I'll have to learn to deal with yer demanding nature, hellion."

He began to give her what she craved, the bed rocking almost violently as his large body labored above hers. She arched to meet each thrust, eagerly keeping time with his pace. Pleasure spiked through her again, too quickly, but there was no resisting it. Like a bolt of lightning splitting the clouds open with a light so brilliant her eyes stung, her release left her gasping on the surface of the bed with her lover groaning out his release in the next moment.

She must have slept because she awoke to discover Quinton toying with her hair. He lay beside her, both of them still on top of the covers. Her heart had slowed, and she shivered as she grew cold now that she wasn't demanding so much activity from her body.

Quinton grunted. "We'll be wanting the bedding now."

He sat up and used one hand placed on her hip to roll her onto her side so that he might free the thick coverlet. But he stopped with it only half over her.

"Ye did nae tell me how that wound came to happen. I want to know."

She knew what he meant but turned onto her good side to avoid conversation. Her passage ached, marking the place he had been but satisfaction was still wrapping her in tranquility so she closed her eyes to dismiss the unpleasant harshness that would certainly arise soon enough with the dawn.

Quinton refused to leave the matter alone. He reached over and cupped the side of her face to turn her attention back toward him.

"Ye'll answer me, Deirdre, or I'll have every man who brought ye to me in this chamber to discuss the matter. Immediately."

"Oh, curse and rot yer arrogant persistence, Quinton. Have no' ye had enough from me tonight?" She rolled over and stood up next to the bed with a hiss.

"I'm the master of this fortress Deirdre and I'll no' have any man serving me who takes a knife to a woman."

He stood up, but Deirdre refused to let the fact that he was so much larger than herself bother her. She walked back to the table and picked up the forgotten ale that Amber had poured into a goblet for her. Lifting it up, she took a long drink of it.

Quinton did the same but he righted the candelabrum and set the candles back in it. He reached for a small box sitting on the table and sparks flew out as he struck a flint stone against a piece of iron. The wick of one candle quickly lit, brightening the chamber almost painfully and illuminating the fact that they were both still nude.

Harsh reality had arrived to sting her with shame before dawn it seemed.

Her nature was a curse… no doubt about it.

"Shall I send one of me men to summon Coalan or no'? The privacy of this chamber is the only reason I'm giving ye the choice lass. If I'd learned of that wound below stairs, me men would already be lined up in front of me to account for it."

"Ye do nae need to threaten me."

He shook his head. "I'm trying to tell ye that in this chamber, I do nae expect ye to keep to any place which the rest of the world says is yers."

She felt her anger dissipating. He was a proud man and what he'd said was far more than she'd ever expected to hear from his lips. Even a wife would not enter his bed expecting to be his equal. She'd only be in his chamber to please him.

"It was no' by design."

"The man's name." Quinton pressed her. She could hear the solid authority in his voice which must have been instilled in him at a young age so he might be the effective laird he was. Highlanders did not follow weaklings. He'd been forged into solid steel by the position he'd inherited else he would have been broken by it. Which only served to make it more of a compliment that he was discussing the matter with her instead of seeking out his men.

"I tried to escape, and Coalan stopped me."

"With a blade against yer flesh?" Quinton sounded aghast.

"Do nae interrupt me when ye ask me a question."

He grunted. "So long as ye never use that tone

with me in front of others, hellion. I cannae have disorder on me land. We'll starve and be overrun by the neighbors because nothing will get finished due to all the squabbling if me men think raising their voices will make me bend."

Deirdre nodded. She was being daring, many would say too much so for her place was lower than Quinton's simply because of her gender. He raised an eyebrow when she didn't continue immediately.

"And… well, Coalan tackled me to the ground, and I think he must have had a small knife tucked into his belt for I did nae even notice the pain I felt was a cut and no' just bruising from being pressed beneath his weight. So let the matter be, it was nothing intentional. I only saw it for what it was when I bathed today."

She raised the goblet once more and drained it.

"Ye have a need to see justice upheld," Quinton muttered.

She couldn't tell what mood he was in for his tone was pensive. His features were guarded and she sent a stern look back at him.

"Aye, I do. Yer man didna intend to harm me, at least no more than what ye had ordered him to do in bringing me here."

"Something ye should thank me for."

Deirdre scowled at him instead, and he stopped hiding behind a stony expression.

Quinton snorted, looking down at the wound. "Only ye could manage that bit of misfortune."

Deirdre put the goblet back on the table. "Ye're the one who sent him after me, so kindly do nae find amusement in the result."

Her gaze finally had time to settle on him. He stood without any shame with the yellow light of the candle washing over his skin. She'd seen parts of men before, but not one entirely bare. Curiosity led her gaze down his length, but she stopped at his cock.

"Are ye never sated?" she demanded.

He laughed at her disgruntled tone. He reached across the space between them and cupped her chin. The contrast between his touch and the night air was startling. It was such a simple touch, but it felt like he had somehow renewed his control over her. A current flowed between them through that touch. He stepped closer, and it felt more correct than anything she had ever felt to have his bare body brushing against her own. Ripples of sensation moved over her skin from all the points of connection until it became as smooth as water submerging her.

"I was nae saying that I've dreamed of ye to get ye into my bed Deirdre."

She drew in a breath that rattled in her throat because his voice was raspy and edged with the promise of more passion. He reached passed her and pinched the candle out, cloaking them in silver star shine once more. A soft sigh pasted her lips in response.

"Aye, we are best suited to the night shadows, ye and I."

He swept her off her feet and carried her back to the bed. This time, he pushed the coverlet aside and sometime during the morning hours they both clung to one another beneath its warmth.

❧

She was a distraction.

Quinton woke every time Deirdre stirred, which was often. She muttered in her sleep, moving away from him. He reached for her, frowning as he did it because he didn't understand why it was so important to have her nestled against his body. It was something worth contemplating but his body was too content with her resting in his embrace to remain awake. He slipped back into sleep, more content than he could recall being in too long a time.

Five

Deirdre woke tired.

She rubbed her burning eyes and her neck was tight, but she stiffened when she lowered her hands and beheld the sight of Quinton Cameron standing in front of his discarded clothing.

He stretched his back, groaning slightly before he lifted his hands so a younger lad might slip his shirt into place.

Her eyes widened, and she sank back down beneath the coverlet until her chin was beneath its edge. Heat flooded her cheeks, and guilt showed up to lash her with its claws over her fall from grace.

She had not even lasted a day…

The boy knew his duties well. He dressed his laird silently and efficiently. Light began to brighten the chamber. Deirdre glanced toward the windows to see Amber pushing the shutters open with a happy smile on her lips.

"Do nae dress yer mistress until Tully sees to her wound."

Amber turned instantly in response to her laird's

command. She lowered herself and snapped her fingers at another girl, who had been working to clear away the supper she and Quinton had eaten so little of.

"Fetch Tully."

Deirdre snorted. It was soft and muffled by the coverlet, but Quinton turned, showing her a frown. She bit her lip but narrowed her eyes to make sure the man knew she was irritated.

"Everyone out."

There was immediate compliance with his command and there was no mistaking that it was an order. The man in front of her was every inch the Earl of Liddell.

Quinton kept his eyes on her, but the moment the door closed behind his staff, he spoke.

"The day has begun, Deirdre. Save that hellion nature of yers for when we are in private."

She sat up, her temper rising above her shame. "If ye do nae care for my nature in the morning light, ye should sleep in yer own chamber."

She shoved the coverlet aside and stood up. "Or better yet, wish me good travel and have done with this notion of forcing me to stay here."

"Why? Because ye think now that I've had ye, I am finished with ye?"

She found an underrobe and struggled into it. "Ye are the one vexed with me, Laird Cameron. I simply think it best to be away from ye so I will nae have to guard each word. I'll no' treat ye like a titled man in the chamber I sleep in. Lovers do no concern themselves with the rules of society."

He chuckled, but it was not a kind sound. She heard his step, light and controlled as he approached her.

She jerked her attention back toward him, tiny pulses of awareness going through her in spite of the bright morning light. She was still too aware of the man.

"Ye are correct about one thing, lass. I am the Earl of Liddell. 'Tis a duty, and make no mistake about that. I've people depending upon me to make sure there is food next winter and protection from any who might want to raid their farms by moonlight. I've very little privacy. Ye'll have to be adjusting to that fact."

"I will nae. Being my lover does nae give ye the right to insist I stay anywhere."

He folded his arms over his chest and looked down at her. "Aye, it does."

Three little words had never sounded so much like an execution sentence. His tone was solid and harsh, without any hint of the tenderness that had seen her succumbing to his advances the night before. She propped her hands onto her hips.

Quinton lifted one finger between them. "Save it, hellion, unless ye want to confess that ye do in fact know who the queen was set to wed and would therefore know which direction to head in. I believe she set herself to wed the black knight of Lorn, but there is no confirmation of that unless ye can provide it."

There was a hint of suspicion in his voice, one which accused her of lying to him. She lifted her chin.

"I did nae lie," she informed him sternly.

Quinton grunted, and in spite of her irritation with him, she felt satisfaction filling her because he believed her. It flickered in his eyes before he nodded. "Ye have nowhere to go Deirdre and even a hellion such as ye are should recognize that taking to the road without an escort is foolish."

He held up one hand when she opened her lips to argue.

"The day is young, and my captains are waiting on the other side of that door for me to see to the things which need doing. So unless ye want them to hear ye crying with passion, save yer argument for when they have finished their business with me and we might have privacy."

He reached out and gripped a handful of her robe over her belly. With a hard tug he sent her stumbling toward him. His mouth claimed hers in a hard kiss that clouded her thinking almost instantly. She struggled to push herself away from him but he held her close and soon, she wasn't able to resist kissing him back. She craved the man too much. There was a raw source of power inside him that bred excitement inside of her. She felt her grip on her self-control loosening and falling away as his mouth moved on hers, pressing her until her jaw relaxed and she opened her mouth. He thrust his tongue deeply inside, stroking over hers and she hooked her hands into his shirt to hold him close.

He lifted his head, and she heard a soft sound cross her lips that was without a doubt born of passion. Satisfaction glittered in his eyes. She growled at him and aimed a brutal shove at his chest.

"Oh… leave me in peace, ye savage."

He snorted at her but allowed her to escape across the chamber. "Ye enjoyed my savageness last night."

"That does nae mean I am no' wise enough to recognize that we'd be better off far away from one another."

"And the temptation to sin again?" he taunted her.

"Exactly. Have ye no shame, my fine earl? That title does nae set ye above God's laws."

His expression darkened, but it was the glitter that entered his eyes that made her pause. Her belly tightened with anticipation because she could feel him losing the fight to go and attend to his duties. As ridiculous as it might be, she was almost sure his cock was rising beneath his plaid. Her gaze slid down before she could master the urge to resist looking.

She heard him growl, "Oh I'm hard, ye hellion."

A second later she was pressed up against the wall. He walked right into her and looped his arms around each of her thighs. With a quick rush of speed, he picked her up and pressed her against the stone wall of the chamber with her thighs spread around his waist.

"Does it please ye, Deirdre, to know ye can raise me cock with yer slicing tongue?" He leaned down and nipped the side of her neck with a bite that was just hard enough to send arousal shooting through her. She jumped, her body responding just as instantly as it had the night before.

He laughed, low and deep, before pressing his mouth against the bite and sucking hard. Her back arched as sensation jabbed into her so intensely she couldn't remain still. Her belly was tightening with desire as her passage began to burn with the need to feel him inside her.

"Quinton, stop this."

He raised his head so that he faced her, and what she witnessed in his eyes stole her breath. Hard need shone in his eyes, and God help her, she was

proud to know she had raised such a fierce emotion
in him.

"And fail to finish what ye began?" he growled
softly at her, a mere inch from her lips. "Admit ye
do nae want me to do that, sweet hellion. Ye bait me
because ye cannae ignore the heat between us any
more than I can."

He pressed his hips forward, and she felt the hard
bulge of his erection against her sex. The fact that her
thighs were spread allowed the folds of her sex to open
and expose the little button of her clitoris. He rubbed
against it, sending shooting spikes of pleasure up into
her passage.

"Do ye want me, Deirdre?" He used his chest to
press her against the wall so he might use one hand to
sweep the folds of his plaid aside and raise her underrobe. "Do ye want me to leave ye unsatisfied?"

His voice was deep and almost unrecognizable. But
part of her knew the sound of her lover. Deep inside
her mind, in that place where she had spent the dark
hours of the night, she recognized the man who could
satisfy her needs.

He brushed his fingers over her open sex, fingering
the center of it before settling on top of her clitoris to
rub it.

"Ye are nae the only one who demands action
from their lover, Deirdre." He sent one thick finger
up inside her, and she shuddered with desire. "I'll hear
ye demand me to take ye, or I swear I'll leave ye here
with the fire burning in yer belly."

"Oh damn us both, Quinton, for the fools we are,"
she snarled at him. But she flattened her hand against

the side of his face and turned it until he faced her. "Take me and kiss me so yer men do nae hear."

It was an imperfect solution for her mind, but her body was happy. His lips smothered the sound that escaped her when his cock nudged its way back into her sheath. Pleasure surged through her with every hard thrust, but what made it impossible to resist were the sounds she heard from her partner. He worked his member, and their kiss smothered his groans of enjoyment. Too soon, satisfaction burst through her. It left her muscles quivering, and she tore her lips away from his to gasp for breath. Quinton buried his face against her neck as he thrust hard against her, and she heard him growl with pleasure. His seed filled her, hot and searing as she clung to him. His chest rose and fell rapidly as he left a trail of soft kisses against her neck.

"Ye intoxicate me, Deirdre." His words were low and deep. At any other time she might have suspected he was mocking her, but she could hear the emotion turning his voice gruff. It touched her even as she was forced to recognize how much weakness she harbored for him.

"Release me, Quinton."

He lifted his head and frowned at her, but his arms allowed her legs to lower. He remained in front of her, his hands cupping her face. "I do nae want to leave ye, for I can see the fight still flickering in yer eyes."

Her legs quivered, but she forced herself to stand. "Would ye rather think me a slut who cannae resist a tumble whenever she spies a man who takes her fancy?"

He grunted and pressed a hard kiss against her lips. "I am the only man ye fancy, hellion."

He moved away from her, returning to the table where his bonnet rested so that the feathers might not be crushed. He picked it up and settled it at an angle on his head. The large brooch that held the feathers was set with an emerald that twinkled in the morning light. It was a symbol of what he was, no mistake about it.

"Do nae look at me like that, Deirdre."

She focused her attention on her overrobe and moved to pick it up.

"Like I used ye because I think myself yer better."

She flinched, unable to dismiss the truth in his words. But she turned to face him, unwilling to duck her chin with shame. "I welcomed ye. I recall that well enough." The gossips might call her many things but they would not label her a coward that laid the blame for her sins on the man that she had dallied with. "I am no' set on making excuses for what I choose to do."

"Stop sounding like we're damned to Hades for enjoying the bodies God gave us."

She tossed her hair over her shoulder and glared at him. "I might tell ye to stop behaving as though I should consider the fact that I warmed yer cock as anything respectable."

He cursed in Gaelic. "I swear ye are the most vexing woman I've ever met."

She snorted with amusement. "Aye, I believe I noticed that fact when ye called me hellion."

He grunted and pointed at her. "Make no mistake Deirdre, calling ye hellion is a compliment. One I'll be happy to explain to ye tonight when we have more time to explore just how much I enjoy yer fiery spirit."

He cast a longing look toward the bed but shook his head. "But duty calls me."

"Fare well."

He aimed a sharp look at her. "Until tonight only, for ye will be here and in case ye have any doubt on the matter, ye're me mistress."

"I did nae agree to such." She insisted.

His lips curled into a grin that was as mocking as it was promising. "Ah... something to look forward to then. I cannae wait for sunset and our debate of the issue."

He pulled the door open, and Deirdre whirled around to hide her body from the men waiting outside the chamber. There was only a small platform at the top of the stairs and it was full. She heard them greet their laird and their steps as they descended the stairs. Bits of conversation floated in through the open door.

"There's a difficulty at the mill. One of the wheels has rotted..."

"Twelve head of sheep missing from the south pasture. We needs hunt down the thieves..."

"The miller's daughter claims she's with child and the father will nae honor her..."

"A letter from the lieutenant general is waiting on ye..."

Deirdre turned and looked back toward the open door, almost pitying Quinton, because she could no longer hear the words clearly enough to understand them but without a doubt, Quinton was still being badgered by the needs of his clan.

That was the harsher side of being a laird. She'd witnessed her own father struggling to care for everything he considered his duty. It would have helped if Robert Chattan had married again so that his lady might have dealt with the matters that were considered a woman's domain. Such as babies who would arrive even without the blessing of marriage. They needed to be recognized by their sires so they might be considered true members of the clan.

But she wasn't Quinton's wife. She growled, because she wasn't his mistress either, no matter what the arrogant savage said.

"Yer wound must be paining ye, Lady Deirdre."

Amber came through the door but paused when she heard Deirdre growl. The girl lowered herself, as did the two girls who followed her.

"Tully will be here shortly to tend ye," Amber continued.

Deirdre shrugged into her overrobe with a snort. "There is no need. I want a bath. Tully can see me in the bathhouse."

She needed to wash the scent of Quinton from her skin. Maybe that would restore her thinking. Deirdre ground her teeth as she left the chamber, because it was simply the truth that she doubted her ability to dismiss the man from her mind.

Curse and rot him!

❧

"Amber, I am telling ye that I wish to wear more sturdy clothing."

Amber looked unsure, but she tightened her resolve and shook her head. "I cannae go against me laird's orders."

"Surely he did nae spend any of his valuable time talking about what a woman should be wearing." Deirdre tried to make her voice more cajoling but Amber still frowned at her.

"He did in fact tell me that he believed ye well suited by silks and velvets." Amber walked quickly across the solar to the bundled fabrics near the sewing table and pointed toward them.

"The laird has even bid me to make everything in the storerooms available for ye if ye find nothing here which ye favor."

"Fine, show me the storerooms." It wasn't that Deirdre wanted to look at fabrics, but she did desire knowledge of how to leave the solar.

Amber smiled, relief showing in her eyes to see her mistress happy once more. Deirdre felt guilt renew its assault on her but for a much different reason now. Berating herself over her lack of control with Quinton was far different than the feeling that was chewing on her now. She'd never had to worry about hurting the feelings of personal servants, for she had never had any. Her father had insisted she and her sisters learn to help one another and not burden the clan by being pampered.

Deirdre felt stifled. The women of the Cameron clan were determined to serve her.

Well, she wouldn't allow it to choke her.

"I am going to walk."

Amber smiled, eagerness shining in her eyes. "I'll be happy to show ye everything, and I know there will be many who will be happy to meet ye. Ye're the first lady the laird has brought to this solar, so there is a great deal of speculation about ye..."

Amber chattered on while Deirdre followed her
through the hallways that made up the castle.
She discovered herself interested in hearing about
Quinton. She shouldn't allow the fact that he'd never
brought another woman to the beautiful solar to
make her feel anything at all and yet, she felt honored
to be allowed to use the fine things.

The man was complex. But his people seemed to
like him well. The castle itself was a maze of hallways,
which connected the towers. Each tower was unique,
having been built at different times. The oldest one
was a simple, Norman one and it was rustic when
compared with the eagle tower. But with the thick
walls connecting them all, Drumdeer was a castle that
would not fall easily.

Deirdre found the workrooms and kitchens more
to her liking and never returned to the eagle tower.
Her fine clothing might set her apart but she had been
raised to be a competent manager of an estate and she
knew every task being performed because she'd done
them herself. The cook finally huffed and brought her
a huge apron to cover her fine clothing.

The woman watched Deirdre with a critical eye
while she helped turn the bread for the evening meal.

"I see yer father had ye taught a thing or two of
value." She declared after a time.

"Aye."

The cook tilted her head. "I've girls who can turn
bread a plenty, what I'm needing is help with the books."

Deirdre dusted her hands on the apron. The
books were considered the lady of the house's duty.
Since Quinton's sister was no longer in residence,

the cook would have had to beginning seeing to the written accounting of what was used every day in the kitchens.

The cook pointed toward an archway, and Amber was already grabbing a candleholder.

"It would be a great help for I need to keep an eye on the supper or we'll all be wearing our teeth down by eating blackened fare."

There was a note of relief in the cook's voice that sent Deirdre nodding with agreement. It was a mark of respect that the woman was willing to allow her near the books. Those written accounts were her duty, and one she would suffer for if they were not kept correctly.

Deirdre followed Amber through the doorway and froze when she gained a look at the cluttered table the kitchen accounts were scattered across. Parchments lay on top of one another with the large books meant for keeping the kitchen accounts open on top of it all. Quills were stuck into numerous items—an apple, a wooden bowl, or a plate—to keep them from having their tips destroyed.

"As ye see, I am a better cook than bookkeeper."

"You shouldn't have to be both," Deirdre informed her. "Someone needs to bring it to the attention of the laird that there are duties his sister did which still require attention."

The cook laughed and so did the five girls peeking through the door frame. A sharp snap from the cook's fingers sent them all hurrying back to their duties.

"Well now, it seems the position of another lady to be telling the laird what he should be doing. That is nae my place."

The cook lowered herself but there was a look of relief on her face as she quickly returned to her kitchen.

Deirdre looked at the mess and discovered herself smothering a soft giggle. It would seem she had found a place at Drumdeer.

"Let's see what sense we can make of this mess, Amber."

⁓

"Where is she?"

Quinton didn't care for how angry he sounded. He wasn't in the mood to examine his emotions too closely. He turned to glare at Coalan, the silence of the ladies' solar sending his ire up even more.

"Somewhere in the castle. She did no' leave."

"Ye're certain of that?"

His captain scoffed at him. "In those clothes? Me men had better be sure she did nae get past them."

Quinton normally had more faith in his men. He didn't care for the fact that he doubted them now but there was something about not knowing where Deirdre was which made him forget why he was normally so sure of things.

The reason really wasn't so hard to put his finger on. He'd spent too much time thinking about her during the day when he had important things to focus on. Instead he'd looked up and wondered what she was doing.

Tracking her through his castle became an interesting journey as he heard tales of what she'd helped with. The spinners claimed she knew her way around a spinning wheel, which was no light praise. His cook smiled when she spoke of Deirdre and commented on the fact that she wasn't easy to fool when it came to how much flour it took to put bread on the tables.

"She spent most of the afternoon in there."

The cook pointed to the back room and he walked through the archway to see the account books neatly stacked. There was a roll of parchments waiting on one side of the table to be entered into the books but they were contained in a basket to keep them from spreading across the tabletop.

"The lady took the books in hand, and I'm right grateful for it," the cook announced.

Quinton turned to look at the woman. "I suppose I should have recalled that my sister was seeing to the account books."

The cook lowered herself. "Ye've more important matters to be concerned with than women's duties."

He caught sight of several maids looking around the doorway and noticed that the kitchen was utterly silent. His people were waiting to see what he'd say about Deirdre doing a task normally reserved for the laird's family.

The fact that the cook had allowed her near the books said the woman respected Deirdre.

Quinton discovered himself grinning as he absorbed the fact that Deirdre Chattan was no pampered laird's daughter. He found the knowledge sitting quite comfortably on his shoulders.

"Yer faith is well placed," he announced before quitting the kitchens to search for Deirdre once more.

When he found her at last, it was in one of the older towers near a set of kitchens used only when there were guests. The rest of the time, it was where the musicians gathered at the end of the day to play tunes on their instruments. The younger folks danced in the center of the room while enough older Cameron people sat on the benches to make the gathering respectable. One of the hearths had a fire laid in it and Deirdre was illuminated by its light. Her silk velvet overrobe shone like a fine jewel as she sipped mulled cider from a common wood mug and nodded her head in time with the music.

When the dance ended and another began, a lad offered her his hand in spite of Amber shaking her head at him. Quinton watched, realizing he was very interested in seeing what she'd do when she didn't realize he was watching.

❧

Deirdre shook her head, refusing the offer to dance. The young Cameron man looked disappointed but she didn't regret her choice.

She was becoming frustrated with the way she compared every man to Quinton. She was acting the fool to do such a thing. Quinton Cameron had received what he wanted from her. Allowing herself to dwell upon him was sure to led her to heartache and disappointment when the man wed himself an heiress.

But she refused the next offer to dance and then another one.

"Do nae ye care for dancing?"

She jumped, her body responding instantly to Quinton Cameron's voice. A ripple of awareness went across her skin, even before she turned to look at him. His grin was too smug for her taste, a glint of victory in his eyes which rubbed her temper because the brute obviously believed she was waiting for him.

"I was just waiting for a man I truly wanted to dance with."

"Is that a fact?" His grin became a wide smile.

Deirdre sat her mug aside. "It is. Coalan, will ye partner me?"

The captain had his hand out instantly but he frowned making her think it had simply been reflex that saw him responding to her invitation. Deirdre didn't allow him to rethink his position but placed her hand in his and gripped his fingers when he began to withdraw it. She pulled the half resisting man toward the forming dance set and smiled at him.

That only gained her a frown from him but he moved in time with the country dance. Coalan abandoned her the moment the last notes were finished, giving her a quick pull on his bonnet before he hurried away from her. But one of the younger men who had tried to get her to dance stepped up and partnered her for the next dance.

The music was lively and the dances put sweat on her forehead. Her thigh ached but she laughed because it felt good to move. But her partner suddenly disappeared when she turned in time and she came back around to face Quinton. He offered her a cocksure grin as he took to chasing her up and down the set in time with the music. His people began to hoot and encourage him with loud clapping. It was only a dance and yet she discovered herself more breathless than she should have been. He caught her up against his wide chest and swung her around in the correct finishing motions of the dance but she felt like it was the first time she'd ever been embraced. Her senses were full of him, the way he smelled, the way he held her against him with just the right amount of pressure.

She stumbled when he set her back on her feet and the room filled with laughter. Her face flooded with color and she offered him a quick courtesy before dashing off and out of the room.

"I see ye do enjoy dancing for ye're blushing."

Deirdre bit back the gasp that tried to escape her lips. She walked farther out into the night, feeling exposed in the light.

"It's warm inside. Spring has truly arrived," she muttered in a sweet tone that even Kaie would have approved of. Quinton lifted one eyebrow and offered her an expression that no doubt he'd used at court when circumstances forced him to appear mild.

"I'm feeling it quite keenly myself."

His tone became wicked and she fought the urge to laugh. "Behave," she muttered but it was the truth that she wished he wouldn't.

"Why should I?"

She propped her hands on her hips. "Ye are intent on being naughty."

"Lads are naughty, I'm a man grown."

She turned and began walking. The darkness suited her mood suddenly. "I've noticed."

He chuckled, the sound soft and enticing when coupled with the shadows. "Good. But I confess I would have enjoyed proving the fact to ye if ye'd declared me a liar for saying it."

He suddenly captured her hand in the dark. She felt the connection between their flesh travel up her arm leaving goose bumps along the way.

"Come lass, let's disappear into the night shadows before Coalan takes his eyes off young Amber long enough to notice I've given him the slip."

"Now ye sound like a lad."

"Nae lass. When I was a lad, I thought having so much attention was something to envy."

She couldn't suppress a short laugh.

He grinned at her and pulled her gently up a set of stairs and then into a hallway. Their steps echoed between the stone walls but only because everything else was so silent. It was the time when the church preached against going out of doors for the demons and witches were at play.

Of course, it was also the time when lovers met. Her cheeks warmed as she felt the sure grip of the man she'd been unable to resist.

Lover…

"Do nae slow down… Coalan knows me better than I know myself at times."

Quinton sounded as eager as a boy on his way to ride his favorite horse between study sessions. He tugged her up a set of stairs and across a section of wall before going through a doorway into a small courtyard.

He sighed when he'd succeeded in pulling her into the center of it. The moon wasn't quite high enough to illuminate it yet but there was enough light from the stars to show her small patches of greenery. She could smell the rosemary and heather and a bird bath stood off to one side, its water appearing glassy in the night.

"Running away from yer captains… is that yer game, Laird Cameron?"

"It is and I'd appreciate if ye'd play along and dispense with the titles."

He stretched out his arms and leaned his head back. She heard a few pops before he straightened back up with a low groan. "Do nae mistake me, Coalan is an excellent man but there are times when I need to breathe." His voice sounded tired but also relaxed. She actually felt privileged to be sharing the moment with him.

"And ye do nae get many of those now that ye are laird and earl?"

He shrugged. "I understand why and expect ye do too."

"Aye, my father is never alone." It was necessary since more than one clan had a reason to plot the murder of a fellow laird.

"I doubt ye were allowed to be either."

Deirdre felt guilt claw its way across her heart. She'd sneaked away from her fellow Chattan women to meet her lover and it had brought shame to every member of her clan. She was the laird's daughter and expected to marry for an alliance.

"It's different for a woman," she remarked.

Quinton captured her hand once again and carried it to his lips. He pressed a soft kiss against it that sent heat through her belly; it was a slow burn, like the coals gave off during the morning hours.

"That was no' meant to make ye feel guilty, Deirdre. I agree with ye that the world is harsher on women for doing the same things as a man."

She tossed her head and went to walk away but he refused to release her hand. Instead he used his grip to wrap her into an embrace with their joined hands behind her back.

"Yer nature is what I find attractive."

She'd somehow forgotten how much larger he was than herself. When she was sniping at him, she didn't seem to recall that he was an entire head taller. She felt small now but her body enjoyed that fact too much. Her nipples tingled before pulling into tight points she feared he felt against his chest.

He growled low and deep and rubbed his chest against hers. "Aye, I enjoy it full well."

She hissed but she wasn't sure if her frustration was aimed at him or herself.

"Of course ye do," she muttered, her vexation clear in her tone. She wiggled free, slightly amazed that he released her.

"Because ye think I brought ye up here for a tryst?"

"Did ye nae?" She walked away and poked one finger into the water of the bird bath. Ripples instantly appeared and ran away from where she touched the water.

"Well… maybe yes but no' only for that reason. If I wanted some meekly obedient bride, I'd have her and she'd most likely sit the day through in that solar without a single protest."

She looked toward him, trying to decide what he meant for his tone was quiet and pensive. He grinned when their eyes met.

"Ye make it sound as though I passed some manner of test by leaving the solar."

He followed her with a lazy pace but she felt him closing in on her with a soft excitement, tightening her belly.

"Maybe ye did for it's a truth I have no' given much thought to what the lack of a lady here is doing to my people. Ye brought it to my attention without saying a word."

She discovered herself fleeing from him in a slow pace while her eyelids actually fluttered. "I would have... spoken up if ye did nae notice... be sure of that." She was trying to sound firm but failed because she was too busy enjoying the fact that he approved her actions.

He stopped, and the moonlight illuminated a frown appearing on his face. "I am nae sure ye would have, for ye do nae think ye belong here."

"As I told ye, Quinton, I would never have gone to Melor if I did nae believe there would be more to our relationship than the lust. I thought he wanted the alliance with my father. I do nae earn my place on my back."

"Does that mean ye'll find the title of being me mistress more agreeable if you perform the tasks a lady should be doing?"

"No," she answered. "But I'll go mad before the end of the week if ye insist I sit in that solar."

"Maybe ye'll discover yerself caring about my people enough to want to stay, for they need ye here as much as I do."

There was a challenge in his voice that snared her

attention. She walked to him, feeling his attention on her as she closed the gap. Reaching up, she slid her hands along the side of his face. She stretched up, tilting her head to one side so she might kiss him.

Quinton met her halfway, but he didn't take command of the kiss. His lips waited on her motions, following her lead as she gently moved her mouth against his. Sensation flowed through her and confidence. She allowed the tip of her tongue to tease his lower lip in a slow motion that drew a shudder from him.

He closed his arms around her, pulling her against him, but not too fiercely. She felt him shaking as he controlled the urge to kiss her as he had always done before. The kiss remained hers, and she shivered with delight as she deepened it. Time ceased to have meaning. There was only the next breath and the next motion of her mouth against his. But she lost her concentration at last, and he seemed to sense it.

Quinton took command of her mouth in that instant. His lips pressed hers until she opened her jaw to allow his tongue to invade her mouth. It was bold, and her body liked it too much. Need began to torment her, and the memory of how much she had enjoyed being satisfied by him made it impossible to resist.

It was Quinton who pulled his lips away from hers. She couldn't read his expression because his face was cast all in shadow now that the moon was behind him.

"I did nae bring ye up here for a quick tumble."

He pulled her over to one of the open places.

"Did yer father ever have a swing strung up for ye?" he asked.

Deirdre saw the twin ropes hanging from a stone archway with a plank tied to their ends. She smiled, unable to help herself.

"When I was a girl… aye, but it has been a long time." She ran her fingertips over the rope, smiling when she felt that it wasn't weathered but smooth. She sat down on the plank, careful at first while she listened to hear any popping that might herald a breaking rope.

"It's in good repair."

She lifted her feet and laughed as the swing took her weight. Quinton caught both edges of the seat and pushed her up into the air. She sailed toward the moon and felt the night air chill her cheeks. When the swing reached its height limit, she fell backward. Her belly tightened, but the hold she had on each rope reassured her so she was free to enjoy the feeling. Her silk robes fluttered around her legs as Quinton gave her another push.

She laughed and heard him echoing the sound. He caught one of the ropes and leaned away from it. She began to turn around him in a crazy circle, which made her just a little dizzy, enough to see her laughing once more. The ropes twisted above her head, raising her up until she was face level with Quinton. He was chuckling softly before he stepped back, and the swing spun in a crazy series of circles to unwind itself. She squealed and held on tight until the swing was once again hanging as it had been when she first sat on it.

"Yer laughter is intoxicating, Deirdre."

"I like it better when ye call me by my name," she whispered.

He offered her a hand, and she placed hers in it, mesmerized by witnessing that he still knew how to play.

He pulled her toward him and nuzzled her chilled cheek with warm lips. "Ye enjoy it when I call ye hellion too, because ye are no' the sort of woman to accept a man who does nae snarl back at ye when ye try to frighten him off with yer spitting."

She wiggled. "That makes me sound like a shrew."

"It's a compliment. Ye know I respect yer strength at the same time that I'm trying me hand at winning yer surrender in me bed."

She believed him, even if she had every reason not to. His embrace opened, but he captured her hand once again and began to tug her back toward the stairs with the hold. She resisted, unsure what to do as desire flared up inside her, but her memory reminded her what happened when men had had enough of their lovers.

Quinton turned to look at her. "Come to bed, lass. It's where we belong."

She realized that he might overwhelm her right there, and that bit of knowledge set her feet to moving. His fingers tightened slightly around hers as they descended into the hallways.

She refused to think. It was a fact that she'd spent too many days considering and chastising herself. She wanted to feel. Nothing more.

A single candle burned in the eagle tower chamber, but Quinton pinched it out. She walked to the window and opened it, allowing the moonlight to fill the room. He slid his hands around her hips and up to her breasts, where he cupped each tender globe before teasing the hard tips with his thumbs.

"Now come lie with me, Deirdre, and I promise to be yer lover until the sun rises and we must face our responsibilities once more…"

❧

Deirdre blinked and wrinkled her nose when she smelled an unfamiliar scent. It wasn't unpleasant, but she lifted her head and felt her eyes go wide when she realized that Quinton was still in bed with her.

Light was streaming in through the windows, but what horrified her was the sound of Amber rustling about the chamber. The girl wasn't looking at them, but Quinton was toying with her hair instead of rising and she realized he was making a point of being seen with her.

He watched her, his eyes full of hard intent and his expression stony. He was at his stubborn best, but she was not in the mood to bend.

She laid her hand on his chest and grabbed a handful of his hair. He snorted before rolling out of the bed and away from her. Amber jerked around at the sound but instantly turned her back on her laird when she noticed that he wasn't wearing a stitch.

Quinton stared at her, a quick flash of surprise lighting his eyes as he rubbed the spot she'd abused. But he suddenly grinned when she continued to glare at him.

"Look after yer mistress well, Amber."

The girl kept her back turned. "Aye, Laird, it will be an honor."

"Yes, it is, but one ye have earned. Lady Deirdre told me how well she thinks of ye last night and asked that ye be appointed to serving her."

Amber clapped her hands together with glee. Deirdre raised a hand to rub at her eyes, because she didn't want to spoil the moment for the girl with her own discontent.

Quinton's words sealed her fate, for there wouldn't be a soul in the castle who didn't hear about it before sundown. Deirdre felt her temper rise, but she was more angry with herself for failing to resist the temptation of spending the night together.

She needed to escape Drumdeer, because she obviously lacked the discipline to resist its laird.

Amber brought her clothing forward the moment she climbed from the bed. Once dressed, she followed the Cameron girl down to the solar, where two other girls had laid out a morning meal for her.

Bells began to ring, and Amber gasped. The girl looked up, horror on her face.

"What is wrong?" Deirdre asked.

Amber didn't answer but hurried to the window and leaned out. The ringing grew louder as all the bells along the walls began to chime.

"The laird is riding out..." Amber answered. "It must have been the letter from the lieutenant general that is taking him away from ye."

Deirdre leaned out of the window too and looked toward the main gate. Two columns of riders were streaming out and down the steep incline. Even from her distance, the yellow, orange, and black of the Cameron plaid was clear in the morning sun. Each man had a sword strapped to his back, Highland fashion.

Quinton rode at the front. She marveled at his daring, but at the same time, part of her would have been disappointed if he'd hidden farther back in the columns. Her cheeks colored as she recalled his words.

Ye enjoyed that savageness last night.

He was right. She was drawn to his strength, even his bluntness. It was a shame, for she had been raised gently, and still she had no taste for the marriage her father had arranged for her. She wished she understood the wildness inside her, but she had to be honest and admit that it had always been her way. She'd hidden it from her father and her kin to appear the image of correctness they deserved, but it had always been a facade.

Quinton was the only man who seemed able to see through her playacting.

"I'm sure he'll be back soon, Lady Deirdre."

"I am no' so certain." But maybe it was fate's way of showing her she was right to think of continuing on to her place with the queen. It would take planning, and she suddenly looked at the Cameron girls all trying to attend her and realized that slipping away from them would be her greatest challenge. She didn't doubt she would have to slip away from Quinton, for the man was every bit as stubborn as she was.

But she would have a place in life that her father might be proud of. Remaining at Drumdeer as Quinton's mistress would not accomplish that. Word would spread quickly now that Quinton had appointed staff to attend her. Deirdre fought the urge to flinch, because her father deserved better than to have his eldest daughter embarrassing him among his fellow lairds.

"Did ye say there was a storeroom below this chamber? I believe I'd like to see it."

Amber wrung her hands for a long moment. "The stores are but one floor below us; I'll pull up the trapdoor."

"Yer service is exemplary, Amber."

The girl beamed before reaching down to pull a section of the floor up. Deirdre was grateful for the fact that the girl was intent on her task because it kept Amber from noticing how delighted Deirdre was to discover a way down to the floor beneath them. She should have thought of it before. The valuable things in the solar were best protected in the tower. It was also reasonable to think no one might be allowed below the solar to keep rumors from surfacing about lovers and afternoon trysts.

"Mind yer step, the stairs are steep," Amber urged her.

Deirdre looked through the opening the trapdoor revealed. True to Amber's word, there were a set of stairs that would allow her to descend to the floor beneath. It was musty looking and dim because the shutters were still closed, but light was penetrating through the seams of the wooden window coverings.

"Amber, there is something I need from the kitchen."

The girl looked up, eager to please. Deirdre ignored the guilt that tried to assault her. She had to find ways to send Amber away from her, or escaping would be impossible.

"I need a morning brew to keep my figure slim."

Amber understood instantly. There was a glint of comradely understanding in her eyes that only two women might share between each other. There were herbs that when steeped in hot water would keep a woman from ripening with child. The church forbade such things, but there were times when it was still the best course of action to take.

"And I do nae want anyone to know. It is a private thing, so go yerself."

Amber nodded, but she looked unsure. "I should ask the laird about that before fetching it. Ye're his mistress, by his own word. I heard and saw it myself."

Deirdre turned to look back out the window to hide the temper that colored her face. "He is no' here. Besides, a man marries for children." She turned to offer Amber a shrug. "Most nobles do nae care so much for the burden of bastards. I've no wish to spend my years worrying that my sons will resent their sire for the fact that they shall no' inherit his position."

Amber abandoned her suspicions. "I'll go for ye." Her voice carried a note of understanding. She left with a determined stride.

Deirdre hurried to descend the stairs, wincing as her wound protested the steep angle of those steps. Once on the floor below the solar, she went and opened one of the windows so more light would fill the room. She frowned when she scanned the room and only found one door. She'd seen it from the other side when passing it on the way to the upper floor. The men set to watching the solar door wouldn't miss anyone leaving from that door.

She shrugged aside her disappointment and began to look through what was in the chamber. She couldn't help smiling, because it was a bit like being a child on the morning of the New Year when gifts were given from parents to children. All around the room were bundles and chests. The scent of rare spices such as cinnamon and cloves gently filled the room. A large fabric loom was leaning in pieces against one wall, just waiting to serve in case the lady wanted to use her time to produce something more practical than a tapestry.

Deirdre began to touch bundles, gently pushing aside the coarse sackcloth that bound them, to see what was covered for protection. There was more velvet and silk, the amount of fine fabric shocking her, for she suspected Joan Beaufort might not have as much herself.

But what made Deirdre smile was the neat stack of wool robes she discovered on one side of the chamber. There were five of them, all sewn in the same design and cut of the same color of wool. They looked new, and she felt her smile fade when she realized Quinton must have had them made in preparation for his bride's arrival. They would have been given as honorary tokens to the girls whom the lady of the manor selected as her personal servants.

That was the position Amber was striving so diligently to gain from her.

She moved the bundle of lady's maids' robes and lifted the lid of a simple chest. It had no lock but was constructed to keep the moist weather away from whatever was inside. She smiled once again when she found the fine boots that had been made to go with the robes. They were only ankle-high, made for inside the castle, but at least they were constructed of leather. She eagerly anticipated being able to wear them.

She had no idea when such a moment might

present itself, but she would have to look for it and hope it came while Quinton was away.

She lifted her head and listened. Soft steps came across the floor of the solar above. Deirdre stood up and climbed the stairs. One of the other girls who had appeared a time or two was setting out a meal on the table. There was still no sign of Amber.

The girl looked up and lowered herself. "The laird says to bring ye yer meals here while he's away."

"How considerate of him."

"What have ye there?"

Deirdre held out the clothing. "Some common robes that I'd like taken to my bedchamber. I'll need something warm to sleep in with the laird away."

"I'll take them."

Deirdre handed off the robes and sat down to avoid having the girl see how relieved she was to be able to get the wool garments someplace where she might use them to escape.

But she missed the look the maid gave her. It was sly and calculated. The moment the girl left the solar, she hurried to a little-used room in one of the oldest keeps. There, hidden among the forgotten things that no one used any longer, was a small writing desk. She pulled a piece of parchment from it and began to pen a letter.

Once it was done, she folded it and tucked it into her bodice. She took the robes to the eagle tower, but only after she slipped the letter into the hand of her cousin, who would take it out of Drumdeer.

She didn't allow her guilt to bother her any too much. Her mother had been a Ross before her father stole her during a raid. So keeping Mary Ross informed of what happened at Drumdeer wasn't so hard a thing to do; it was only a letter, after all, and the lady paid well for the information.

❧

Amber returned empty-handed from the kitchen.

"The cook refused me. She said it was a sin to prevent the laird's seed from taking root, because God placed him in his position. I went to the brewmaster, but he turned me away as well."

"I see." And she did. There were traditions in the Highlands older than the church. When the laird fathered a babe, it was considered good luck for the clan and a sign that God favored them. The farmers would all anticipate a good harvest if she conceived, and there would be weddings among the Cameron girls, because their mothers believed it was a blessed season.

And she would be guilty of bringing a child into the world who would bear the stain of her sin for its entire life.

Well… she would not sit idle and wait for it to happen. Since she had failed so miserably to resist allowing Quinton into her bed, she'd just have to devise a way of escaping the cage he'd closed about her.

She had to… it was her duty to her conscience.

❧

"Hold!" Quinton held his hand up, and the men behind him reined in their horses. In front of him, he could see the dust rising, telling him there were horses on the road behind the hills.

"Most likely Hay retainers," Coalan announced.

"I agree." But Quinton still felt his palm itch to draw his sword. He watched the road, waiting to see what colors the men approaching were wearing. The letter he'd received from Archibald Douglas had been full of threats. The man was desperate to stop the queen from marrying again, and Quinton doubted he was the only Highland laird who had gotten such a letter.

The Douglas were always happiest when they could manage to stir up the clans and pit them against one another, because it meant they wouldn't unite against the Douglas.

That was exactly why he'd made it his personal mission to keep the clans from fighting. Quinton didn't trust the Douglas, and he never would. Scotland needed her king, not the Douglas growing powerful enough to depose the young James II, because they felt there wouldn't be enough unity among the other clans to do anything about it.

"It's Roan McLeod."

Quinton relaxed, and so did Coalan. Roan McLeod was the eldest son of the McLeod laird. His father was old, and Roan led the clan, even if he wasn't laird just yet. He was also the man who had been set to wed young Kaie Chattan. Quinton had had the duty of telling him the girl harbored a true calling to serve the church. Some men would have kept her anyway because of the alliance she would have brought with her, but Roan had released her, despite his father's displeasure.

"And what brings the Cameron riding out

today?" Roan asked when he'd closed the distance between them.

Quinton grinned and reached into his shirt to pull the letter from Archibald Douglas from the pocket sewn to the inside of the garment.

"Well now…" Roan reached into his doublet and produced a similar letter. "Have one of those myself. What do ye make of the fact that our good queen seems to be making her escape?"

"I caught a lass wearing Joan Beaufort's gold and silk."

Roan's expression hardened, and he edged his horse closer, but the stallion took offense at being urged so close to another male horse. Quinton snorted and dismounted. He didn't care for the position of weakness being on his feet put him in, but Roan followed suit, and it was clear from the man's face that he liked it even less.

"Me men caught Deirdre Chattan on the road in the queen's clothing." Quinton informed his fellow laird.

Roan cursed. "I wish I'd known that, for I passed a couple of nuns riding up to the high ground, and I thought their horses mighty fine for their sackcloth robes."

Roan snorted and growled when he realized Quinton was grinning. "They will have made it to the black knight of Lorn's castle by now. Why do ye find that pleasant news?"

Quinton eyed the man. "Because I think the Douglas are going to find it harder to plot against the rightful king with the queen wed again."

Roan relented. "Aye, it is better for the McLeod and the Cameron. I agree." He suddenly grinned. "So what have ye done with Deirdre Chattan?"

"I kept her. After all, by wearing the queen's clothing and never identifying herself, she allowed my men to labor under a misconception. I couldnae have my lads working so hard for naught, you understand."

"Certainly no'," Roan agreed with a smirk.

"She's secure in one of me towers, where such a delicate female belongs."

Roan snorted with amusement. He bent over and braced his hands on the tops of his thighs as he shook with laughter. Quinton raised an eyebrow.

"What? Do ye nae believe me?"

"Oh aye…" Roan wiped a hand across his face. "I've never known ye to be a liar before, but I'll admit I'm tempted to argue with ye about whether or no' Deirdre Chattan is delicate."

"Well, ye have me there. She's a hellion."

Roan grunted. "Most men would say that word like a curse."

Quinton shrugged. "I am nae most men."

"No, ye are nae, but she isna just any woman. She's Chattan's eldest daughter, and her dowry went to the church. A fact ye helped bring about. What do ye plan to do with her?"

"Why do ye ask me in that tone, Roan McLeod? What should I do with her?" Quinton demanded.

His fellow Highlander stared him down, offering him no quarter as the tension thickened between them. The men waiting on them grew quieter as they noticed the stand off. Roan suddenly chuckled, amusement returning to his eyes.

"Well now, Quinton. Seems a true shame that ye need to be asking what to do with a fiery lass like

Deirdre Chattan. But I suppose I could give ye a few instructions on what a man does with a fine woman like that after sunset—"

"Choke on them," Quinton replied. "I shared her bed last night, and since I've confirmed the queen is now another man's problem, I plan to return to warming myself next to Deirdre's spirit. So forget ye know where she is, man, for ye will nae be making amends with yer father for giving up yer bride by taking Deirdre. She belongs to me."

Roan snorted and pointed at him. "I agree it's a good thing the queen is settled, for it means I can get on with finding a way to deal with Robert Chattan, but I do nae for one moment believe Deirdre would agree she belongs to ye. No' after one night; no man is so memorable."

Roan began to return to his men, but Quinton reached out to stop him. "What do ye mean 'settle accounts with Robert Chattan'? His daughters are taken now."

"No' the one whom Ruth Hay bore him."

"And how does yer father feel about ye wedding a bastard?"

Roan shrugged. "Erlina would nae be illegitimate if her mother wed Robert Chattan, now would she?"

"I hear the woman refused him."

Roan grinned. "Well… ye see… so much time has passed, I feel the two should be reunited so they might discuss the matter now that tempers have had time to cool. Think of it as a Christian duty I'm about. The two really need to wed and wipe the blight from their souls, as well as legitimize their daughter."

Quinton frowned. "The Hay will nae take it kindly if ye take one of their kin. Ruth Hay is Laird Kagan Hay's aunt."

"Does nae change the fact that I need her and Robert Chattan wed because me father has asked little enough of me in this life. He wants a Chattan alliance through my marriage, and I cannae be taking Kaie away from the church."

"Ye could take her, and the church would no' be able to argue with ye since she was contracted to ye, but I respect ye for no' forcing the girl into yer bed. She has a true calling."

"I seek more from my marriage than just what me father wants," Roan muttered, the frustration clear in his voice.

"That's plain enough, or ye would have kept Kaie Chattan instead of granting her plea to go to the abbey."

Roan grunted. "Well, it's time for the church to repay my generosity and help me see Ruth Hay and Robert Chattan wed."

"What does Robert Chattan have to say on the matter?" Quinton asked.

Roan suddenly grinned. "I have nae asked the man. I sort of figured he'll find it harder to argue with me if he is blinded by the sight of his beloved at the time I ask him."

Quinton grunted, but determination flashed in Roan's eyes. He offered Quinton a wink. "Ye'll also be owing me a debt of gratitude for keeping Robert busy while ye're settling the details of just what Deirdre is to you."

"Is that a fact?" Quinton demanded.

"It is, for it would certainly put a strain on yer courtship if her father showed up at yer gate."

"That it would," Quinton agreed.

Roan McLeod wasn't in the mood to budge on his plans. Quinton recognized the firm look in the other man's eyes. Roan wasn't laird yet, but his father's health was poor. The fact that Roan wanted to please a man who wouldn't likely live through the winter was a testimony to how much honor he had. Ruth Hay would be facing that determination, but Quinton wasn't worried Roan would harm her.

In fact, it had long been a mystery why she had run from Robert Chattan, for the two had been set to wed. Some liked to say it was because she had borne a daughter, and at the time Robert hadn't been laird of the Chattan. His father had been a strict man who believed Ruth failed in her duty when she birthed a female child. Rumor was that Robert's father had forbidden the marriage until Ruth produced a son who would carry on the Chattan line. Such a practice hadn't been unheard-of in those days; it was still in practice in some places. It was a custom many claimed came from hell's army and the Norsemen who had settled in the Highlands instead of taking their plunder back to their frozen countries. A laird only wed a woman who had already given him a son, because when it came to the laird's bloodline, there might be no chance taken on a marriage that would not yield male heirs.

But Ruth Hay had run from Robert Chattan, not been put out by his father, so the mystery persisted. She'd never married another either, and the alehouses were often filled with the gossips debating just why.

"Good luck to ye, Roan McLeod, but I do nae owe ye, for if I'd nae told ye of young Kaie's calling, ye'd have a weeping wife to keep ye company tonight," Quinton informed him. Owing favors could get a man in trouble fast, and he wasn't interested in accumulating debt if he could avoid it.

Roan frowned. "Fair enough. I am thankful for that service."

Roan turned his stallion, and his men followed. The dust rose up as they headed toward Hay land. Quinton smiled, for the first time content with not having anything pressing to keep him away from home.

"Drumdeer!"

Deirdre heard the bells ringing. A bolt of excitement raced through her, banishing the gloomy spirits she'd spent most of the day enduring.

"The laird is back," Amber announced. "No doubt he could no' stay away for even a night, because ye are here."

"Amber, that would be foolish for me to allow ye to believe." Deirdre meant to instruct the girl on what was proper, but Amber was on her feet and out of the small chamber behind the kitchen before she had the opportunity to mention how improper her relationship with Quinton was.

She battled more guilt, because she was now setting a poor example for the Cameron women. No doubt the church would want her locked in the stocks for her immorality.

Of course that would be amusing if Quinton landed there along with her.

She smiled at her own jest, for there was no possibility of it becoming a reality. Quinton was a noble. The priest might lecture him, but there would be no physical chastisement.

No, such a painful corrective measure would be reserved for her.

She shook her head and dipped her quill into the inkwell once more.

"How can I believe ye missed me when ye are paying more attention to that book than the fact I have returned?"

Deirdre jerked her hand away from the ink before she spilled it. "Do nae surprise me like that, Quinton Cameron," she declared as she rose from her seat. "I might have ruined the ledger, and it has taken me two days to make sense of it."

He looked surprised, and for a moment, she watched irritation flicker in his eyes over the tone she used. But his gaze swept down her body, sending heat into her cheeks. The low neckline of the overrobe granted him a full view of the swells of her breasts. His lips curved into a sensual grin as his attention settled on the creamy display.

"I should annoy ye more often, lass, for I like that pose ye've assumed full well."

Giggles erupted from the kitchen.

"Oh… I need decent clothing, ye insufferable man."

He raised his attention to her face, a question in his

eyes. "Insufferable?" He clicked his tongue in reprimand. "Now, lass, ye cannae complain about what ye reap from the seeds ye sow."

She stood straight to minimize the amount of breast he might see. "Is that so? Well, Quinton Cameron, I'll—"

She never finished, because the man reached across the narrow table and plucked her off her feet in a moment. He tossed her up and over his shoulder, to the delight of the maids peeking around the arched doorway. She sputtered, but he smacked her backside, and the sharp *pop* bounced between the walls of the kitchen while he carried her through them.

"Ye're a beast," she whispered so only he might hear her. A soft chuckle was her response as he strode through the hallways and up the stairs to her chamber, with her hanging over his shoulder.

"And ye are a hellion," he declared once he'd tossed her into the bed she'd spent too many hours thinking about. It bounced as it took her weight, but she only managed to push herself up to her elbows before Quinton joined her.

"And my lover," he whispered against her ear. His voice was hot and full of intent, which sent her body quivering with eager anticipation. She turned and embraced her lover.

Damn her reasons for needing to avoid his touch.

※

"Ye need to listen to me, Quinton."

He lifted one eyelid and growled softly, "We've communicated quite well for the past few hours, Deirdre."

"I want some different clothing, and yer people will nae allow me to have it without your approval." She detested having to ask him for such a thing.

He cupped one of her breasts and rubbed his thumb back and forth across the nipple. "I like ye just like this."

The man wasn't taking her seriously. His voice was lazy and still gruff with drowsiness.

"Quinton..."

He rolled over her, pushing her down into the bedding and sealing her demands beneath his kiss. Her mind abandoned thought a few moments later.

         ❧

Simon Smithson heard the door open with a squeal from the rusty hinges. His men all tightened their expressions. He stood up first, stepping forward to face whatever their fate was going to be. He didn't allow himself to dwell on the stories he'd heard of how the Highlanders liked to toy with their prisoners before killing them.

He'd take everything as it came.

Cameron retainers pushed him and his men out of the cell they'd inhabited for the last week and through the musty dungeon. Simon blinked as the sunlight hurt his eyes and blinded him. When his vision finally returned, he discovered himself facing the Earl of Liddell.

"Ye're free to go."

Simon frowned, wondering if he'd heard the Scot correctly.

"Get off me land." The earl pointed Simon toward his horses, their fine leather saddles still on the animals' backs.

"That's right. Ye leave with what ye came with," the earl continued.

"Then where is the lady?" Simon asked. His men hissed at him, fearing his impertinence might gain them the hanging the earl seemed willing to spare them if they left.

"She's a Scot and belongs here."

"She's earned a place with my mistress, and I should take her with us."

The earl glared at him, narrowing his eyes. Simon didn't retreat, even when the Highland laird looked like he was considering running him through.

"Do you truly believe only Scots understand duty?" Simon asked. "The lady was in my charge."

"Well then, you'll be leaving with almost everything ye came with, for the lady belongs to me," the earl announced. "Take yer men and go before I lose me patience."

Quinton watched the English escort leave through a small side gate. They didn't open it very often, but it would allow the captives to ride down a road that was deserted.

"I did nae expect them to ask for the lady," Coalan said.

"They cannae have her."

Quinton was repeating himself, but he didn't care if anyone thought him deranged for it. Deirdre would be staying.

❧

Mary Ross enjoyed many things—fine things and refined items—but such a lifestyle required attention to details. She looked at the letters that had come in from Drumdeer and other castles where she had informants. She selected the one from Drumdeer first because Quinton was still more important than any other man. She opened the letter and began to read, but quickly lost her good humor.

She crumbled the edges of the parchment as her hands began to clench tight with her anger.

The bitch!

No one would take her place in the eagle tower solar.

No one!

Mary paced around her own fine solar, wrinkling her nose at all the things her husband had provided for her.

She wanted none of it. Drumdeer was where she longed to be, and it had been too long since she had been directed by her family to wed a more powerful man. She had been waiting forever for him to die, and yet he lived. Quinton still loved her; such was the reason he'd not married. She knew it, actually felt it inside her heart, and it gave her comfort every time she was forced to tolerate her current husband.

But she couldn't stand idle while another woman called herself Quinton's mistress.

She suddenly stopped, a thought forming in her head. Mary hurried back to her letters, scanning the pages again to make sure she understood everything her spy was saying.

Well… if the Chattan girl wanted her place with the queen so badly, Mary would make sure the queen called for her. She looked about to make sure her attendants were still in the outer chamber where she had sent them. Once she was sure they were not peeking through the doorway, she opened her writing desk and took out a very fine piece of parchment.

One worthy of a queen.

⸎

"Ye've impressed my household."

Deirdre smiled, unable to stop her lips from curving. She was pleased to hear such a compliment from Quinton, for the man didn't hand them out without a solid reason.

She turned around and looked at him. "Oh my, so this is what you look like by the light of day."

He tilted his head but shrugged. "Aye, I'm guilty of avoiding ye after sunrise, but I enjoy the night hours full well."

She pressed her lips into a pout.

"Och now, I did nae mean it like that. Ye're a handsome woman, Deirdre, but ye have a stubborn nature. I was letting time soften yer attitude."

"Leave it to a man to call a woman stubborn when she is only attempting to do the right thing," Deirdre accused him, but her tone lacked true disgruntlement.

He crossed his arms over his chest. "If it includes leaving Drumdeer, ye can call me an unmovable ass, but we're nae discussing it."

"Clothing…" she hissed at him. "I want a say over what I wear, Quinton."

He shook his head. "Ye'd slip past me men too easily."

She slapped her hands down on top of the table where she'd been working. "Ye cannae simply keep me." Even as she spoke the words, she knew he could do exactly what he wanted. He was laird; no one would go against him.

His blue eyes were dark, contemplating her while he frowned. "I think we'll go back to seeing one another by moonlight, lass."

"For how long, Quinton?"

He stopped at the doorway and looked back at her.

"For as long as it takes for ye to admit ye belong with me."

He was gone before she could utter a retort. The kitchen was silent as the laird walked through it. Deirdre couldn't sit down, because her temper was rising so fast. She felt as though it would leave blisters on her cheeks, it raged so hot.

"Some lasses would be thankful the laird is willing to shoulder the responsibility for keeping them. It makes things easier between the lairds if the man is the one making such decisions."

It was the cook who spoke, filling the doorway while rubbing her hands on her apron. There was a look on her face that came with her years of experience. Deirdre sat down, defeated by the logic in the woman's words.

It was more than that, though.

Deirdre felt the walls pressing in on her. What bothered her most about how she felt was the fact that part of her was relieved. Days had passed into weeks and longer, until a month had gone while she was at Drumdeer. The castle was growing on her, and her will to leave fading.

Her father's face rose from her memory—the disappointment she'd witnessed in his eyes when she departed for the abbey and her place of shame. She couldn't take her own happiness again at the expense of her sire.

She mustn't, for she feared she'd be unable to live with herself if she did.

❧

"God damn Douglas," Quinton growled as he reread the letter in front of him. The messenger who had brought it to him looked rather bored. Obviously the lad had seen similar responses to his master's letters.

"I'll be there," he announced. "Tell yer kin the Camerons will be coming."

The lad pulled on his bonnet and hurried down to where his horse was waiting. Quinton snorted and stood.

"I suppose it will be good to get out of this room." But it was the truth that he'd rather stay. Riding the hills by night was no longer drawing his attention as it once had. The confrontation he'd had with Deirdre weighed on his mind as he strapped his sword onto his back and descended to the yard.

He did not want her unhappy.

That thought gnawed on him as he rode out to meet the Earl of Douglas.

❧

The bells rang long before sunset.

Deirdre sighed, because her mood was melancholy, and it muddied her thoughts. The day stretched on endlessly, but she refused to leave her duty, in spite of not accomplishing very much. Once the day was finished, she walked to the bathhouse and indulged herself.

But once she was clean, the only place to go was her chamber. The place held too many whispers of the nights she'd spent there with Quinton. She realized she missed him, and the idea of not seeing him that night hurt.

She frowned and forced herself to climb to the bedchamber. She would not wander through the hallways looking lovesick. Her escort trailed her, and she was happy to leave them behind the solid door of the chamber. At least they did not hear her sigh when she stared at the empty chamber.

A soft knock interrupted her thoughts.

"The cook thought ye'd care for something before supper." The girl offered her a nod before sitting a tray on the table. She never pulled the cloth off and was gone in a flash.

Deirdre felt a touch of suspicion tingle down her spine as she reached for the cloth. When she pulled it away, she discovered a plate of bread and cheese and fresh summer berries.

But there was also a letter.

Her name was clearly written on it, and she picked it up. It was sealed with wax, but there was no signet pressed into it. She broke through the dried wax and unfolded the parchment.

Deirdre…
You have served me well. Your place is waiting for you if you will journey to the black knight of Lorn's holding to serve me.
Joan Beaufort

Deirdre held the letter close to her chest for a moment. She knew where the black knight of Lorn called home. He was a powerful man, and it made perfect sense that the queen would have chosen him to wed.

"Mistress…" Amber was out of breath and stopped in the doorway to pant. "I did nae realize ye'd be leaving the accounts before supper."

She hurried into the room while Deirdre turned to hide the letter from her. "It is no difficulty, Amber. I simply longed for a bath, and I'm no' yet accustomed to having anyone tending to me."

Deirdre looked about for a place to conceal the letter from Amber's attentive eyes.

"Who brought ye food?" Amber sounded suspicious, and she looked at the plate with a frown on her lips.

"I do nae know the girl's name. I've seen her at least once before."

Amber scoffed before realizing she had allowed the sound past her lips. "Forgive me, mistress, but I'd prefer ye only partake of what I bring ye." Amber picked up the tray and walked toward the door with it.

Deirdre might have argued with her for being so protective, but she took the opportunity to slip the letter beneath the cushion of the window seat.

"I'll be back with supper for ye, mistress; the cook won't begrudge ye eating a bit early since the laird is nae here." There was a knowing gleam in her eye that sent Deirdre toward the window seat the moment the door shut. She pulled out the letter and read it once more.

Her heart suddenly protested, but she ignored it. Hadn't she sworn to keep her heart as cold as stone? Well, she had, and even if there was much to like about her life at Drumdeer, there was still her father's honor to consider. She looked at the bed she'd shared with Quinton, and felt tears sting her eyes.

She went across the chamber to the opposite window to check for any sign of Quinton's return.

She had to remain firm in her choice. It was the only honorable one. The last time she'd taken a lover, it had been because he'd promised her marriage. A bride didn't always have to be a maiden, so long as there were wedding vows later. Quinton had not promised her a wedding, nor was the man willing to listen to what she wanted from their relationship.

She felt the sting of that shame keenly. Maybe if she could shoulder the weight of that burden alone, she might follow her heart and stay. But to become his mistress would shame her father and her clan. She refused to do it, even if her father had always pronounced her guilty of that crime. Melor Douglas had deceived her into yielding her innocence to him.

But Quinton had not, and unless he was prepared to offer her more, she would leave him now that she knew where the queen was.

Amber returned with a cheerful smile. "The cook outdid herself tonight. You'll enjoy supper."

Deirdre hurried to conceal her troubled emotions, but not before the girl noticed the gloom darkening her features.

"Do nae fret, lady. The laird will return; he always does." Amber hurried to lay out the supper.

"Thank you, Amber. I am well for the night, simply tired."

The girl smiled with relief. A flicker of wicked understanding flashed in the girl's eyes. "Ye have been keep up late quite often, mistress."

Deirdre felt her cheeks heat, but she nodded. "Aye, so I am going to seek my bed early. Good night."

Amber left the chamber, and the moment door closed, Deirdre hurried to the table where a small writing desk sat. She opened it and pulled a clean sheet of parchment from it. Quinton deserved an explanation, and she penned him a few lines.

> *Quinton,*
>   *I've gone to take my place with the queen. Remaining with ye is something I'd like, but it will no' bring honor to my name. I must think of my father.*
>   *Deirdre Chattan*

She looked about the chamber but settled on leaving the letter on the chair that he used when eating at the table. A quick glance toward the window sent her heartbeat accelerating. She went to the bed and began to rearrange it. She pulled the seat cushions off the chairs and pushed them beneath the coverlet to make it look as though she were in the bed. The sun was beginning to set, and she felt her chance for escape sinking with it. Once the gates were closed for the night, she would be imprisoned. The castle was large, but not large enough to hide in if it was discovered that she was missing.

The clothing she'd taken from the solar storerooms was still sitting in the bedchamber. Deirdre had carefully pushed it behind the silk clothing Coalan had given to Amber from the queen's horse. She picked up the ankle-high boots and pushed her feet into them. She fought back frustration as she laced them closed, but smiled with satisfaction to at last be wearing proper footwear. If she never wore another pair of silk slippers, she would be content.

She returned to the door and pulled it open in nothing but the common underrobe and boots.

"I need Amber. Go and fetch her, please." One of the lads pulled on the corner of his cap before starting down the stairs. Deirdre closed the door and forced herself to count to one hundred so the first retainer might reach the bottom of the tower.

She opened the door again and looked into the startled face of the remaining retainer. "I cannae wait for Amber. My leg pains me too much. Fetch Tully quickly."

"But, lady… I cannae leave my post."

"Do nae be ridiculous… ye are here for me. Fetch me what I need, and quickly. I'll bar the door if that puts yer worries to rest. Now go."

The youth opened his mouth to argue once more, but Deirdre lifted her hand and pointed him down the stairs. He shut his mouth with a snap and took the stairs at a run. Deirdre had to control the urge to run across the chamber. She couldn't risk having her steps heard by the youth. Such would certainly betray the fact that her leg injury had healed very nicely, but it was the only excuse she could think of to get both men away from her door.

She counted as she shrugged into the wool overrobe and covered her hair with the plain veil that matched the serving attire. She grabbed the bread and cheese from her supper and tied it up in a linen napkin.

She turned her back on the warm stew in spite of the rumble of protest from her belly. She reached out and pinched out the candles before hurrying out of the chamber and pulling the door closed behind her. She ran down the steps, her lungs threatening to burst before she made it to the bottom of the eagle tower. Time seemed to slow down, each step taking three times as long to pass over as it normally did. At the bottom floor, she turned and forced her pace to become even as she moved toward the long stone hallway that connected the tower to the rest of the castle. She looked down, trying to appear haggard and worn by the day.

Most of the inhabitants were in the great hall, enjoying the last meal of the day and conversation with their friends now that their duties were finished. Retainers remained on watched on the walls, but they faced outward, scanning the darkening hills for signal fires.

Inside the stable, only a few young boys remained. They were the newest members of the staff and therefore had to sit watch while the older boys and men got the chance to enjoy supper in the hall. The boys were gathered around the remains of the blacksmith's fire. They broke bread with one another while one of them tossed a set of dice.

She passed them and took a mare that was in a stall at the far end of the stables. There was no time to saddle her, only to slip the bit into her mouth and toss a blanket over her back. With a soft pat to gentle her, Deirdre pulled her gently from the stables and toward the main gate. A few people were still passing through it, on their way down to the village for the night. She muttered a prayer before leading the mare forward toward the open gate.

~❦~

Tully arrived first. She frowned when her soft rap failed to gain any answer from within the chamber. A moment passed as the young retainer became increasingly nervous.

"She's waiting on ye to tend her leg," he insisted, gesturing for her to enter the chamber.

Tully opened the chamber door a mere two inches and saw that the candles were no longer burning. Amber froze behind her, and the two retainers followed them.

"My lady?" she whispered. "Do ye need me yet tonight?"

There was no answer, but the small lantern that hung outside the chamber door for the retainers to see by cast its yellow light over the bed. The lump beneath the coverlet was plain.

"She's sleeping," Tully whispered.

"But the lady insisted that she needed ye."

Tully lifted one weathered hand to silence the lad. She looked into the dark chamber, staring at the bed for a long moment.

"I hear that noble ladies change their minds quickly. She's gone to her bed, and that will heal her leg better

than anything I have to offer." Tully firmly closed the
door and nodded.

"Let her be, and do nae fret. Ye did as she asked."
Tully looked at Amber. "Find yer bed, child. Ye look
as though our fine lady works ye hard."

"It will be worth it if she names me her chief lady's
maid. Such would make me family proud."

The two lads set to guard the door both stared at
one another as Tully and Amber descended the stairs.

"I do nae understand ladies," one announced.

"Nor do I. Do ye want to play cards?"

One began to deal out cards on a tiny table that
sat near the door. It was a good way to pass the time
as well as keep their wits keen throughout the long
hours of the night. Their duty was to guard the door,
so they would.

❧

Deirdre had to suppress the urge to move to fast. She
trembled like an autumn leaf ready to fall. Retainers
watched those crossing out of the castle, but only
with mild interest. In the servant robes, she passed
through easily. It seemed too simple, but her muscles
ached from the tension. She waited until she was
several hundred feet from the gate before mounting
the mare. The animal might look old, but it still had
strength and took to the road in a graceful canter.
Deirdre leaned low over the neck of the mare,
tucking her veil close to her face as she headed away
from Drumdeer.

It was a bittersweet moment, filled with a sense of
accomplishment, but also remorse. She refused to turn

her head and look back over her shoulder. Honor was not about making the easy choice.

She rode through the night, using the moon to keep her direction true. She avoided the village, the memory of how Coalan had captured her too vivid in her mind for her to risk being seen. By dawn, she could see that she was still on Cameron land, because the men working in their fields wore the same yellow, orange, and black plaid Quinton did. She slid from the back of the mare to give the animal a rest.

She found a small river to allow the animal to drink. She lay down, intending to close her eyes for only a moment while the mare drank its fill. But sleep smothered her intentions, taking control of her the moment her body was at ease. Her will ended up succumbing to the needs of her body and the warm weather. The grass felt perfect against her cheek while the scent of new plants made her sleep deep and restful.

Riding all night didn't normally bother Quinton. The dawn showed him his castle, and it was a fine sight, made even better by the knowledge that Deirdre was inside. He didn't make the mistake of thinking she was waiting on him. Well, he wouldn't say she'd admit she was anticipating his return.

But part of him wanted her to.

He paused, holding his stallion back while he contemplated the towers turning gold in the rising sunlight. His stallion snorted, eager to return to his stable.

He was itching to find his bed too—the one he'd shared with Deirdre. He cursed the time it had taken him to return, for it had cost him the dark hours of the night. Those hours when he might have pulled Deirdre close and there wouldn't have been any fight left between them. Now that the day had begun, she'd be ready to spit at him once more. He'd been ignoring her attempts to talk. Maybe that was cowardice on his part, but avoiding any possibility of her talking her way into leaving him was what he wanted. He didn't understand his need for her, but he knew that he dreaded seeing her leave.

His cock stirred even as he regretted missing the opportunity to simply savor having her near.

He chuckled softly, amused by his own contrariness. He set his heels into the sides of his stallion, and the animal surged forward toward Drumdeer.

Beware, hellion…

☙

Amber struggled to stifle a yawn on her way into her mistress's chamber. It wouldn't do for the lady to think she was not up to the challenge of serving her. She opened the shutters and listened carefully for any sounds from the bed, but the chamber remained silent.

Too quiet, really. Tension began to creep through her, and she turned to look at the bed with suspicion. The feeling that something was not right refused to leave her. It twisted in her belly, making her move toward the bed in spite of the fact her mistress had yet to call for her.

A snap made her jump and sent her heart pounding at a frantic pace. She turned to find her laird standing behind her. Amber pressed a hand over her lips to seal her cry of surprise inside. Her laird winked, and she lowered her hand while staring at him in confusion.

Try as she might, she couldn't recall seeing Quinton Cameron, Earl of Liddell and laird of the Cameron, ever do anything as playful as wink. He grinned at her and chuckled softly while gesturing her toward the door.

"I'll wake yer mistress up, lass," he whispered when she passed him.

She had to lift her hand and press it against her lips again to avoid laughing while she was still in the chamber, but once she made it down the first few steps, she giggled. The girls on their way up to help her looked at her with confusion on their faces.

"Let's go to the hall. The laird just returned."

Understanding dawned on them all, and knowing gleams entered their eyes. A few more giggles floated up the stairs to amuse the men outside the chamber door.

Quinton grinned, anticipating Deirdre's annoyance with him waking her up. But the idea of what that fiery temper might be used for sent him toward the bed. He needed her before the demands of his station began to nip at him once again. In fact, it was amazing how strong his desire was to seek her out.

"Ye'll have to admit that I wore ye out or that ye remained awake waiting for me last night, since ye are still in bed," Quinton muttered softly. He tugged his shirt over his head and tossed his boots aside.

"But I am no' complaining. The idea of waking

ye up is most pleasant...." He crawled into the bed, sending his hands beneath the covers in search of his lover.

All he encountered was cold sheets. He searched the bed, disbelief coursing through him. He felt her loss like a cut, and it stung too much to contain. He bellowed with rage, while throwing the bedding to the floor to make sure his mind wasn't playing tricks on him.

But Deirdre was not in the bed. He stared at that certainty as rage began to burn inside him so hot, he knew without a doubt why some men went insane over women.

She'd left him, and it hurt.

So fucking badly, he wished there were a man taking her from him, because he wanted someone to kill.

❧

Amber was pushed into the wall by Coalan as he rushed up the stairs in response to his laird's cry. It was one of rage; there was no mistaking that. People in the yard heard it, and more Cameron retainers took the stairs at a run in their efforts to get to their laird's side. Amber followed, horror flooding her when she reached the top floor and found only men inside the chamber. The bedding was strewn across the floor, proving that her mistress was nowhere to be found.

"Saddle fresh horses and do it fast, because I'm riding out!" Quinton roared. He turned a deadly look toward Amber.

"When was the last time ye saw yer mistress?"

The men surrounding their laird parted, leaving her facing him. There was no hint left of the teasing man who had winked at her. Fury danced in his eyes. He snarled as he shoved his foot into one of his boots, but it was the word "mistress" that stiffened Amber's spine. She wanted the position of lady's maid, and it wouldn't be given to a coward.

"Just before sunset. The lady claimed that she wanted to eat here." Amber looked over at the table where the forgotten meal still sat. Coalan knocked the linen cloths covering the dishes aside to see what lay beneath. But Amber was the one who knew exactly what was missing.

"She took the bread and cheese... and one cloth," she announced, but a hint of silk velvet visible over the table made her pause and lean down to pick up the discarded overrobe. It was wrinkled from having been lying in a puddle on the floor all night long, and the delicate slippers were beneath it.

"What is she wearing?"

Amber crossed to the large wardrobe that contained all the finery Deirdre had arrived with. She had hung each robe there herself, and she counted them twice before turning back to look at the laird.

"Nothing is missing, no' a single veil."

Quinton grabbed his shirt and pulled it over his head. "Well, I sure as hell hope the men on the gate would have noticed a naked woman walking through it. Find out who gave her the clothing I forbid her to have."

There was a gasp from one of the girls who had

followed Amber. Every head in the room turned toward her. She turned white, shaking visibly beneath the weight of so many stares.

"Speak up, girl. Tell me what she's wearing and how she came to have it. I told ye to keep her in her silks for a reason."

The girl shrank beneath the tone her laird used, but one of her friends shoved her forward with a hiss.

"I… I… well… the lady… she found the stack of… of… maid's robes that were made for… yer bride… in the storeroom, beneath the solar… She bid me bring them here, because she'd be needing something warm to wear while ye… were away."

Quinton tilted his head and suddenly lost a great deal of his rage. Oh, he was furious, no doubt about it, but he just couldn't help but be impressed by Deirdre's cunning. He propped his hands on his hips.

"Well, lads… she will nae get far on bread and cheese. Someone get down to the stable and see if she took a horse. The rest of ye, out until I've finished dressing."

There was a shuffle toward the door, but Coalan remained. "Why are ye intent on following her, Laird?"

Quinton pulled his bonnet on and shot his captain a knowing look. "For the same reason yer eyes follow young Amber around like a toddler watches his mother." Quinton secured the cuffs of the shirt with a soft growl. "And I don't care to admit it any more than ye do, Coalan, so kindly grant me the privacy to deal with it in me own way."

"Riding out after her isna private."

Quinton grunted. He wanted to curse the man

for arguing with him, but Coalan was in his position because he didn't shirk away from facing him when his mood was dark.

"Well now… if ye're of the mind to let me ride out alone, so be it."

Coalan made a low sound in his throat. "No' while I've got breath in me body," he announced. "Hate me all ye like, Laird, but I'm going with ye. I do nae need those cursed Douglas trying to claim Cameron land because ye went and got yerself killed before having a son."

Quinton snorted. "I rather like ye, Coalan. Why else would I forget to mention ye were the one who left that wound on my mistress's leg?"

Quinton pointed to the unsheathed dagger that was tucked into his belt.

Coalan looked stunned, his expression becoming perplexed as he thought about what his laird had said. Rage suddenly darkened his complexion.

"It's nae a good habit, I know, but it's never caused a problem before…"

"It was nae intentional, and ye might like to know that Deirdre was the one who told me such."

"That does nae excuse me actions." Coalan took the dagger and pushed it into the top of his boot where it belonged. There was look of self-incrimination flickering in his eyes that Quinton had to respect. Every man made his own choices and the best men held themselves accountable for their actions.

"I'm going after her, and I do nae want to think about why." It was honest and harsh. Call him a

possessive bastard, fine. But he was going to chase
Deirdre down, and maybe, after he caught her, he'd
be able to understand why the need was threatening
to burn him alive.

No one noticed the maid who lingered in the
bedchamber. She offered the bare chamber a smug
smile. Wasn't it just like a noble laird to dismiss a girl
like herself and never see her? She shrugged and reached
down for the letter that was sitting on the seat of the
laird's chair. Thank goodness she'd seen it first and
shoved the chair beneath the table in time to keep it
hidden. She picked it up and tucked it into her bodice
before swiping some dishes off the table and carrying
them through the doorway. No one paid her any mind,
and she smiled brighter, this time with victory.

Someone pushed her.

Deirdre moaned, her head aching from too little
sleep. She didn't want to rise yet.

The next nudge was harder.

"I'm tired, Quinton Cameron… go away… I need
to sleep, no' to deal with yer demands."

"Now there's an interesting bit of information."

Deirdre's eyes flew open, because the male voice
didn't belong to Quinton, and it was far too smug for
her comfort. She scrambled to her feet but discovered
that she stood facing several men who were all intently
staring at her. Their plaids were green and cranberry,
giving her a slight bit of relief because they belonged
to the Hay clan.

But only a tiny amount of comfort, for the Hay

clan and her own were not friends, not since her father had been handfasted to the laird's sister. It had happened when she was very young herself, and she didn't recall much of what had caused her father not to wed the girl.

"Who are ye to Laird Cameron?"

The man who spoke wore a bonnet with three feathers sticking straight up. She stared at them for a moment, cursing her lack of luck.

"That's right," he continued. "I'm Kagan Hay, and I want to know what ye are doing wearing the crest of the Earl of Liddell so plainly but without any escort near ye."

Deirdre looked at her overrobe and noticed the carefully embroidered crest of the Earl of Liddell placed prominently on the sleeve. She'd been so excited over finding the robes that she hadn't looked at them completely. It had been a grave error on her part, for to wear the crest was to use the authority of the earl. A person might be hung for such an offense if the nobleman demanded it.

"I'm on my way…"

"Oh aye… I can see that ye clearly rode the night through, for that's about how long it would have taken ye make it to me land from Cameron's." Kagan's gaze swept her from head to toe. "And it explains why ye were dead to the world about ye too. Now answer me. Why are ye wearing that shield?"

Kagan Hay loomed over her, his dark eyes as hard as the sword he had strapped to his back. His men aimed similar looks at her, condemning her before she even had the chance to speak.

Well, she hadn't come so far to be stopped by men who only wanted to help out a fellow laird. She raised her chin and faced them with every bit of fiery spirit Quinton had ever accused her of having.

Some curses had good uses after all, it would seem.

Six

"IT IS NOTHING FOR YE TO BE CONCERNED ABOUT, Laird Hay," Deirdre informed him. "Unless ye are so possessive of yer land that no one might sleep upon it without yer permission."

A hint of amusement entered his eyes. "I would nae say that about me, but I'll admit I am rather defensive of me fellow lairds. Wearing that shield carries the authority of the Cameron clan."

"Ye think I do nae know such a thing? Well, I do, and there is no need for ye to stand in me way while I've places to be going." She was being brazen, but there was no way she was going to get past Kagan Hay without demanding it. He was clearly no fool. That didn't mean he couldn't be handled by the right woman.

"I've places to be," she informed him and went to walk past him, but he hooked a hand around her upper arm and held it tight while he studied the shield.

"These were made for Quinton's bride to use. The Ross shield is below the Cameron one."

"Release me."

Kagan Hay shook his head. "I think no', lass. Ye do nae belong in this clothing, but ye must have been at Drumdeer to get it. Yer comment when I woke ye told me that much."

There was a knowing glint in his eyes that sent heat into her cheeks.

"I never said that I was nae at Drumdeer, only that I've places to go. I'm Robert Chattan's daughter, and I have been granted a place by the queen."

Kagan released her. Relief surged through her, but it didn't last long. Kagan's expression had darkened dangerously.

"You'd have something to prove that, if it were so."

Deirdre pulled the folded parchment from her bodice.

Kagan wasn't impressed. "This isna sealed."

"The wedding never took place, so there is no reason for anyone to be so concerned about me wearing an overrobe that means nothing."

"Robert Chattan's daughter would know better," Kagan informed her. "A daughter of any Highland laird would know that wearing the arms of any clan is the same as the plaid. Ye're making a statement about who ye are, and if ye wear that crest and are nae loyal to the Earl of Liddell, ye might be intent on doing harm by using the respect other men have for him."

He gripped her arm once more. "So ye're coming along, because I'll no' be leaving ye loose to poison one of me fellow lairds. Do nae worry. I'll send a letter up to Drumdeer."

"I am Robert Chattan's daughter. Send yer letter to him." But the men riding with Kagan Hay didn't believe her. They cast suspicious looks at her, because Kagan had made a good point. Wearing the crest on her arm would grant her entry into any castle in the Highlands. Quinton's position was that high. No one would want to risk offending him by refusing her shelter. Failing to see the crest had been a grave mistake on her part. Kagan could lock her away in a cell, and none of his fellow lairds would think anything wrong with it, for they would agree that she might have been about murdering one of them under the protection of the crest.

"Are ye now? Well, that's one thing—I know someone who can help me prove whether or no' ye are telling the truth. There is no need to risk sending one of me men onto the land of a clan that is nae friendly with the Hay."

"My father is nae feuding with ye."

"But we are nae friendly either. If ye were his daughter, ye'd know that."

Kagan took a length of leather from one of his men. That same man grabbed her forearms so that his laird might tie her wrists together. Kagan knotted the leather but tested the binding to make sure it wasn't too tight. She stared for a moment at the bindings, disbelief holding her in its grasp.

Her luck was rotten, and that was a fact.

Deirdre snorted at him. "What's yer concern, Laird Hay? I thought ye have already judged me guilty. What matters a bit of pain?"

He slipped one fingertip beneath another loop of the leather. "It matters even if ye are a liar, because I am nae a bastard who does nae care how me decisions affect the people I make them about. Besides, ye might be telling the truth, and I'd hate to have the Chattan raiding me land by harvest moon because I treated their laird's daughter badly."

"Ye men think of naught but fighting."

Kagan Hay grinned at her. "If the words ye spoke when ye woke are true, ye know Quinton Cameron thinks of other, more pleasing things too. I confess to having the same tendency from time to time. It might be interesting to see which man will thank me the most for sending him news of just where ye are."

"I am no' Quinton Cameron's wife or even a Cameron. Ye should send word to me father."

Kagan's face became serious. "I understood very clearly what ye are to Quinton, and the fact that ye are wearing this robe tells me he liked having ye enough to give ye freedom among his private possessions. I think he will be looking for ye, for ye would nae be on the road alone even if he'd discarded ye. Quinton Cameron is an honorable man who would nae place a lass in such peril. So ye stole that robe with the intention of doing something that he would no' approve, and that is a fact. Robert Chattan's daughter or nae, I will no' allow ye to roam free on me land."

"Untie me, and I'll happily leave yer land."

"Nae, I'm taking ye to me aunt Ruth. If ye are Robert Chattan's daughter, she'll tell me." He nodded toward his men. "Ye need no' fear ye will be treated unkindly on the way. Me men will mind their hands. I give ye me word on the matter."

It was more than she could have expected,

considering the circumstances. But Deirdre hissed because she didn't want to find anything about Kagan Hay that she liked. It would be much better if she remained angry over her new status as a prisoner once again.

Yet she had to admire the fact that he wasn't a brute. *Ye enjoyed Quinton being a savage…*

She tried to ignore her thoughts, but there was little else to do. Kagan put her on the back of her mare, and they rode for the rest of the day. He didn't take her to her father's land, but that would have been too much good fortune to hope for. Her father and the Hay clan were not on the best of terms. She wouldn't call it a feud, but it was as close as it might have been before fighting began.

Her father had loved a Hay woman. Deirdre had heard only bits of the tale because her father didn't like to talk about it. Whatever had happened, it had set the Hay clan against the Chattan, and now she was heading into the heart of their territory.

Her luck had returned to being cursed.

Kagan didn't take her to a fortress or a castle or even a tower.

He stopped his men several hours after sunset near a large house. It was two stories high and built of solid stone. He dismounted and used a fist to pound on the door.

"Take a rest, lads. Ye've earned it—but I need to know if our fair lady told me the truth of who her father is."

There were several mumbled responses that left no doubt in her mind about the fact that Kagan men's didn't care for having her in their midst. One of them reached up and pulled her off her mare.

"Who's causing such a fuss at this hour?" The door opened, and a woman stood there. Deirdre stared at her in wonder, for the candle she held illuminated a face that was beyond fair. She was a beauty, and no mistake. Kagan's men instantly transformed from a disgruntled group into charming men who looked as though they had not just spent endless hours in the saddle.

"Kagan Hay. I'd say I was happy to see ye, but I'm no', and the church tells me that lying is a sin."

"So is being sharp-tongued, Erlina," Kagan informed her, but his voice was rich and kind. Deirdre felt her eyes widen; the man could be quite charming, it seemed. "I need to see yer mother for a moment. The matter is important."

Erlina opened the door wider in invitation. "How could I have ever doubted that anything ye sought might be otherwise, Laird Hay?"

Kagan paused in front of her. "Because ye are yer mother's daughter and too devastating to the male gender."

Erlina shook her head. "Earthly beauty should be ignored. The priest tells me so often."

"Aye, while he's admiring ye."

Erlina laughed. It was a delicate sound with a hint of wickedness that earned her admiring glances from Kagan's men. A few of them were bold enough to hold their hands out in the hopes that she might place her own in theirs for a kiss, but she refused them all by keeping her hand against her chest.

"Go on with ye all. Me mother is near the fire." Erlina frowned when the light showed her the bindings on Deirdre's wrists.

"And best ye hurry, Laird, for I do nae care for what ye bring into me mother's house. This is no' yer castle, and we don't need any ghosts of prisoners disturbing our sleep."

Kagan turned and hooked Deirdre's upper arm. "As I said, the matter is important."

Only a few candles were burning in the house, but their light allowed Deirdre to see that it was furnished well. The air smelled fresh, and there was no musty scent of rushes rising from the floor.

"Mother, Laird Hay is come to pester ye."

Kagan's eyes narrowed, but Erlina merely offered him a sweet smile in response. Kagan pushed her into the room with the fire burning in the hearth, and she felt the heat on the tip of her nose.

"What nonsense is this?"

The woman who spoke was obviously Erlina's mother. She might have been older, but she was just as fair as her daughter. She looked at Deirdre's bound hands and frowned.

"There's a reason I do nae live in yer castle, Nephew. I have no liking for cages or seeing ye use them on people."

The woman didn't look at Kagan. She stared at Deirdre, her frown deepening until her forehead was furrowed. She suddenly snorted, the sound striking Deirdre as harsh, considering how refined she appeared.

"God's breath, ye look like yer father. I hope yer mother's ghost haunts him for that sin. Ye'd have done better with her looks."

"Whose child is she, Ruth?" Kagan asked softly.

Ruth turned her attention on him, and her look was not friendly. "I'll nae say his name. Ye know well I've sworn never to say that name."

Kagan grunted. "But ye never said why."

Ruth lifted her chin, and her expression smoothed, her feelings disappearing behind a perfect smile. "I do nae have to. Why did ye bring her here? Are ye thinking to end the conflict with the Chattan by having her to wife? I've heard all the Chattan daughters are contracted. Did ye steal her? That will only cause us trouble with the clan ye took her from."

"I did nae steal her. I found her on the road, wearing the crest of Quinton Cameron on her sleeve."

Ruth turned and stepped around Deirdre to look at the sleeve in question. "The Ross girl never married the earl."

"Exactly why I'm suspicious of her. But she claimed she is Robert Chattan's child, and ye are the only one I know who could confirm that for me. If ye say she is the daughter of Robert Chattan, then she is nae intent on murder by wearing the Cameron crest. As laird, it's me duty to think about matters such as those."

"I agree. We do nae need more trouble that will begin feuding."

Ruth circled Deirdre. It became an effort to maintain her poise, but Deirdre stood firmly in place; ducking her chin might damn her completely as guilty of everything Kagan suspected her of. Ruth stared into her eyes before making a small sound beneath her breath.

"Clearly Quinton Cameron has finally found a woman who is nae frightened of him or all his noble power." Ruth looked toward Kagan. "As I told ye, she's more her father's daughter, and she spoke truthfully about what blood is in her veins."

"Why did nae ye wed my father, and why will ye nae say his name?" Deirdre demanded. Ruth frowned at her, but Deirdre shot her a stern look in return.

Ruth didn't answer, but Erlina laughed, which drew Deirdre's attention.

"I'll tell ye who I am, Deirdre." Erlina smiled sweetly while her mother growled softly. "I'm yer sister—yer bastard half sister."

❧

His men were waiting for him to admit the trail had gone cold.

Quinton ground his teeth and cursed, but there was nothing he could do. Deirdre had made her escape.

It hurt.

He snarled and muttered a few more words that no one might approve of, because it fucking hurt. He didn't want to return to Drumdeer without her, but he had no way of knowing where she had gone.

But he wasn't giving up. If she could wound him, he'd have her back. No matter how long it took him to find her.

❧

"I've never heard of another sister. No' ever a single word," Deirdre muttered.

"Of course ye haven't," Ruth informed her. "Robert is a stubborn goat who will nae give me any quarter until I submit to his demands to wed him." She flounced down on a chair near the fire with a huff. "Which I will nae do."

Kagan looked at Deirdre, which fired her temper. "Oh, do no' ye dare look to me to explain this, Kagan Hay. I did no' even know I had another sister or that ye were dragging me up here to be identified by a woman who is family because she bore my father a child. I knew the Hay and my kin were untrusting of each other, but I never suspected it was because one of yer kin refused to wed my father as though my father is beneath her."

"I never insulted his offer of marriage by saying it was unworthy," Ruth insisted. There was even a note of hurt in her voice.

"What is all this shouting about?" Another young woman appeared in the doorway. Deirdre turned to look at her and gasped. She was the mirror image of Erlina. She walked into the room, wearing only a sleeping robe.

"I cannae sleep while the lot of ye are yelling."

Deirdre gasped. Her mind worked frantically. She suddenly understood.

"Ye were afraid of my grandfather harming yer daughters."

"What do ye mean?" Kagan demanded.

Deirdre looked back at Erlina and her twin sister. "My grandfather was a superstitious man. I was young when he died, but I remember him telling me that twins were cursed and that there was no way to know which one was good or evil. I watched him order a pair of twins drowned, but the mother escaped with them before it happened."

"But it does nae change the fact that he was laird of the Chattan at the time my daughters were born, and there was no way I was going to let that demon know I'd given yer father a set of twins," Ruth said. "So I came home before he discovered I had birthed a second daughter, and I refused yer father when he tried to entice me back with an offer of marriage."

"So ye just let me father think ye detested him?" Deirdre demanded. Ruth looked away, staring into the fire instead of answering.

"Mother?" Erlina spoke up. "I want to know the answer to that question myself. Ye always made it sound as though my father cheated on ye with another woman."

"Oh, enough, out of all of ye," Ruth announced. "I did what was best for me daughters. I do nae need any of ye standing in judgment over me. If I'd wed Robert, one of ye would have been smuggled out of the castle in a basket of laundry to grow up somewhere without any notion of what blood runs through yer veins. And what if I'd been found out? Ye both would have been drowned. He wasna the only man in the Highlands who believed twins were bad luck."

It was true. Deirdre shook her head, because her grandfather had believed in all the old superstitions. "My father does nae believe such old folklore."

Ruth pointed at her. "How do ye know for sure? Yer mother never gave him a pair of twins. Just because he does nae order any others born on his land to be killed, does nae prove he would welcome a set of his own. A laird cannae have his position questioned." She suddenly sighed. "Besides, it was done long ago, and by the time yer father was laird, it was past undoing."

"Ye mean that ye did nae want to trust him," Deirdre insisted. Maybe she was mad to make such an accusation, considering her circumstances, but at the moment, shock kept her from thinking about what she said.

Ruth surprised her by nodding. "Aye, ye're right. But mark my words, girl. Ye do nae learn what true fear is until ye have tiny new babies depending on ye for their lives. A mother learns what being afraid means when she finds her heart full of love for her children."

There was a truth in Ruth's words that sobered everyone in the room. Erlina crossed the room and sat down next to her mother. Her sister followed, and Deirdre fought back tears to see the pain her grandfather had caused them.

"What is yer name?"

Erlina raised her head from where it had been resting on her mother's shoulder.

"Her name is Shylah."

Deirdre felt anger flickering inside her for the time with her sisters her grandfather had denied her. She knew it was wrong, but it was hard to force her temper aside. She turned on Kagan and lifted her bound hands.

But the brute shook his head. "I think I'll leave ye secure for the time it takes to get ye to Strome tower."

"But ye know I'm no' a threat."

Kagan smiled, and the sight of it sent a ripple of apprehension through her.

"What I think is that since ye're kin, 'tis my duty to see ye are well provided for."

"What ye mean is ye want to see if Quinton Cameron will offer ye something of value for my return."

"Will he?" Kagan asked bluntly.

"He'll give ye nothing. He's already forgotten me. Why do ye think I left him?"

The smile faded from Kagan's face. He contemplated her good and long before shaking his head.

"Maybe, but then again, maybe no'. A woman will do a great deal to protect those she loves. Even leave a man she loves, because remaining as his mistress would shame her clan. I know for a fact Quinton didn't contract ye, so that means ye took him as yer lover and stole that clothing to escape Drumdeer."

He looked past her to Ruth before he let out a soft whistle. "Let's ride home, lads. It will certainly help to ease tension between the Chattan and us to have the man know his daughter is being cared for inside Strome tower."

∾

Strome tower was an old Norman fortress. It lacked the refinements of Drumdeer, and if there were any touches of decoration, Deirdre couldn't find them. Kagan was welcomed home by the ringing of the church bell and several more which were set onto the walls.

Once he and his men rode into the courtyard, the huge gate that kept the castle secure at night was lowered back into position with ear-splitting groans.

He slit the leather binding her and turned her over to an older woman by the name of Peg.

"Find her something to do, Peg. She'll be staying awhile."

Peg looked as bewildered as Deirdre felt by Kagan's words, but Deirdre had plenty of time to ponder them.

❧

She discovered her nights filled with dreams of Quinton.

Deirdre did her share, laboring along with the other maids to keep the tower clean and food on the tables. She worked harder than some, but it wasn't because Peg ordered her to.

No, she tried to exhaust herself so that she might sleep without remorse tormenting her. Her plan failed her too many nights to count. Tears that she managed to avoid by keeping her mind on her labors could not be fended off once she was lying in the narrow cot that Peg had moved into the room Deirdre slept in. Once she was no longer forcing her body to move, the only thing she could do was keep her tears silent.

"A strange thing happened today."

Deirdre bumped her head into the top of the hearth she was clearing ash out of. She turned a hard look on Kagan Hay.

"Ye did that just to be mean."

He shrugged unrepentantly. But his gaze studied her while she took the time to look at him in return. The man had dark hair to go with his dark eyes. She waited for any sort of attraction to stir inside her, even the mildest amount of lust, but nothing tingled across her skin.

Deirdre dusted off her hands, excitement finally arriving to send her blood moving faster through her veins. It felt like she had been sleeping for months, frozen in place while Kagan forced her to remain in his tower fortress.

"For Christ's sake, what do ye want of me, Kagan? It cannae be my fine abilities as a servant."

He grinned at her. "Actually, from what I hear, ye work harder than most of the girls I pay to keep this castle."

She groaned. "Fine. I'll sit on me arse, even if it bores me to death if that is what it will take to make ye stop holding me here."

"It might be interesting to see how long ye could stand doing naught. According to the letter I just received from one of me kin on Cameron land, ye lasted two days in the solar before ye found a way to escape." He held up a folded parchment, and she failed to mask how much she longed to read about Drumdeer. She realized she was looking at the letter like a hungry colt and glanced away, but it was too late.

"Quinton is searching for ye."

Her heart jumped. "Well, he should nae be," she snapped. Fear suddenly threatened to choke her. Quinton was a powerful man, and there were many lairds who would relish the opportunity to have something to press him into favoring them.

She shot a hard look at Kagan. "I have a place waiting for me, and I long to take it. I am nothing to Quinton Cameron."

"He claimed ye were his mistress."

"And ye believe such nonsense?" Deirdre hid her

fear by turning to look at the pile of ash waiting to be removed. She scooped it up and dumped it into a large bowl to take outside for soap making.

"Why should I doubt it? I hear he said it in front of his captains."

She forced down the lump in her throat. She might be weak enough to tumble into Quinton's embrace, but she was strong enough to face down Kagan Hay. She turned to glare at him.

"I am sure there are women who actually believe that a man like the earl might be besotted by them, but I am nae so whimsical."

"But ye are dropping weight. Yer face is thinner." Suspicion coated his words.

Deirdre stood and propped her hands on her hips. "Because I'm worried Joan Beaufort will nae wait forever for me to arrive. Surely ye can understand I want to make me father proud by gaining a position that will bring honor to his name."

"Considering ye shamed him by taking a lover and ruined his plans to wed ye to Connor Lindsey, that would certainly make sense."

Deirdre picked up the bowl of ash and balanced it on one hip. "Connor is wed to my sister Brina, and they are well pleased with the union. It is time for ye to allow me my freedom so that I may also please my father."

Kagan Hay shook his head. "Keeping ye ensures that yer clan will nae raid mine, and I will nae set ye loose when it's possible Quinton Cameron might come for ye once I tell him ye're here."

She left the room and made her way down the steps until she was outside the larger tower.

She was truly foolish…

Her position was precarious, and she had been consumed with her own worries. She needed to be more concerned with how she might be used against Quinton. Or her father. Kagan Hay had good reason to want to make her father suffer for the fate that had befallen his aunt. Highlanders held grudges longer than anyone else. Even if it had been her grandfather who began it, Kagan might decide to begin raiding her kin in retribution.

The thought of blood being spilled sickened her.

She reached up and ran her fingers over her cheek. Maybe she was thinner; she wasn't sure. Well, she would have to begin eating more. She'd never see the outside of Strome tower if Kagan continued to suspect that Quinton might want her back.

But do ye still want to go to serve the queen?

Deirdre didn't care for how much she disliked that idea. She had risked everything for it, and now, she dreaded it. She shook off the feeling and forced herself to recall that honor was a thing easily preserved.

She'd made her choice, and she would be content.

೧೪೪

Summer grew warmer, and still Kagan held her inside his fortress. They had more visitors, and one morning, Deirdre arose to find the kitchens in a frenzy. Wagons were hauling fresh meat and other stores up into the yard, while the cook shouted at her staff. Maids scurried to please her, but she only continued to snap her fingers and call out more orders.

"What goes on here?" Deirdre asked Peg.

"Archibald Douglas, the lieutenant general himself, was sighted on the road. He sent a missive up to the laird that he's going to be joining us for supper. The cook is running mad with preparations for it."

The smell of roasting pork floated through the hall, and Deirdre suddenly gagged. She clamped a hand over her mouth and ran toward the garderobe. Her belly heaved, refusing to be quieted until every bit of food she'd eaten was lost.

"Ye don't care for roasted pork? Pity that, it will be a fine treat, I'm thinking," Peg informed her when she returned. "Still, there will be plenty of other things to enjoy. But I fear we'll have to suffer this day first."

The hours flew too quickly and yet not fast enough, for Deirdre watched for the approach of the promised visitors with eager anticipation. She fought to conceal her growing excitement but couldn't help but smile as she thought about how many people would be moving in and out of the gate.

It was the opportunity that she had longed for. The waiting felt impossible to bear now that she could feel an end nearing. The sun seemed frozen in position for hours at a time. At last the bells began to ring, and she ran up the stairs of the tower to look out the windows with the other Hay women.

Archibald, Earl of Douglas, seemed to enjoy making a large impression. His men held long pikes with banners flying the earl's colors. The sound of trumpets and drums floated to her as he rode closer.

She had to resist the urge to laugh, for Quinton would have been in the yard before anyone heard him coming. That was the way of a Highlander. They masked their movements, blending into the pace of life around them so they might be more effective in defending their land.

For all that Archibald Douglas was also a Highlander, it was obvious he preferred the ways of court.

Kagan greeted the earl in the yard while servants hurried to bring a huge chair into the hall. Deirdre descended to the kitchen with the rest of the maids to discover the earl's men poking their fingers into everything the kitchen staff had labored so hard to produce throughout the day. The earl's men broke pieces of pastry off pies and tasted them, ruining the delicate shapes that were constructed to please the eye before the food was tasted.

They sniffed and licked and chewed mouthfuls of stews and sauces while armed retainers stood watching suspiciously. Every maid was lined up against the wall while the earl's men ran through the kitchen, and the cook began to cry.

At last, the oldest man among them grunted. "I am satisfied, no poison," he announced and turned to walk away, leaving them the task of salvaging the feast for his master. Deirdre began to carry plates of fresh fruits out to the banquet tables with the other girls, but she ran into two of Kagan's retainers.

"The laird says ye're to come with us."

"I've been given a task to do." She brushed around them, the sight of the people streaming in and out of the hall beckoning to her.

But the retainers followed her. One reached out and hooked her upper arm the moment she sat her platter down.

"Do nae be making a fuss. Being Chattan's daughter will nae gain ye any favor with me."

"Unhand me. I've work to do. Ask the cook. She needs all of us now," Deirdre insisted.

"She'll make do with the good Hay lasses. Ye are to be locked abovestairs so that ye do nae slip past the gate during the upheaval of the earl's visit." The retainer began to pull her across the stone floor toward a side doorway. "That is what me laird says, so it will be so."

"What is amiss there?"

The hall fell silent. The retainer pulling on her froze as everyone turned to look at them.

"Can't yer men wait until after supper to toss the skirts of yer serving lasses?"

Kagan tried to reply, but Deirdre snarled, her temper gaining the upper hand.

"Take yer hands off me." She grabbed a plate off the table and used it as a club against the man holding her arm. He released her with a growl.

"Chattan bitch," he cursed as he raised his hand to slap her.

"Hold!"

The Earl of Douglas's voice bounced off the walls, and the retainer lowered his hand. Deirdre felt tension tighten along her shoulders as Archibald Douglas stood up and braced his hands on the table in front of him.

"Bring her here."

Deirdre stepped forward, avoiding the hand the Hay retainer tried to hook around her upper arm once more. She kept her chin level as she moved up the center aisle. Kagan sat next to the earl, a dark look on his face. She refused to lower herself before the man.

The earl narrowed his eyes. "Ye are either foolish or simple to risk offending me, girl."

"The Douglas have never dealt honestly with me." Rage edged her words, but there was no fear. If the man wanted to have her hanged, so be it. She'd still spit in his eye and tell him the truth about his kin. Melor Douglas had lied to her and shamed her.

The earl should have taken offense. Instead he began to chuckle. The men sitting beside him all grinned.

"Ye must be Deirdre Chattan," Archibald Douglas declared. It wasn't really a question, but Deirdre tossed her head and answered, "I am, and yer nephew is a liar. He broke his word, which he swore on the honor of yer colors. So I will nae lower myself before any man wearing them, because there were men with him when he did it, and no retribution was made to my father. That is nae worthy of me respect, so ye shall no' have it."

There was a rumble from the Douglas retainers, but the earl held up his hand, and it ceased.

"Well now. I agree that every man should be upholding the honor of his clan. I'll be seeing me nephew soon, and he'll be accounting for that. If the man is going to seduce maidens, he'll have to do it without dishonoring me colors."

There were snickers in response, but Deirdre maintained her stance. She stared straight at Douglas, refusing to be broken by his bluntness.

"He was making war against Connor Lindsey through me. Do nae think I'm so naive no' to know that now. Such knowledge only deepens my disgust."

The earl frowned, the amusement leaving his eyes.

"I might find myself agreeing with ye, except for the fact that Connor Lindsey just used yer sister to take something from me that I treasured. Young Brina used the robes of the church to deceive me men, so I believe that evens out anything I owe yer father for me nephew's actions." The earl sat down and contemplated her as a king might. "It seems that Robert Chattan raised daughters who are surprising in their courage. I can only imagine how the church is faring with yer sister serving it. The penitences must be increasing daily."

Kagan grinned, but Deirdre wasn't in the mood to savor the compliment. There was something gleaming in the earl's eyes that made her wary. The man was plotting. He was king in everything but name, ruling through the young James. Except that the king was not with the earl, and that meant something important had drawn him away from wherever the boy was. Archibald Douglas wouldn't risk losing control of the boy for just anything.

"How is His Majesty?"

The earl growled softly, "His Majesty is safely residing in Edinburgh. Something I intend to make sure remains the same. William Crichton is calling his men in, and I'm here to crush him before he threatens the king."

There was a flurry of whispers behind her. The news of possible fighting wasn't welcome. Mothers looked at their sons with fear in their eyes, while wives moved closer to their husbands. The men couldn't show their fear, but she saw more than one man reach down to ruffle his child's hair in an attempt to stay close to life.

The earl grunted, regaining everyone's attention.

"Ye are another matter, Deirdre Chattan. Yer sister Brina took something of mine—"

"Connor Lindsey's sister is a person, no' a belonging, and she belongs on her father's land as sure as any child does," Deirdre interrupted him. Kagan made a slashing motion with his hand, but she refused to heed the warning.

"Highlanders keep the women they steal, and that's a fact too," the earl snarled. "Laird Hay, why is she in yer tower?"

"I found her on the road wearing the Earl of Liddell's arms on her clothing," Kagan responded.

"So… ye were at Drumdeer." The earl leaned forward. "What are ye to Quinton Cameron?"

Deirdre fought the urge to look at Kagan. For some reason, the man was keeping silent on the matter of what he'd learned about her. The earl snorted.

"It doesna matter. I'll find out soon enough." He snapped his fingers. "Ye are no longer a child, so I can keep ye, Deirdre Chattan, and maybe I'll solve the problem of me nephew soiling the Douglas honor by having him wed ye. I warned Connor and yer father that they would nae be the only ones making alliances through marriage. Finding ye here is the turn of luck I need to restore balance."

Horror flooded her. Her throat felt like it was swollen shut. Douglas retainers closed in on her quickly, hooking their hands around her arms and pulling her away. The thought of having Melor for her husband sickened her. She was firmly shut behind a solid door before she recovered enough of her wits to respond.

She cursed, words that should have made her blush, but instead all she felt was a sure sense of their being deserved.

※

The Douglas retainers took her to a small storage room close enough to the hall for her to hear a few scattered notes of music drifting under the door from the feast. The door was a sturdy one, and she heard a bar being lowered into place on the outside to lock her in.

The room itself was small. If she stood in the center, she could touch each wall with her fingertips when her arms were outstretched. That was comforting, because it was dark with the door closed. Some light came in from under the door, but it wasn't enough to brighten the black corners.

She shivered and hugged her arms close. The hours of the night stretched out in front of her with the promise that they would be long ones. She listened, fearing the unknown and the possibility that there might be rats sharing the space with her.

She'd prefer that to having to wed Melor Douglas.

A soft snort echoed off the close walls. Truly, there was no pain worse than a broken heart, for she had nothing but scorn left in her for the man she had once believed herself in love with. He was a sniveling child who had used his bloodlines to gain what he wanted.

But the Earl of Douglas could wed her to him.

Sickness threatened to turn her stomach at the idea. Instead of Melor's face, her memory offered up an image of Quinton. Without meaning to, she was comparing the two men and noticing all the reasons why Quinton was superior to Melor.

She shouldn't.

But she couldn't seem to stop herself from considering the way Quinton went after what he wanted without dishonesty. Oh, the man had run her to ground, there was no doubt about it, but he had done so without misrepresenting what he wanted. She'd known from the first time he kissed her in her father's house that Quinton Cameron desired her—in his bed or anywhere else they found themselves consumed by passion. Her face warmed as she recalled just how much she had enjoyed being pressed up against the wall with his body against hers.

But she frowned, because she couldn't stop the dread from following that memory with the warning that it might be the last time she ever touched Quinton. That turned her cold. Pain slashed its way across her heart.

She ordered herself to stop feeling so deeply.

She'd promised herself that she'd never allow a man to affect her in such a manner again. But her logic had failed her.

Muffled sounds came from outside the door. She couldn't understand the words, but the tone was one of argument. A moment later the bar lifted, and the door was opened.

"Be quick," one of the retainers barked.

Peg stood firm in the face of his gruffness. "As I told ye, lad, I'm an old woman, so I cannae understand what yer worry is."

The retainer looked in at Deirdre. "Ye stay there, or I'll deny ye the comforts yer friend has brought ye."

Peg carried a lantern that cast its yellow light into the room. Deirdre stared at the single candle with longing, unable to dismiss just how welcome the light was. She stepped back, and the Douglas retainer grunted approval while he waved Peg through the door. Deirdre bit her lower lip when she realized how shiftily she had given her submission when faced with hardship. Ruth's words rose from her memory.

There was a hook set into the stone wall, and Peg hung the lantern from it as she muttered.

"This is a storeroom for apples and other autumn-harvest foods. The cook keeps it clean, and it's mostly empty now. So ye need no' fear that the rats have been allowed to nest in the corners."

Two girls followed Peg. One sat a rolled pallet on the floor before she left as quickly as she'd come. Peg snorted.

"There are those who somehow think the earl would care if ye are brought comforts." She set a basket covered with a cloth on the table before pulling a heavy cloak off her arm. "As if the man is thinking about ye at all while the feast is being laid before him."

"Out, woman. I said ye could bring the things, no' stay and chatter," the retainer said. "I've me orders from me laird, and I do nae plan on doing anything less than the duty I've been charged with. Out with ye."

Peg nodded. A small shaft of panic went through her as Deirdre realized she was going to be shut in alone once more. It made the last moments with the older woman quite precious.

"I'm grateful, Peg, for the fact ye thought of my comfort."

The older woman humphed beneath her breath. "Ye should nae have to be, but yer manners are pleasing."

The door closed behind her, and the bar lowered into place once again. The lantern was suddenly a dear friend, its light almost cheerful.

Now that there was light, she could see what else the room offered. Along one side, there was a ledge that might be used for storing sacks of autumn apples. At the moment, there was only a single, half-full sack sitting on it from last year's harvest. There were no windows, because it was built behind the hall. She picked up the pallet and unrolled it on top of the ledge. It was only a coarse sackcloth filled with chaff, but it would certainly be more welcoming than the stone.

She picked up the sack and looked inside. A dozen apples lay at the bottom of it, slightly overripe from the months that had passed since they were picked. She carried them to the table and sat on a stool. The basket held bread and cheese. A small gourd contained water, and there was a slice of the roast pork. She sat the gourd carefully on the table so that the water wouldn't spill. Tension robbed her of her appetite, but she forced half the meal down.

Who knew what the next few days might offer her?

The music beyond the door played on. Deirdre discovered herself pacing the small confines of the cell until the music ended and the hall grew quiet. She resisted pinching out the candle but finally forced herself to lie down. Sleep didn't come easily, and when it did, she dreamed of Quinton Cameron.

⚘

"A Highlander keeps the woman he takes."

The Earl of Douglas lifted one silver eyebrow in response, but Kagan refused to be ignored. Deirdre Chattan appeared in his yard with Douglas retainers tugging her toward a mare.

"The Chattan woman is mine. I found her, and I brought her here. She stays," he insisted.

"Do nae make me take her from ye by force, Laird Hay." Archibald Douglas shot him a hard look. "Me men are inside yer fortress, so it will nae be too difficult."

Kagan growled, and the earl chuckled in response.

"Ye do nae care for that, do ye?"

"Piss on ye," Kagan snarled. "I'm beginning to understand what fired the lass up so much that she scorned ye there in front of all."

"Ye think I lack honor like me nephew Melor?"

Kagan didn't shrink in the face of the earl's rising fury. "Ye rode through me gates as a guest. Threatening me is a violation of that trust, and taking any woman I consider mine is dishonorable."

The earl surprised him by nodding. "Ye're right about that. But ye're a fool if ye think I have nae heard Quinton Cameron fancies the girl his mistress."

Kagan stiffened, and the earl grinned.

"That makes it more of a matter between earls," Archibald continued. "Ye're also a fool if ye think I am nae keeping me eye on the fact that Robert Chattan has been making alliances that his eldest daughter might further by becoming Quinton Cameron's mistress."

"A mistress is no' a wife. No laird goes to war over his mistress," Kagan insisted.

The earl shook his head. "Ye do nae know Quinton

Cameron very well. I do. The man has pride, more than his share. When that bride of his ran off before the wedding, it cut him deep. He's never discussed the topic of taking another bride since, nor has he called any of his bed partners his mistress. This Chattan girl is important, and I will no' be standing by while the Chattan, Lindsey, and Cameron make an alliance that can threaten the Douglas."

Kagan Hay didn't care for the way he felt. He could feel his temper straining against the leash he'd been forced to put it on since the Earl of Douglas arrived.

Archibald Douglas turned to watch his men preparing to leave. Deirdre Chattan lifted her chin when she caught the pair of them watching her. The sun lit her honey blonde hair and made it glow.

"Ye see, Kagan Hay? Ye're looking at her now like a hungry pup. That woman is the sort who men will fight over."

"She's pretty enough, I admit that, but I do nae make my way in this world by using women."

Archibald laughed and took a leather gauntlet from a lad who stood holding them out. He pushed his hand into it so fast that the leather creaked in the cool morning air.

"Maybe ye say that now, but if I left her here, ye'd begin to think about wedding her, because it would settle the tensions along yer border with the Chattan. The harvest moon will be full by next month, and when the raiding begins, ye'd think about taking her to the church. Admit it. Men use women to forge alliances. Ye are no more noble than the rest of us when it comes to securing yer land."

The Earl of Douglas mounted his stallion, and his men gained their saddles too. The yard was full of the sound of leather and metal while horses snorted in response to bearing the weight of their riders. Deirdre was the only oddity among the retainers, but she looked as regal as a queen.

Kagan suddenly grinned. Aye, he did have to agree with Douglas on one account: she was a woman who drew men to her. She was as bold as the Highlander blood that ran through her veins. Strength radiated from her, and he suddenly regretted not getting to know her better while she'd been beneath his roof. Marrying for peace was the way the Highlands maintained their balance. He'd been foolish to overlook that opportunity.

But that didn't mean he couldn't wise up.

❧

Deirdre had decided she detested horses.

Or at least riding them.

Two days later, she was close to attempting to kill the Earl of Douglas if the man didn't end their journey. Of course, the retainers who rode with him would no doubt make that task impossible, but her temper burned hot enough to make her think about it.

At last, Restalrig came into sight. She'd only heard about it from those who went to court to serve the queen. Her father had forbidden such a service, believing the court to be a den of vipers and sin that would corrupt her.

Melor Douglas had been raised at court, so she found herself agreeing with her father.

The towers of the fortress rose several stories into the air, with thick walls enclosing them. The village was built up around it into what was more of a city. Merchants had signs hanging above their doors to advertise their wares. Wagons pulled around corners to make way for the earl's men, and people leaned out of upper-floor windows to watch them as they passed.

The earl didn't stop but rode straight through the gates of his castle, taking her along with him.

Deirdre growled. Locked within another stone fortress. It was vexing enough to kill her. But at least she was able to slide from the back of her mare. She gave the creature a kind pat for the service it had given her, but she admitted that she was happy to be standing on her feet.

Maybe her stomach would settle now, but it was unlikely, considering how dire her circumstances were. She couldn't seem to recall what it felt like to be at ease, without tension knotting her shoulders and making them ache.

"Welcome to Restalrig."

Deirdre turned around to discover a huge man standing behind her.

"I'm Troy Douglas, and me uncle has charged me with yer care, Mistress Chattan."

He didn't sound any more pleased with the task than she liked hearing it. He had dark hair and green eyes. He grinned when she stared at his eyes.

"Got those from me mother; she was Irish. Which accounts for why she named me Troy; the Irish have a whimsical nature, and my father was infatuated with her."

Troy extended his arm. Deirdre sighed but began walking, because the idea of being forced into the tower disgusted her.

"My uncle claims ye have a way of slipping out of castles without being noticed." Troy offered her a hard look. "That will nae be happening here, for I have no intention of having to tell me uncle ye are missing."

"Of course no'. I am, after all, a person of such importance."

Troy laughed, his face splitting with a smile that made him quite handsome. "Well now. We cannae be arguing with what the earl wants."

Deirdre scoffed at him. "I've argued with the place one earl put me in, and I will no' hesitate to do the same with yer uncle."

"I'm beginning to understand why my uncle told me to see to ye."

Troy took her deeper into the castle and then up a set of steps built against one of the walls that enclosed it.

"I personally have no liking for locking a woman up who has committed no crime, but I must obey me uncle."

Deirdre froze, unable to force herself to continue walking toward another cell. "Where are ye taking me?"

Troy stopped, distaste evident on his face. "No place as bad as what ye are thinking."

But she would be going to wherever he was intent on taking her. She could see the resignation in his eyes. She forced her feet to begin moving once more, but her neck felt like there was a noose around it.

"This is the countess's solar and gardens. She is nae

at Restalrig , so ye may reside here, providing ye do nae destroy her finery." Troy offered her a hard look. "I'd have to rethink me kindness if ye did that sort of thing."

"I am nae a child who needs lectures on her behavior," Deirdre growled at him.

The brute only laughed in response. "Oh, I've noticed ye are a woman grown. Have no doubt about that."

He winked at her before turning to leave. The snort she let out only ensured that the last sound she heard from the man was his chuckling.

Deirdre turned to face another solar. It was grand and furnished with finery, but she didn't care for it. Instead, she discovered herself longing for the one in the eagle tower. Everything in front of her appeared gaudy by comparison.

But there was an open door on the far side. She walked toward it, curious as to why she had not been shut in. Beyond the doorway, she could smell rosemary and heather. There was another door set into the wall, but it was closed. A set of narrow stone steps led upward, and she climbed them, to discover herself on the top of one of the square towers.

It had been transformed into a garden. Plants grew in planter boxes, and there were even two large trees in the center, providing shade to a pair of benches placed there. She went to the edge, where there was a four-foot wall to keep anyone from stepping over the edge. It was a sheer drop down to the yard below, nothing but smooth stone.

Two birds sang from somewhere in the tree, making

her turn around and face the garden once more. It was like a dream—a place of beauty and tranquility hidden inside her imagination, in spite of all the reality that surrounded her.

"My wife insisted on having this built."

Deirdre jumped and stumbled into the wall that edged the garden; Archibald Douglas laughed and pointed at the wall.

"I made sure that was included so no one would fall off."

He walked into the garden and sat down, looking haggard. She stared at the lines marking his forehead and the dark circles beneath his eyes.

"Age is a bitch that I hate," he announced bluntly. "Much like the choices that are needed to build empires."

"Is that what ye're doing by keeping me here, building yer empire?" she asked.

Something flashed in his eyes. "Exactly." He grunted, but it was more a sound of approval than annoyance. "I told Laird Hay that ye were a rare woman. Ye're clever."

"If I were clever, as ye say, I'd never have fallen for yer nephew's lies."

The earl shook his head, but a look of longing appeared in his eyes that silenced her.

"We were all innocent once, lass." His words were edged with regret. "Now ye understand what the world is really like. Some crumble when they get kicked in the jaw, but others pick themselves up and become stronger. They take the sting and pain and use them to fortify themselves."

There was a glow of appreciation in his eyes that

sent prickles of nervousness through her. He was the sort of man who kept what he liked, and she'd rather have his disgust than impress him enough to be of interest to him.

"I want to leave this fortress." Deirdre stepped forward. If he was going to admire her strength, maybe she'd get what she asked for.

He grinned at her. "I see why Quinton likes ye."

"He does nae like me much at all." The words were past her lips before she thought about them. A sudden protective urge took control of her, and the way the earl was watching her doubled it.

"Ye're the first woman he's called mistress since his bride ran off six years ago. I recall it well ye know. Mary Ross had his heart in her little hand, and she crushed it in front of all for a man who had an older title than Quinton's. Mary is quite the cunning little bitch. Her husband is old enough to be her grandfather, but she spreads her thighs for him because of the connections it brings to her kin. I wonder if ye are nae very much like her, enticing Quinton to make amends with yer father. Ye might be worth a great deal to the man."

Fear clenched her belly as a gleam entered the earl's eyes. Six years was a very long time for a man as powerful as Quinton to have avoided finding another bride with a dowry and connections. She couldn't help but feel complimented, even if her pride still smarted at being called a mistress. But she was sickened by the greed flickering in Archibald Douglas's eyes. She'd never thought to be used against Quinton, and she hated the man in front of her for making it plain that he would use her to press Quinton.

Well, she wouldn't let that happen without a fight. Deirdre scoffed at the Earl of Douglas.

"Ye're going to be disappointed. The gossips at Drumdeer can say what they will. That doesn't mean those words came out of Quinton Cameron's mouth."

Archibald snickered at her.

"I know what he said. I make it my business to know everything about my fellow earl, and I trust me sources. Quinton is a powerful man, and any woman who can snare his attention is worth having in my possession if I'm lucky enough to come across her."

"Oh, for Christ's sake! I am no' Quinton's mistress just because he said such a thing. I'll be the one deciding if I'm any man's mistress. Make no mistake about that." She tossed her head. "I sneaked out of his castle after he said that, so think on that before ye decide I'm his woman. No man likes it to be known that a woman left him, especially an earl. I wager he's thinking he's well rid of me."

"I bet he'll be riding up here to see what it will cost him to have me give ye to him. That's the only reason I'm even waiting on deciding what to do with ye. Quinton has many things that I want."

The earl's words were hard and sharp, just like the look in his eyes. He'd order her throat slit if it brought him enough gain. Even seeing that truth didn't make her cower. She lifted her chin and stared straight at him. If she was going to die, she'd face her fate with courage.

The earl pointed at her and stood up. "That's exactly why I think I'm right. Ye're fearless, just like he is. Melor does nae deserve ye, because he was too blinded by his lust to no' see that wedding ye would have been a better strike against the Lindsey than just taking yer virginity."

"I should no' have even given him that."

The earl snorted with amusement. "But ye did, and the fact that Quinton still wanted ye tells me he will be riding up here to negotiate with me. He's interested in ye, and no' just the things that would come with contracting ye through yer father. That's why I took ye from Laird Hay. I'm going to wait a bit to see if Quinton comes for ye."

The earl became silent, contemplating her from narrowed eyes.

"And if he does nae?" she demanded. It might not have been the wisest thing to ask, but her temper refused to allow her to accept his treating her like a thing to be traded for his personal gain.

"Ye're still Chattan's eldest daughter. Ye have uses. I just need to decide which is best for me."

"My dowry went to the church, because Connor Lindsey took my sister Brina, who was promised to it."

The earl shrugged. "And ye think that will stop me from having it back if I wed ye to one of me kin? The church knows that maintaining balance with the right men is essential to its survival, Deirdre Chattan. They'd give me compensation. I've no doubt about that. But I'll be waiting to see what I can get from Quinton first."

"It will be naught. He will nae come for me; he has too much pride to chase a woman who scorned the place he offered her."

She fired her words at the earl's back. He didn't turn around but continued walking until he disappeared down the steps. She heard the door at the bottom open after he pounded on it and then close.

Quinton couldn't come for her—he mustn't.

She covered her mouth, her knees refusing to hold her up as horror flooded her. Pain slashed across her heart as she faced the terrible reality of what escaping Quinton might mean. The Earl of Douglas might even kill him once he was inside the walls of Restalrig. It wouldn't be the first time some powerful laird had died while sleeping beneath the roof of another powerful laird. Too much of history was written in the blood of those who were murdered so another family might rise to power.

"*Do nae come…*"

She whispered the words, and it felt like they were branded into her soul. But her heart hoped that he would.

And that sent tears down her cheeks.

Quinton cursed and then cursed some more. The door hit the wall because his men entered his study so fast. Coalan looked around, searching for any threat before he abandoned the fighting stance he'd taken.

"That limp-cock bastard Douglas has her!" Quinton crumpled the letter in his hand and threw it violently across the room.

"That son of a mongrel bitch is waiting to see what I will give him for her!"

Coalan picked up the letter and placed it back on Quinton's desk. "I'll tell the boys to make ready to ride."

"I did nae tell ye to do that." Quinton was snarling, but Coalan faced him with a calm expression that only infuriated him more. "What makes ye think I'm going up to Restalrig?"

"The look on yer face," Coalan announced. "My laird."

He pulled on the corner of his bonnet and headed for the door. Quinton felt like the man had delivered a solid punch to his unprotected belly. He sat back, trying to breathe while his men left.

The letter remained, and Quinton ground his teeth as he stared at it.

Damn Douglas for the bastard he was, and damn himself for a fool the pain in his chest declared him to be.

Not since Mary Ross had shown her true colors had he felt even a twinge from his heart. He swore again. Viciously and long. Mary Ross, with her perfect face and delicate body, had enthralled him. He'd set eyes on her, and she'd begun a dance that kept him mesmerized by her charms.

It had never crossed his mind that her mother might have taught her every trick known to womankind to snare him. He'd been grateful after she'd run away from him, and determined never to let a woman control him again.

The letter refused to be dismissed. It drew his attention like an open flame.

Just like Deirdre…

Her face haunted him, as did the scent of her hair. He found it hard to look at the eagle tower now and swore every time he awoke in the middle of the night searching for her.

Damn him for a fool.

He stood and grabbed his sword. He was going. Coalan was right, and that pissed him off too, but he crossed the room and threw the door open. Coalan already had the Cameron retainers assembling. They did it with the swiftness he expected of his Highlanders. Coalan stood, looking too sure of himself, or at least too confident for Quinton's unstable emotions.

"I'm going because that bastard Douglas is only using her to get at me, and I will nae have any man thinking that I would stand by while innocents suffer in my name."

Coalan held out the reins without changing his expression. Quinton grabbed them with a snarl.

"I'm going because I will nae have it said that anyone escapes me before I'm good and finished with them."

Coalan mounted his own horse, still silently listening to his laird. Quinton swung up into the saddle and frowned at the look on his captain's face.

"I'm going because…"

His stallion snorted, tossing its head as it felt the agitation of its master. Quinton reached down to soothe the beast, but it refused to be placated, because it could feel the unrest boiling inside him. He could say what he liked, but the animal knew him too well.

"I'm just going… and that's all ye need to know!"

❧

Melor Douglas enjoyed being important.

He rode up to Restalrig with a smile on his lips

because his uncle had summoned him. Considering how many nephews Archibald Douglas had, it was a good thing to be remembered by the old man. The retainers allowed him in, and he left his horse in the care of the stable lads because he didn't want to keep his uncle waiting. Archibald was getting old, which meant it was a good time to be remembered, for it might mean he'd see an inheritance. He was looking forward to the old man's death, and so were many of his kin. Archibald had enjoyed his power too long.

"Well, I see that ye did nae waste any time in getting here."

Melor offered his uncle a respectful lowering of his head. "Ye are nae a man to be kept waiting, even if ye are me kin."

Archibald laughed and shook his head. "Ye've got a smooth tongue, but I already knew that."

Melor grinned and took a mug of ale from a serving wench. He sat down in a comfortable chair, enjoying the fact that he might sit in the presence of his esteemed uncle. There were plenty of men noticing the honor from across the hall, but his uncle merely watched him take a drink from the mug.

"That isna a good thing when ye are using that skill to shame the Douglas colors, boy."

Melor frowned, his neck tightening.

"Yer quarrel with Connor Lindsey should no' have been settled by taking his woman."

Melor spit on the floor. "If he cannae hold what is his, so what if I take it before someone else does?"

Archibald nodded his agreement. "That would be agreeable to me, if ye had nae lied to the girl."

"What does it matter what I say to a woman?" Melor groused.

Archibald glared at him. "Ye swore on yer colors that ye'd wed her, and there were witnesses. Those are my colors too, boy, and her father is a Highlander."

"Connor Lindsey was bastard born, and he should never have inherited the lairdship. That land was to be mine."

The earl grunted. "Aye, that's a sore spot, to be sure, but Connor is laird of the Lindsey, and it's a done thing now."

"Deirdre Chattan has gone to the church, so that is finished as well," Melor declared.

His uncle frowned, but there was a gray pallor to his skin that Melor had never seen before. He leaned forward to get a better look, only to have the earl pound the tabletop with a fist.

"I'm no' dead yet, boy, so save yer gawking. Ye're here to answer to me on the fact that ye shamed yer colors, and it is nae something that I will tolerate from any of me kin."

"She was a stupid girl who failed to keep her thighs closed." He snorted. "She wasn't the last woman I fucked."

"I'm more concerned about whose bed she went to after ye ruined her father's arrangement with Connor Lindsey."

Melor frowned. "Deirdre Chattan went to the church."

"No, lad, Quinton Cameron took a fancy to her."

Melor straightened, and his uncle nodded.

"That changes things, now does it nae, lad?" Archibald eyed his nephew with growing distaste.

"Quinton Cameron is a powerful man. If he weds that girl, it will unite Chattan and Lindsey with the Cameron. They'd match us in number."

Melor spread his arms out. "So what do ye want me to do about it?"

Archibald coughed, the sound drawing Melor's attention to his face once again.

"Nothing." He barked loudly to make sure every man heard how strong his voice was. He refused to admit he was growing ill. Shivers moved across his skin, but he wasn't willing to allow those little tremors to make him seek his bed so his kin might begin circling him like a fresh kill. One of them was likely to smother him so they could inherit his power all that much quicker.

"The girl is here."

"Here?" Melor stood, agitation clear in the way he couldn't remain still. "Why?"

"Because I wish it so. Ye were summoned because I may decide it best for ye to make good on yer promise and wed her, for the sake of Douglas pride."

"I do nae want her for a wife."

The earl coughed again, this time long and rocky.

"And ye think that matters?" Archibald stood, but his legs quivered. He leaned his weight on the tabletop. "Ye'll wed her if Quinton Cameron does nae show his face and offer me something better than the alliance I'll gain by having Robert Chattan's daughter married to me nephew. Now get out of me sight, and mind yer tongue when ye're looking to ease yer lust. The Douglas colors are mine. Disgrace them again, and I'll have ye shipped to France."

The earl coughed again, and this time, there wasn't any doubt that he was sick. But he sat back down in his chair, refusing to relinquish the high table. He was the Earl of Douglas, lieutenant general of Scotland.

He did not sleep during the day.

Instead he picked up a quill and began to pen a letter.

Indeed, he was a powerful man, and he made a habit of knowing everything about every other powerful man. Quinton Cameron was no exception. Mary Ross had been keeping track of the Earl of Liddell since she had wed the Earl of Braunfield, and it was possible the woman might offer him something of value to make sure Quinton didn't get his mistress back.

Archibald laughed when the letter was finished. He sealed it and snapped his fingers at a messenger.

He'd have the most gain possible for the girl, and he didn't care where she ended up. After all, she was only a woman—a creature created to ease a man's cock and give him sons. There were only a few women he dealt with, and Mary Ross was one of them, but only because she was the Countess of Braunfield. Her husband was an old fool who liked having a pretty treat in his bed.

Archibald chuckled, but it turned into a rocky cough once again. He watched the messenger leave with the letter, and he smiled. He was still the earl, and no fever was going to keep him from making sure he gained more than anyone else involved with the fate of Deirdre Chattan. In fact, he was going to enjoy watching Quinton try to negotiate for her. Quinton had never bowed his head to him, not completely. Oh, the man respected him, true enough, but he had never accepted that Archibald was superior to him.

That was a joy he would have, or Quinton Cameron would never see Deirdre Chattan again.

⁓

"A letter, Lady Braunfield."

Mary Ross held up her hand, and her attendant placed the letter gently against her palm. She smiled, mildly interested in what the letter might contain.

Life was so often boring.

But the seal of Archibald Douglas snared her attention. She looked around before breaking it and reading the contents. Her face was red when she finished the last line.

"What is it, my lady?"

Her attendants knew her too well, and they clustered around her. Her temper was flaring, and she reached out to slap the closest cheek.

"I am the mistress here. Ye do nae demand anything of me."

Her attendants all lowered themselves, but that didn't erase the curiosity from their eyes. Mary ground her teeth and read the letter again.

The words demanded action, and she felt herself rising to the challenge. In fact, she was desperate to move past where she was in her life. She smiled at her attendants and waved them forward. They all came with smothered giggles. Each girl was from a noble house and knew very well that scheming had its place. Any woman who wanted more from life than being used by a man had to plot carefully, or she'd never gain anything for herself.

"It's time for us to take a hand in our fates, ladies."

Mary laughed; she was suddenly so happy. The future would be bright and full of wonderful things for her. All she need do was rid herself of the past.

She planned to do so quickly.

"Help me dress. I want my husband in my bed tonight."

Seven

DAYS PASSED IN A RHYTHM THAT THREATENED TO drive her insane. Deirdre was grateful for the space the garden gave her to walk, but she quickly tired of every inch of it. The door only opened twice a day, for maids to tend the room. The retainers forced her up into the garden while the girls did their tasks. Meals were left behind once the girls had left, and Deirdre found them of little interest because the silence of the chamber was almost too much to bear. She began to wake often during the night because she had done little to tire herself out. She marked each day with a stone that she placed in a bowl, but the sight of the increasing pile made her melancholy.

But that didn't make her happy to see Troy Douglas when he arrived before dawn. The man appeared through the door under the stairs and frowned darkly at her. He didn't carry any lantern, but the moon was full.

"What do ye want?" she demanded as she pulled the bedding around her. Disgust went through her as she considered what most men wanted at that time of the night. Her skin turned cold at the very idea of have him in the bed with her.

He lifted a hand and made a slashing motion. He tossed a pile of clothing down beside her and sat on it so that his face was inches from hers. He caught her forearms to keep her near.

"If ye value yer life, be quiet. The earl is dying."

She froze, icy dread filling her. "What happened?"

"Fever, and there are plenty who lay the blame on yer shoulders by saying ye are casting spells up here. This is boy's clothing, and yer only chance to avoid the retribution being plotted against ye. Bind yer breasts before ye put the shirt on. I plan to sneak ye past the gate as a lad."

He stood and left the chamber. She could see his large form standing near the doorway beneath the staircase. He put his back to her, and she kicked the bedding aside. Horror filled her as she tore her under-robe off and reached for the strip of fabric lying among the clothing. She wound it around her chest and pulled it snug to flatten her breasts. Then she struggled into the shirt. Her fingers fumbled the laces, and she ordered them to perform. Panic was trying to take control of her, but she forced it aside with the grim possibilities of what might happen to her if she failed to make use of the opportunity Troy was giving her.

The kilt was harder to put on. She struggled to fold it and get it belted around her body. Sweat appeared on her forehead as she laced the knee-high boots and knotted the leather ties firmly. She finished by shoving her hair into the bonnet and pulling a section of the plaid up and over her head to help disguise her feminine face. She hurried toward the man who was waiting in silence.

"I've got one chance to get ye away from Restalrig." He leaned close so that his words remained only a whisper. "I'm riding out to fetch a wise woman, and ye're going with me men." He pulled the door open and stepped through.

"Why are ye helping me?" She shouldn't have wasted time asking, but part of her needed to know.

"Snaring the attention of Quinton Cameron does nae make ye a witch, and I will nae stand by and watch while ye are burned."

She gasped with horror, and Troy turned around to face her. "Did ye think I'd go against me uncle for any other reason?" In the dark passageway, it was impossible to see his expression, but she would have sworn that she could feel his anger radiating through the air. She heard him begin moving again and followed him down the stairs. He opened another door that was so narrow he had to go sideways through it, but he paused before she was able to follow him.

"Keep yer head down and make sure that kilt does nae flap up while we're riding, to show off yer soft thighs. I pray to God that ye noticed how yer father's men ride with their laird, because yer ability to do the same will be the only thing that saves yer life. No' a single soul must guess yer identity, for I'll be forced to bring ye back if that happens. I've a mother who would suffer if I admitted to helping ye."

"I understand. Thank ye."

He turned his back on her, and she followed. Her heartbeat began racing as they passed through a hallway and then down another flight of stairs. She could hear the sounds of horses now. They snorted in the dark, and she could see the shapes of Troy's men waiting beside the animals.

"Let's ride, lads. Me uncle has nae time to spare."

Troy swung up onto the back of a horse, leaving her to find one to ride herself. Young boys held the reins of the one horse that didn't already have a rider. She reached out and took them and mounted, while the rest of Troy's retainers were doing the same. It felt as if everything she did was wrong, each action screaming out her gender. It felt as if every step the horse took toward the gate was impossibly slow. Her teeth ground together as she battled to keep her face down and make the distance to freedom. True fear gripped her, and she realized that she had only been playing games before. Her other escapes had been nothing compared to the one she was engaging in now.

There was true danger in being caught now. Not the threat of having her choices taken from her, but the blunt reality of having her life taken. Every quibble that she'd had with Drumdeer and the abbey suddenly seemed so childish.

The gate guards didn't raise any alarm when they passed beneath them. Relief surged through her, but the men riding in front of her and behind her still kept her muscles tense. Troy led them through the village streets and off into the fields, which were full grown with crops now. The night breeze made the drying stalks brush against each other, while the moon lost its glow and the horizon turned pink.

Troy didn't slow the pace; he kept them moving until Restalrig was no longer in sight. The few wagons and travelers on the roads made way for them, the Douglas plaids they wore carrying authority that had the farmers pulling on the corners of their bonnets in spite of the fact that the earl was not with them.

But Troy suddenly put his fist into the air, and they all skidded to a halt. The horse raised a dust cloud—the summer was fully upon them now. As it settled, Deirdre bit her lip to keep a gasp from escaping. Coming up the road was a force of men over a hundred strong. The Douglas retainers cursed as the Cameron plaids identified who was approaching. They looked toward Troy, waiting for the command to run into the hills where they might be impossible to catch.

Troy stood steady. His men glanced at each other behind his back, but they didn't argue against his will. Deirdre found herself holding her breath, waiting for the Cameron retainers to get close enough to recognize her.

Quinton might well leave her on the side of the road.

She suddenly fought to hold back tears. Pain slashed through her, but she couldn't ignore the truth. She'd left the fine chamber he'd put her in, and the news had spread far. There weren't many men who would take back a woman who had done that. Especially one who wasn't his wife. Quinton had his pick of bed partners, and more than one family would encourage their daughter to take advantage of his interest because of the station it would give them.

She had no right to think he'd welcome her back, but at least she was free of the Douglas.

She just didn't understand why she hurt so much.

"Troy Douglas." Quinton's voice sent two of those tears down her cheeks. But they were tears of relief, and she wiped them away quickly before the Douglas men noticed. She'd be a fool to think she still couldn't be run through. Quinton would be close enough to watch her die, and nothing else.

"Quinton Cameron," Troy responded with a touch of arrogance. The Douglas retainers grinned when Troy didn't use Quinton's title. It was a brash move that gained them all narrowed looks from the Cameron retainers.

Quinton snorted, a grin curving his lips. He moved his stallion forward. "Ye always were a bold one, Troy." Quinton's tone made it clear he was giving a compliment, but he was also challenging Troy to join him away from his men.

Troy didn't hesitate. He kneed his stallion forward and never looked over his shoulder for support from his men.

Quinton wasn't in the mood for conversation. He moved his stallion close to Troy Douglas and growled.

"All right, I'm here, so get on with whatever ransom yer uncle is demanding. I'm warning ye, lad. I do nae have the patience for games." It wasn't the smartest thing he might have said, but he wanted Deirdre back.

"I would nae tell ye what my uncle wanted, even if I knew," Troy commented. "I'd be a poor excuse for a man if I didna honor the colors I was born under."

Quinton frowned. "Fair enough. Where is yer uncle?"

Troy looked between the two groups of men and

lifted his hand toward the Douglas retainers. Quinton's eyes narrowed with suspicion.

"Are ye truly planning on setting yer men against mine?" It would be suicide, but a fine way to start a war. It would be easy to say he had attacked the Douglas over the fact that Deirdre had run off with Archibald. Every feud in the Highlands had conflicting tales about just how the fighting started.

But Troy signaled his men to fall back. Quinton felt surprise move through him, but he mimicked the motion. Both sets of retainers didn't care for the order their lairds gave them, but after a sharp look from Quinton, Coalan nodded before pushing the Cameron back.

Troy looked back at him after making sure that the Douglas were far enough away not to hear his words.

"My uncle is dying. He might already have died in the time I've been on the road."

Shock held Quinton in its grasp. Troy nodded firmly to assure him that he'd heard correctly.

"Fever took him a few days ago, and it is nae relenting. I sent for a priest, but I would nae have done that if I had thought it would have the effect that it did upon yer lady."

Quinton felt a chill run down his back. There was something sickening his stomach, which he finally recognized as dread, the sort that he feared. "Speak up, man. I warned ye that I have no patience for games in this matter. What happened to Deirdre Chattan while she was in the care of the Douglas?"

"My uncle went to talk to her in the garden my aunt had built on one of the tower roofs. There were many who claimed she cast a spell on him while there was no one to witness the event."

"I swear to Almighty Christ that I'll reduce Restalrig to rubble if ye allowed her to be burned." Quinton fought the urge to pull his sword and run Troy though. It was a blinding need that threatened to control him completely.

"I did nae allow me kin that chance." There was disgust in Troy's tone, and his expression told a story of a man who was torn.

Quinton held on to his own control as he waited to see why the other man was so agitated. Troy cursed low and long before shaking a fist toward Quinton.

"I am no' a traitor!" He leaned forward, his lips curling with a snarl. "If she were nae a woman, I'd never have interfered in me uncle's orders. But…" His words trailed off, frustrating Quinton.

"But what, man? Spit it out."

Troy snorted. "But it's a fact my uncle is an old man, and the aged fall sick. It does nae take a witch to make that happen. Just do nae ye be thinking I'll do anything like this again. I'm proud to be a Douglas."

He turned and whistled. "Boy… get up here!" He looked at Quinton. "Call up yer youngest. I need this to look good."

Deirdre knew whom Troy was calling. The other Douglas men looked at one other before turning their attention toward the back of the line where she sat. One of them snapped his fingers.

"He must mean ye. Everyone else here has a beard, lad."

She kept her face down, but nodded and gently

kicked the sides of her horse. The Douglas watched her move forward, some of them grumbling as she went.

"Troy needs men at his side. Must be that damn Cameron forcing him to only have a lad to guard his back."

"The Earl of Liddell no doubt wants to keep us from bringing the wise woman up, so our laird will die…"

"Look, boy! If ye are all the laird will have, do a good job of it. Ye're a Douglas… remember that."

Except that she wasn't a Douglas or a Cameron. Deirdre raised her face the moment she cleared the last Douglas retainer. She bit her lower lip to still its trembling. She was a pawn between powerful men, but the truth was, she was nothing if one side decided she was worthless.

Quinton might do that very thing.

Troy cursed as she drew closer. But the man turned toward Quinton.

"Now pull yer sword and tell me to retreat, but do nae be thinking I'll ever hand over what ye want so easily again," Troy declared.

Deirdre watched surprise flicker in Quinton's eyes. She felt his gaze as surely as if he'd reached over and touched her. He muttered beneath his breath, "I will nae forget this." His words were low and directed at Troy.

"I do nae want yer promises. Just get her out of here, and remember I did it because I will nae see another woman burned."

Deirdre felt the blood drain from her face. Troy grunted and lifted a fist into the air. "Now make it look good, Cameron, because I do nae need me own kin pissed at me."

Troy turned, and in spite of the distaste evident in his expression, he swung his fist at her head. He struck her against the side of her head, the force of the blow knocking her off the horse.

"Bitch!" He swore, loud enough for his men to hear. "I should have listened to me uncle when he told me ye were crafty in the ways of escaping! How the hell did ye get into me ranks?"

Deirdre hit the ground and rolled, out of instinct. Pain went through her shoulder, but she continued rolling, to clear the powerful hooves of the horses. When she staggered to her feet, Quinton had his sword leveled at Troy's throat.

"What did ye think, Douglas? That any woman I'd care anything about would be easy to contain? She's mine because she's a true hellion!"

Deirdre heard horses approaching, and she was suddenly pulled off her feet by a grip on the back of her plaid. She landed across a saddle, her chest taking most of the impact as her nose was pressed against the yellow, orange, and black of a Cameron plaid.

"I'm taking my woman, Troy Douglas, and if ye want to live to see sunset, ye'll stay off me trail, for I swear I'll order ye all run through, down to the last man."

Horses snorted, and men cursed, but she couldn't see much of what was happening. The rider who had her turned his horse away from where Troy and Quinton were fighting. She bounced in a tangle of arms and legs for long moments before she was suddenly pulled up and deposited onto another horse.

"Wrap yer thighs around that saddle, lady, because we're about to ride hard, unless I miss me guess."

It was Coalan who spoke to her, and she realized she was surrounded by Cameron retainers. The horse was one of the spare ones that they always took in case of accidents when they rode out. She gasped when she looked back toward Quinton. His sword was the only thing between him and every Douglas who rode with Troy. They faced him with ugly snarls on their lips and hatred in their eyes.

"Fine… take the witch! Ye are welcome to her, but mark my words…ye'll be dead as soon as she turns her evil against ye!"

Troy looked at her and spit. His men followed suit before he turned and rode away from them. Quinton hesitated only a moment, making sure that none of the Douglas had the notion to reverse course and try to put a blade through his back.

He turned and kicked his stallion into a full run. Coalan leaned over and grabbed her horse's bridle, while he turned his own in the opposite direction. In a blur, the entire force of Cameron retainers all reversed. Coalan hadn't been exaggerating either. They rode hard, leaning low over the necks of their mounts while the sound of pounding hooves rose to a near-deafening level.

Quinton didn't ease the pace until they had put a great distance between the Douglas and themselves. Even so, he still pressed his men hard, and she struggled to stay in the saddle. The sun set, and still he did not stop them. He continued on until the towers of Drumdeer came into sight.

For a place from which she had made such an effort to escape, Deirdre found herself very happy to see it once again.

❧

Quinton took her into the eagle tower himself. His hand was hooked onto her arm as he pulled her up the stairs without a single word. Holding back her temper became almost impossible, and only the quick pace he set kept her from blistering his ears where others might hear.

But that control shattered the moment he shoved in the door of the sleeping chamber.

"Get yer hand off me!" she snarled and flung her body into the room to break his grip. It worked, because he'd been pulling her and hadn't expected her to pass him.

He shoved the door shut. "Mind that temper of yers, Deirdre, for I've had the devil's time chasing ye."

"No one forced ye to do so, and my father will certainly no' be looking to ye to keep any contract between us."

Quinton snarled, "What is between us is personal, hellion, and I am no' finished with ye. Be very sure of that."

Her temper deserted her, leaving her staring at him in confusion. Her emotions were suddenly a tangled mess she failed to understand. But one thought surfaced that did make sense.

"Ye had no right to announce I am yer mistress. That's my choice to make."

"It's bloody mine too!" He was on her in a moment, his huge body moving faster than lightning. His touch burned like it too.

He grabbed the belt holding her kilt in place and released it. "I hate seeing ye wearing that bastard's colors."

The Douglas kilt puddled around her ankles, but that didn't satisfy Quinton. "In fact, I hate seeing ye in anything I did nae give ye."

"But that's—" She let out a shriek as he gripped both sides of the collar of the shirt and tore the garment in half.

"That's what I feel, and ye are nae the only one who has the right to speak their mind once we are closed inside this chamber, Deirdre. Ye'll bloody well hear me feelings as well."

He dropped the ruined sides of the shirt and sent his hands into her hair. The bonnet fell off, and he groaned before he buried his head in her hair. His hands cradled the back of her head while he inhaled deeply.

"I do nae ever want to see another man's things on yer body, for I swear I wanted to strip ye the moment I saw that blasted Douglas plaid."

He didn't give her a chance to reply. He held her head in place while he pressed kisses against her neck and across her jawline until he claimed her mouth. Sensation flowed down her body, heat burning along her skin. Each kiss was like a brand, and she reached for him, unable to hold her hands away from him any longer.

His kiss was savage. He angled her head so that his mouth fit against hers. But that wasn't enough for him or her. She opened her mouth, and he thrust his tongue deeply inside it. A moan surfaced from her and then another one. Her nipples hardened, and the fabric of his clothing irritated them. She longed to feel warm skin against hers. She clawed at him, seeking the ties holding his clothing closed. Frustration made her fight her way free of their kiss.

"I hate yer clothing as well," she informed him. Her tone was bold and demanding, and she yanked on the tie that held his sword at his shoulder while she spoke.

He laughed, low and deep. It was a dark sound, dangerous, but she enjoyed knowing exactly what sort of man he was. It was his nature that bred such heat inside her.

"I like the sound of that order."

He pulled his clothing off as quickly as he'd shed hers. She quivered as he bared his flesh, and excitement flared through her. There was no thought in her mind except the need to be pressed against him once again. She reached down and yanked on the tie holding her boots closed while he smiled at her effort.

It was a hungry smile that promised her raw passion. The idea of it stole her breath. Her passage suddenly felt empty, and her clitoris throbbed for attention. He scooped her up before she finished with her boots, and carried her to the bed.

"Ye seem to be having a little difficulty with those boots." He laid her down and pulled each boot off her while the bed supported her weight. But he paused once they had been tossed aside. He stood looking down at her, frowning.

She could see the hurt glittering in his eyes. She'd stung him by rejecting him.

"Ye wounded my pride too, Quinton." She sat up and pulled the tie off the end of her braid. With her fingers, she freed the long strands of her hair. "But I am no' too proud to admit I still cannae resist the temptation of lying with ye."

He snorted before placing one knee on the bed. "We make a fine pair, Deirdre, for I cannae walk away from ye, and I would have given that bastard Douglas anything he asked for ye."

He placed his hand on her breast, cupping it while his lips thinned and flames flickered in his eyes.

"Any goddamned thing he asked…" Quinton growled the words, his frustration clear. But he leaned down and captured the hard tip of her nipple between his lips.

Heat spiked down her body. She arched up, curling her hands into his hair as he sucked upon her. She'd never thought her nipples might be so sensitive. Pleasure flooded her, but it only fanned the flames of need burning inside her. She was impatient once more, almost frantic to have him inside of her. She lifted her leg and wrapped it around his to pull him toward her.

"Oh no, hellion… I plan to make sure ye have a good reason to stay with me…"

He hovered over her, his breath teasing her lips while the tip of his cock pressed against her open sex. But it was the look in his eyes that drew a whimper from her. There was no mercy, only hard promise in the blue orbs.

"I'm going to prove ye will never find another man who can satisfy ye as I can…"

He pushed her thighs wide, and she gasped with need, but he only pressed them wider, until her knees were up to her waist on either side of her body. He slid down her body until she felt the brush of his breath against her sex.

"What are ye doing?"

He stroked the insides of her thighs, sending delight up her body once more.

"Proving that I am yer master, Deirdre…"

His voice was rough again, but the word "master" drew a snarl from her.

"No one is my master—"

She sucked in her breath as he leaned down and sucked her sex. He closed his mouth on top of her folds, where her clitoris was sheltered between the delicate tissues. She cried out—there was too much sensation to contain inside her. His mouth felt like it might burn her, but she lifted her hips, because it was a torment she had to have more of. She was suddenly poised on the edge of climax but unable to tumble into the vortex.

"I will be yer master, hellion… have no doubt that ye might snarl at me, but yer flesh will always crave my touch."

He thrust two thick fingers into her sheath with his words. Her body convulsed with the need to come, stalling her ability to refute his words. Instead she clawed at the bedding and growled at him, but her hips lifted for him, her body eager for the penetration.

"Most men will gladly let their partners suck them off, but they don't bother to return the favor."

Her eyes opened wide, and she sat partially up with the aid of her elbows. "Ye cannae mean…"

"I do," he assured her.

He moved his fingers again, pumping them several times, and she fell back against the bed, unable to resist the need to lift her hips in unison. But her clitoris begged for the touch of his mouth once more. It was wicked—it must be—but she felt like the need might drive her insane. She felt his breath against her delicate folds first this time. A moan surfaced from her as every second felt like an hour.

"The idea is tantalizing… is it nae?"

"*Yes.*"

He chuckled, but she felt him lean down and capture her folds once more between his lips. The tip of his tongue slipped between the folds that shielded her clitoris. The first touch sent her jerking away from him. The sensation was white-hot, and she cried out, but it wasn't quite enough to give her the release she was desperate for.

"No' yet, lass… I'm going to enjoy listening to yer pleasure…"

He used his free hand to spread her sex open. Her clitoris was now completely exposed, and he growled with approval. She felt the soft vibrations of that sound as he applied his mouth to her flesh. Time stopped as she was caught in a storm of sensations, each one too intense to separate from the next. He toyed with her clitoris, using the tip of his tongue to rub it until she was snarling with the need to climax. But he refused her that release, switching at the last moment to sucking on her. All the while, he continued to probe her sheath with his fingers, his at pace lazy, denying her the friction she craved.

"Goddamn ye, Quinton! I cannae take any more…"

"Then have yer pleasure, lass… and know it's my touch that gives it to ye…"

His words were savage and so hard she might have

taken offense at another time. For the moment, it was exactly what she needed to hear, the solid determination to see her satisfied. He returned to her clitoris, sucking it harder than before, while his fingers finally worked at the pace she needed. Her spine arched and it felt tight enough to snap, but she didn't care. All that mattered was the shattering of the bubble of pleasure that had remained so maddeningly out of reach. It burned a path through her, making breathing impossible as she twisted and strained while it assaulted her.

"That is why ye belong to me, Deirdre. No man will ever enjoy making ye moan as much as I do."

He covered her, his arms going around her body, but he didn't thrust into her body. Instead he rolled over, stopping when his back was flat on the bed. He cupped her hips, holding her above his erect member before slowly lowering her onto it.

"Now prove ye are me match. Ride me."

Anticipation lit his eyes. Power surged through her, a confidence she'd never expected to feel. Her knees were set on either side of his body, giving her a good position to control the pace.

He chuckled at her. "Ye like the sound of that, do ye nae?"

She lifted herself up until only the head of his member was still inside her, and then allowed her weight to take her back down. She leaned down and braced her hands on his chest, the position allowing her to rise and press down with more confidence.

"I do."

He grinned at her, and she yelped when he smacked one side of her bottom.

"Then ride me, lass. Let's see if ye can stay in the saddle when yer stallion begins to run free."

"Watch me."

He laughed and smacked the other side of her bottom. "That's the idea. I'm going to enjoy the sight, I promise ye."

He released her hips and cupped both of her breasts. But he was far from still. His hips thrust up every time that she plunged down, his member penetrating deeply with the aid of her body weight. The look of growing enjoyment on his face urged her to move faster. She wanted to push him to the same limits that he'd wrung from her. The need grew inside her, just as the desire for deeper satisfaction did. She was in control of the angle that his member entered her body, and she leaned farther forward to increase the amount of friction against her clitoris.

"So that's how ye like it... hard and fast..."

"As do ye," she growled at him, hating the fact that he was in control enough to study her. He returned his hands to her hips, urging her back down the moment that she lifted off him.

"Ye may think ye want to control me, but the truth is..." He clamped her against him, his member deep inside her sheath, and flipped her onto her back. The bed shook, and she slapped at his shoulder.

"I wanted to stay in the saddle!"

"But ye also enjoy knowing I'll take ye."

He whispered his words against her ear, holding her neck with one hand while pinning her beneath him. His hips drove his cock into her with frantic motions while he kept the angle the same she'd had atop him.

"Ye need to know yer lover will satisfy ye. Admit it, Deirdre. Ye'll never be content with any man who does no' take ye."

She couldn't answer him, because her body was once more twisting and straining toward satisfying the need that was burning inside her belly. She felt his seed beginning to flood her and strained toward him in a final motion to unleash her own pleasure. Her thighs held him against her as her body shuddered along with his. Pleasure was so bright; it burned away everything else while it controlled her.

She ended up with Quinton sprawled on top of her. His chest labored as fast as hers to catch the breath they'd both lost. The bed creaked ominously before one of the ropes snapped, and they both fell through the frame to the floor.

The door burst inward; the men outside rushed in to investigate the crash.

Quinton laughed like a lunatic. He looked at her, assuring himself that the mattress had buffeted her fall before laughing louder.

"We need a better bed, lads!"

He reached through the frame and dragged his plaid over her before scooping her up in his arms.

"I know right where one is."

He strode from the chamber without a care for the fact that he was bare arsed.

"I can walk, Quinton."

He tilted his head but never slowed his pace. "Aye, but ye tend to take yerself places I'd rather ye did nae go. So I think I'll keep ye for the moment."

He descended the stairs and then walked through

one of the hallways as bold as could be. Maids shrieked when they looked up to see him striding so confidently with nothing on but the plaid draped across her.

But it was the giggles following them that stoked her temper. Once the shock wore off, the inhabitants of Drumdeer enjoyed their laird's antics full well.

"Ye're doing this on purpose," she accused him.

"Ye helped me break the bed ropes, lass. I remember it well, but if ye like, I can ask the lads what they think—"

"Do nae ye dare," she hissed and reached for the plaid that was slipping all around her with the motion of Quinton's pace.

He climbed several flights of stairs before entering a chamber that was without a doubt the master's. He tossed her on the bed and jumped on it at the same time. She yelped, but the ropes only groaned slightly, in spite of the way he continued to test them by jumping.

"Stop it, Quinton. I trust yer word on the matter."

He sat back on his hunches, his expression growing serious.

"But ye do nae trust me on any other matter. Now that's the truth, is it nae?"

She sat up but hugged the plaid close to cover herself. "Oh… do nae be demanding something from me that ye refuse to grant me in return."

"What are ye talking about, woman? I gave ye everything, and ye ran away as though I'd insulted ye."

He left the bed and walked to a table that stood against one wall. There was a glass bottle there, which he grabbed without any concern for how rare such glass was. He yanked the leather cap off its narrow top and poured a measure of dark liquid into a goblet.

"Ye did insult me when ye so boldly announced I was yer mistress."

He swallowed and shook his head. "We'd spent the night together, proving that ye're just as attracted to me as I am to ye. Damn and curse yer stubborn nature, Deirdre. Ye cannae deny the heat that burns between us."

"That does nae mean ye may assume something like that without asking me if I agree." She tossed off the plaid and stood. He was distracted by the sight of her so boldly walking nude across his chamber. A tiny surge of power went through her, and she reached for another goblet and held it up for some of the wine he was drinking. "Ye are nae my master, Quinton Cameron."

He offered her the wine, accompanied by a low chuckle that promised her a battle. But he replaced the cap and watched her take a long drink of wine.

"That's a discussion I would be happy to have with ye, as often as ye demand it of me."

There was no mistaking the fact that he planned to have those conversations in his bed. He placed his goblet on the tabletop and offered her a grin that sent a shiver down her back, but her pride refused to yield.

"Our troubles are nae in bed, Quinton."

He reached for the goblet and drained it. "Agreement between us, at last."

Deirdre lifted the wine but wrinkled her nose when she inhaled its scent. Her belly turned queasy, and she hastily set the goblet down.

"Ye do nae care for French wine?"

"No' tonight, it seems." She wrapped her arms around herself, suddenly feeling chilled. Quinton scooped her up before she realized his intention.

"Stop carrying me about, Quinton."

He placed her in the bed and covered her with the blankets, no remorse in his eyes at all.

"I find a certain satisfaction in knowing exactly where ye are, Deirdre."

He stood and walked toward the door.

"That does nae mean ye may keep me in that solar like some exotic animal ye've decided to keep as yer pet."

He shot her a hard look before opening the door. "Bring us something for supper. Anything the cook has hot will be welcome, and a drink for the lady. She cares nae for wine."

He closed the door with a hard shove before turning to contemplate her. She suddenly didn't care for how vulnerable she felt lying in his bed. She pushed at the bedding and heard him growl. A moment later he was sitting on the bedding, trapping her in the process.

"What is yer quarrel with enjoying what I give ye, Deirdre? Do ye fancy walking among those who might harm ye?"

"Nay," she announced as she struggled to sit up, and then hissed when she realized his attention had shifted to her bare breasts the moment she achieved her goal.

"Are ye now going to tell me ye want to argue about the fact that I enjoy the sight of ye, woman?"

"Nay."

"No… no… Do nae ye have anything else to say?"

He propped his hands on either side of her, pinning her against the headboard. "I would have killed to regain ye."

He smothered a word of profanity and pushed away from the bed. He gave her his back, hiding his emotions.

"Well... I do nae want that either, but I'm grateful ye took me away from the Douglas."

He stared silently at her, and his face was flushed. "How could ye go to the Douglas, Deirdre? Do ye detest me so much ye felt ye needed the protection of another earl?" Betrayal edged his words, and she felt each one like a dagger.

"I did nae go to the Douglas..."

He snorted and turned his back on her once more.

"Do nae ye dare give me yer back, Quinton Cameron. Ye'll hear what I have to say." She kicked the bedding off and stood. He turned to face her the second her feet slapped against the floor. Rage flickered in his eyes, but she faced it without flinching.

"I did escape yer castle, but I was on me way to take me place with the queen when Kagan Hay found me."

"Are ye saying that bastard gave ye to the Douglas?" Rage had flickered in his eyes before, but now, his tone was deadly.

"It was nae like that." He opened his mouth, but she held up her hand, and he shut it with a snarl. He turned and pulled a door open on a wardrobe that stood off to one side and tossed one of his shirts at her. She shrugged into it and rolled up the cuffs because the sleeves were so long.

"Now, tell me how it went before I set me mind to killing the wrong man."

He was trying to listen to her. Maybe it wasn't about whether she was his mistress, but it was the beginning of a better relationship between them.

"I failed to notice there was a shield on the sleeve of the overrobe I wore."

"Aye, they were made for me bride, and the details were nae overlooked, even if her honor was lacking." He suddenly frowned. "Did Laird Hay suspect ye of wearing my shield under false pretenses?"

Deirdre nodded, earning a snicker from Quinton, who seemed perfectly at ease in nothing but his skin. He sat down and took up his wine once more. "A laird has to think of things like that, lass. Another good reason for ye no' to be traveling alone."

She didn't care for the way he was justifying his actions.

"Nor does it make it right for ye to have locked me up."

Quinton sat forward, but Deirdre stopped him with a single raised finger. "Do ye want to hear the rest of this tale or nae?" There was a glimmer of something in his eyes that promised her retribution later, but he nodded. "Laird Hay took me with him to have someone he knew tell him if I'd lied about my name. Someone who had known me as a child…"

She suddenly paused, looking down as she considered Ruth and the secret she now knew about her half sisters.

"He took ye to see his aunt Ruth."

Deirdre lifted her attention again. "Ye knew about her?"

Quinton didn't falter when he answered. "And yer half sister. I know about her."

"Well, why did nae anyone ever tell me?" she muttered with exasperation.

Quinton chuckled. "Most fathers don't share news about their bastards with their legitimate children—or at least the daughters."

Someone rapped on the door, and Quinton called out, "Enter."

The timing was perfect, for she chewed on the knowledge of Erlina and the second daughter Ruth had birthed. It was her duty to tell her father, but she battled with whether she should leave Ruth in peace.

Supper was simple, but her belly grumbled as she smelled the porridge a sleepy-eyed maid had placed in front of her. It had to be past midnight, and the meal was an odd assortment of things. A wedge of cheese, fresh spring berries, and bread that must have been baked that morning. Quinton wasn't interested in the food. The moment the door closed, he began questioning her again.

"What are ye hiding now, Deirdre?"

She faced him with a frown. "Why do ye always assume that ye have the right to know what I'm thinking?"

One of his dark eyebrows rose. "So we're back to that, are we? Yer list of things that I am no'. I am no' yer father—thank Christ for that, considering how much I enjoy being between yer thighs."

Deirdre growled at him, "Do nae be blasphemous. We are sinning enough to tempt heaven's wrath."

She began to eat the porridge, too hungry to care if the man was unhappy about her attitude. He toyed with the round of bread but ate little of it, while she scraped her bowl clean.

"So is that why ye left me? Because ye cannae bear the sin of being me mistress? Is that why ye deserted the protection this castle grants ye without any idea where ye were going?"

His tone was quiet now, and she realized it mattered to him if she was ashamed of their relationship.

"I told ye that the queen had sent for me."

"Told me how?" His tone expressed his disbelief, but also the fact that she'd wounded him.

"I left ye a letter."

She suddenly couldn't bear the thought of hurting him, and she quivered because she realized her words had the power to do so.

"I left because I cannae shame me father." She stood, feeling caged by the walls. "I am sick unto death of nae being trusted. And why... because... because the men of this world all think a woman should be innocent and chaste until the day she weds. Then she must become the opposite and please her husband, or suffer his mistresses... oh... ye will never understand."

She paced in a circle, unable to look at the brooding man who watched her and judged her. He'd happily lie with her, but not allow her the choice to remain by his side.

Choice—she'd left the abbey seeking it...

The chamber went dark, the candles being pinched out. Her skin prickled with awareness as she turned in a circle to try to see Quinton. He was there, and she could feel him closing in on her. She yearned to have him near, and yet that close proximity frustrated her. Her feelings were in a tangled mess anytime he was about, but it was worse when they were separated.

His arms suddenly encircled her, pulling her close and keeping her confined when she wiggled. He stood behind her, his hands soothing her with long strokes as she failed to contain the tears that felt like they were falling from her heart.

"I understand, lass…ye're sick of being told yer very nature is wicked. Ye're wrong about me no' understanding that. I do, for there've been too many times I've listened to the same accusation. Dawn will be soon enough for us to argue about what place ye have here. For tonight, it's beside me, and that pleases me greatly." He placed a warm, soft kiss against her neck. "I need it to please ye too."

She shivered, sliding her hands along his forearms, each fingertip delighting in the feel of his body so close to her own. She savored the moment, smiling as she heard him inhale the scent of her hair. She could feel the steady beat of his heart against her back, and it fed the need that had gnawed at her since she left him.

"It pleases me, Quinton."

He picked her up and carried her to his bed. He joined her, snuggling against her as she tried to roll away and sort out her feelings. Quinton refused her that space, and somehow, the darkness made it accept-able to cling to him. Exhaustion claimed her, and she slept, but her dreams were full of questions that she didn't have good answers for.

❧

Quinton left Deirdre sleeping in his bed. It was a relief to see her head pillowed on the creamy linen he'd slept on too.

"Coalan, I've a task for ye."

His captain was waiting outside his chamber for him.

"Deirdre claims she left a letter for me." Quinton shot a hard look at his man. "Find out what became of it, but do so quietly."

"Aye, Laird."

Every castle had its spies, and Quinton wasn't prideful enough to think his own holding was an exception. If anything, there were men who had reason to watch him simply because noble titles were becoming so scarce. It was a fact that he lived with, but he'd be damned if he'd allow them to manipulate Deirdre.

He would slit their damned throats first.

❦

"Shh…"

Deirdre wrinkled her nose; she was still tired, but her mind refused to let her return to slumber now that she knew there was someone nearby. She opened her eyes and heard feet shuffling. Thick bed curtains enclosed her. The bed was huge, and her memory returned in a rush. Quinton was long gone, but someone was moving around the chamber. She reached out and moved the curtain a tiny amount to see who it was, because she was still wearing only Quinton's shirt.

"Good morning, Lady Deirdre." Amber stood directing two other girls who were cleaning away the remains of the meal she'd shared with Quinton. "I'm sorry if we disturbed ye, but there are a great many who are waiting to see ye, if ye are ready to rise. The laird said yer duties might wait a bit this first day since ye arrived so late last night. That has no' stopped the Cameron women from hurrying here to gain some of yer time."

"My duties? What do ye mean, Amber?"

Amber pulled the curtain aside so that Deirdre might leave the bed. "Aye, ye heard me correctly. The laird said ye'd be taking up the women's issues, and the word has already gone out. There are three midwives here to see ye on matters of importance, and several mothers who want to discuss their daughters marriage contracts with ye and—"

"Amber... please..." Deirdre rubbed a hand over her eyes and reached for the goblet of water. Her belly rolled, but after quick bite of bread it quieted.

"I'm sorry, Lady Deirdre, but it has been too long since we've had a mistress to see to the matters that a woman should. I'm as excited as everyone else. There are simply things that only women should be discussing."

"I'm no' yer mistress, Amber."

The girl refused to back down. She stared straight at her with confidence on her face. "The laird said ye were, and that ye were to be allowed to go wherever yer duties take ye."

"He did?"

Amber nodded, and Deirdre fought the urge to smile. She lost. Her lips rose, and Amber grinned brightly.

"Well then. Let us begin."

Maybe she was surrendering to the fact that she was Quinton's bed partner, but at least he was trying to meet her in the middle. It was something more than she'd had, and she discovered that it lightened her heart in a way that she hadn't believed possible.

Trust.

It was the first trust she'd had since her father had discovered her relationship with Melor Douglas. Deirdre dressed and went to see the midwives, because Quinton might have given her his trust, but the respect of the Cameron women would have to be earned.

She was eager to begin doing it too.

Quinton ground his teeth and sat looking at his hall. At the long trestle tables, his men sat in front of their supper, but they kept their voices low tonight. His pride strained under the weight of their glances and the way they looked toward the door to see if Deirdre would join him at the high table and take her place as he had directed.

Damn the woman.

She was the only soul living on his land who argued against her place, and God curse him for a fool, he allowed her to continue doing so.

She suddenly hurried into view, her face flushed as she came up the aisle at a fast pace and offered him a quick courtesy before coming around the high table to the seat by his side.

Deirdre froze when she looked into Quinton's eyes. They were cold. So cold that she shivered and looked away, only to discover that every man in the hall was staring at them. She was halfway into the chair but felt too stiff to finish sitting. With so many eyes upon them, it seemed like some sort of commitment that, once completed, would be binding for the rest of her life.

"Sit down, woman."

Her bottom hit the seat, and the hall filled with whispers. Her face flamed, and her throat felt like it was swollen shut.

"Ye belong here, at suppertime. Do nae make me wait on ye."

It was only the number of stares still on her that made her hold her tongue. She suddenly forced her emotions down and presented the assembled company with a smooth expression that would not have offended a nun. Being a laird's daughter meant she had been trained in the art of poise, even if her father had refused to send her to court. She offered Quinton a soft smile that meant nothing, but had to fight back the urge to frown when he returned it with an equally false expression.

The meal stuck in her throat and dragged on forever. But at last Quinton stood up, and half his men did too.

"Good night, lads."

He reached down and closed his fingers around her wrist. The hold infuriated her, because it was too possessive by far. But she allowed him to take her from the hall and up the stairs to his chamber. The moment they were behind the closed door, she snarled at him.

"Do nae ye dare spit at me, hellion! I've given ye everything this day."

She backed away from him but propped her hands on her hips. "Ye have no reason to be so angry over a few moments of tardiness."

"I thought ye'd used the freedom I gave ye to leave me again."

Deirdre stiffened. "So ye do nae trust me as I thought when I heard ye had given me duties here…" Disappointment slashed across her newfound happiness, cutting her deeply.

"I've plenty of reason to think ye'd take to the road again, Deirdre. Ye do nae have the right to look so stricken."

She drew herself up and blinked away the tears of hurt burning her eyes. "Well, I've plenty of reason to be distrusting of any man who only offers me a position in his bed, but I did no' toss any accusations at ye because another man played me false in the past."

Quinton crossed his arms over his chest. "I've offered ye more."

"Aye, that's true, and then ye nearly had me clamped back into yer prison solar for refusing to go and find me supper before the last midwife who came to see me was dealt with."

He drew in a deep breath, obviously fighting for control. "All right. I understand why ye were late to supper."

"But ye are no' offering me an apology."

He gritted his teeth. "What do ye want from me, Deirdre?"

"The same thing ye are so furious over no' receiving—respect."

His forehead furrowed with confusion. "I set ye above every Cameron woman today."

She nodded. "That's trust, and I am grateful for such. Happy even, this morning, so much so I made sure I did nae place my own comfort above the duty ye allowed me to take responsibility for." She shook her head. "But that is nae respect."

"We have no' had enough time together for respect to grow, Deirdre." He tempered his tone now, the anger fading from his eyes.

"It will never grow without ye learning to trust a woman again. Ye are no' the only person in this chamber who has been played falsely by the person they thought to wed. Ye'll have to trust me no' to leave, even though the chance is mine, or we have nothing."

He drew in a deep breath. "We have plenty between us—plenty of heat."

He closed the distance between them and cupped the sides of her face with his hands, but she flattened her fingers against his lips to prevent his kiss from clouding her judgment.

"Desiring me and respecting me are two separate issues, Quinton. I will never be content to stay with ye if I cannae trust ye to want more from me than the passion ye share once we are in bed."

His hands dropped away, and she could see him battling to understand her. But he shook his head and stalked away from her.

"I swore I'd never let another woman into me heart, Deirdre. Ye're seeking affection, and that is something I can offer no woman. I can give ye much, though, tenderness and a position that will be as good as the one ye sought with the queen."

The words were torn from his soul, but it felt like they were ripped from her heart.

"If that is how ye feel, it is time for me to return

to my father's house." She had to push the words out, past her longing to remain with him, because she knew separation would tear her in two.

Quinton stiffened. "No." He made a slashing motion with his hand. Deirdre propped her hands back on her hips.

"I sneaked past yer men once. What makes ye think I cannae get a letter to my father if I wish it?" Casting a challenge at his feet in his present mood wasn't the wisest choice she might have made, but she was too hurt to rein in her words. "I'll no' stay with a man whom I do nae want to stay with. I have no' agreed I am yer mistress. That is my choice alone."

Quinton chuckled at her, but it was not a kind sound. He stepped up to her, looming over her while his eyes narrowed.

"I am yer lover now, lass, and ye consented to it. That was one of yer options, was it nae? I like having ye in my bed quite well. Summon yer father here, and I'll be happy to complete the business of making ye me wife, so ye will have nowhere else to hide from me and warming me bed will be yer duty."

She stepped back, pain gripping her heart.

"What bothers ye, Deirdre? Did nae ye begin this entire game looking for a better catch than yer father contracted for ye? Well, here I am, ready to give ye what ye seek. Be satisfied and cease this struggle between us." His face was set into an ugly expression that horrified her with just how greedy he was accusing her of being.

"That is no' how I came to yer bed. I never used yer desire to try to secure yer title for myself. I am no' a whore who looks for the price she will earn for her favors. Ye are mean beyond belief to say such a thing to me." She shook her head. "Ye are no' the man I took as my lover. If ye use my father to force me to wed ye, I swear ye shall have only cold submission in yer bed."

"But ye said ye left to take a position that would bring honor to yer father, Deirdre. Is that nae what ye swore ye were about when ye sneaked past me gate?" He grunted. "Well, I'm offering ye a position that will please him."

"I never intended to earn my place by prostituting myself. That isna what lovers are."

She lost the battle to hold back her tears. They streamed down her face as she searched his eyes for the man she had been unable to resist. Quinton suddenly jerked, his gaze moving over the wet tracks that marked her cheeks. He reached out to smooth them away, but she stepped away from him, wrapping her arms around herself as more tears flooded her eyes. He clenched his fingers into fists.

"Damn it to hell and back. What do ye want of me, Deirdre? I cannae offer ye my heart; it is *dead*."

"I thought mine was too." She whispered the words but felt like each one was branded into her soul. She turned and headed for the door.

"Where are ye going?" he demanded.

She stopped, cringing at the idea that he could force her to stay with him. She dreaded thinking that he'd insist she remain in his bed against her will, but he was master of the castle. No one would interfere with his will.

"To the eagle tower."

"For how long, Deirdre? Ye burn for me as surely as I do for ye."

She looked over her shoulder at him. "I want more, and ye should too. Think on that, Quinton, for ye loved once and knew the joy. I, for one, am no' content to live without it."

He roared the moment she left. The sound echoed up the tower and startled the birds nesting in the eaves. But she didn't let it stop her. She loved him. May fate have pity on her, she loved him, and if his heart was dead, hers would join it.

So she couldn't stay. Even lust wasn't strong enough to keep her with him. Lust wasn't enough. Not nearly enough.

Eight

Dawn seemed determined not to arrive. Deirdre breathed a sigh of relief when the horizon turned pink. Her bed had offered little comfort, even if someone had fixed it. Her mind dwelled on her conversation with Quinton. She wanted to go to him and take what he offered.

It was so tempting, too much so, really, because it came with a bitterness that she could not stomach. Admitting that she loved him only made it impossible to lie with him if he did not return her affections.

Many would call her a fool for that.

She sighed and sat up. There would be plenty who would tell her to take what he offered and hope for a brighter future.

It was almost enough.

But she found her pride unwilling to settle, unwilling to take less than what she would give in return. It was such a whimsical notion, and most would accuse her of being touched by madness for having it. Women loved, but men rarely did. That was a harsh fact of reality. She'd been taught to avoid letting affection creep into her heart until after she wed, because love so often led to ruin for a woman.

But she loved Quinton.

So she dressed and opened the chamber door. Cameron retainers stood there, and they climbed to the solar behind her. She walked straight to where a writing desk stood. Inside it were parchment and ink. She picked up a quill carved from marble and her hand began to shake as she noticed the fine details that Quinton had selected for the woman he loved. Envy rose inside her, but it was a sad sort, and she tightened her grip on the quill.

She wrote the letter to her father three times. Her tears ruined the first two, but she finished the third and sealed it with wax, but she left the seal of the Earl of Liddell sitting in its box instead of pressing it into the hot puddle.

She would not use Quinton's name. She hadn't gone to his bed because of his title, and it still stung that he failed to understand how his proposal insulted her.

She sighed and forced herself to stand up and walk toward the door of the lady's solar. The retainers outside pulled on their caps the moment she opened the door. Forcing her hand out, she offered them the letter while gritting her teeth. If they noticed, they didn't remark upon it, only took the letter with another pull on their bonnets.

It was done.

She forbid herself any more tears. She was no longer a girl, but a woman who had made her choices and had to live with the results. She sighed and leaned against the window looking out over the ripening fields. Four months seemed so long, and yet it had been so little time.

"I told ye what I'd do if yer father arrived."

She jumped and turned to face Quinton in a swirl of her skirts. He held up her letter, one of his dark eyebrows raised.

"Is this yer way of telling me what ye want, Deirdre? I thought ye had more courage than that. Ye've never lacked the spine to face me."

"Stop being so insufferable, Quinton. Or can ye nae believe that I do no' fancy yer title more than I want yer affection?"

He lost his mocking look, his face becoming impossible to read. Deirdre tossed her hands into the air.

"No, I do nae believe it, but I admit that ye've raised me curiosity."

"Do nae toy with me, Quinton. No' about this."

He wiggled the letter between his fingers. "But what can ye expect me to believe? That ye would summon yer father and expect him to just take ye and no' demand that I wed ye? Perhaps ye've no' heard that my bride only beguiled me because her mother pointed me out as the most titled man in sight." He winced. "She did a fine job of it, weaving her charms around me until I fell on me knees at her feet. I think she would have wed me too, except the Earl of Braunfield arrived at court, and her mother pointed her ever-so-well-trained daughter toward him instead, for the connections the man had."

It was a horrible tale, but not an uncommon one. She sighed, refusing to allow her temper to rise when the situation was so pitiful.

"I never mentioned the idea of marriage between us, Quinton. It is true I've decided being lovers is no longer to my taste since I cannae have yer affection. If ye are going to be cross with me, do it for the right reason."

He drew in a deep breath, closing his eyes for a moment. She moved toward him, reaching up to place her hand against his cheek. His eyes opened instantly, and for just a moment, hope flared through her, because he looked at her with such longing, she was certain his heart still had life in it.

"Let's go back to bed and engage in the sort of conversation we are best at."

She took her hand away. "That will solve nothing."

He caught her hand and put it beneath the pleats of his kilt against his erection. Heat spiked through her, burning away her reasons in a flash.

"It will relieve the heat licking at both our insides. The attraction between us is uncommon, lass. I'll admit that freely. Ye are more than a tumble to me. I've fucked other women, but I never called them my lover. Ye are that, Deirdre. Do nae doubt that means something important to me."

"That is nae love." She pulled her hand free and heard him growl.

"I'll treasure yer love, Deirdre. 'Tis a gift I am no' blind to."

She turned to stare at him, temptation renewing its urging for her to take what was offered.

Her pride still refused, and she shook her head.

"Send the letter. I need an escort home so no more of yer neighbors will try to use me against ye. I'll tell ye this, Quinton Cameron. It's a disgrace the way yer fellow nobles try to take advantage of ye through anything they think ye fancy. Well, I'll no' be a part of it again."

His lips suddenly split into a grin that completely baffled her.

"Ye are beginning to show the makings of a fine countess, Deirdre. Yer understanding of me life is admirable. So I will no' be sending this letter to yer father." He walked over to the writing desk where the candle that she'd used to melt the sealing wax still burned. He touched the edge of the letter to it and held it while it caught fire. He dropped it to the stone floor once more of it had been consumed.

"I believe we could both benefit from time together to explore our compatibility."

"Are ye insane?" she demanded. "Ye must be the only laird in the world who is nae happy to be rid of a woman ye have already had."

He flashed her another smile that was arrogant enough to make her hiss.

"And ye must be the first woman without a dowry who turned her back on a titled husband," he insisted. "Rewrite that letter, and I'll let me men take it to yer father, but I swear I'll keep me word, for I am nae finished with ye, Deirdre. If I see yer father riding up to me gates, I'll be happy to sit down with him and draw up contracts between us."

Shock held her silent while he closed the distance between them. "And ye are nae finished with me." He stroked her cheek, sending a shiver down her back. "Admit it…"

Damn her flesh to hell…

He noticed her reaction too. She saw the knowledge flare in his eyes a moment before he captured her mouth in a hard kiss. He cupped the back of her head while he angled his face to press his lips solidly against hers. It was a hard kiss, but also an intimate one. He stopped just short of crushing her lips, giving her a taste of his tongue that wrung a moan from her.

The cold night alone suddenly seemed like a month. Her body wasn't interested in being held back by her pride any longer. She kissed him back, giving him everything he demanded of her.

He reached down and hooked her thighs with his arms, lifting her up as he carried her across the chamber to press her back against the hard stone wall once more.

The memory of what he'd done the last time he'd had her in the same position set fire to her. She whimpered as need clawed down the inside of her passage.

"That's right, hellion; ye recall exactly how much ye enjoy my touch."

He pressed a hard kiss against her neck that sent sensation flowing down her body. Her nipples contracted as she hissed at him.

"I want more."

He raised his face to lock stares with her. "So do I."

A moment later, her feet touched the ground, and he pushed away from her.

"Which is why ye'll be staying." Satisfaction shimmered in his eyes for a moment as he contemplated her. "And ye can feel that hunger gnawing at ye, for I'll no satisfy ye until ye come to my chamber."

He crossed the room, and frustration spiked through her. "Well, ye'll be waiting a long time for that to happen."

He paused at the door and grinned at her. "Then I'll have to set my mind to thinking of ways to encourage ye, Deirdre Chattan."

She leaned against the wall the moment the door closed behind him. Her body quivered as excitement flowed through her. An insane urge to giggle almost gained control of her, and she slapped a hand over her mouth to ensure that she remained silent. She'd like to swear that she'd never go to his chamber.

But the fact was, she doubted herself.

Deirdre made sure she was not late to supper. It wasn't really a task when she realized that she'd been looking over her shoulder for Quinton most of the day. She jerked her head about, because she was sure that she heard his step behind her. His promise rose from her mind endless times during the afternoon as she recalled exactly how he'd looked when he spoke.

The man always kept his word.

She shivered again, in spite of the fact that he was nowhere near. Just the memory of the sound of his voice was enough to elicit the response from her flesh.

As tempting as it was to snub him by not sitting by his side, she was wary of what such an action might prompt him to do. Quinton was a Highlander through and through. She had no doubt that one action from her would gain a response.

She decided on attending supper because she knew all that would happen at the high table was teasing, and she'd stand up against that well enough.

But she froze in front of Quinton, because the chairs that they had sat in the night before were gone. Instead he occupied one side of a double seat. There would be nothing between them at all except their clothing, and the man was wearing only a shirt and a plaid.

She'd feel his warmth and smell his skin...

She shook her head and completed her courtesy while casting her gaze toward the floor to tear it away from him.

"A fine evening to ye, sweet Deirdre. I swear the day was too long." He patted the seat beside him with anticipation flickering in his eyes.

"I came to tell ye that I will nae be dining in the hall tonight... and to give ye my apologies personally. My duties are demanding."

"Ah... well then, we'll withdraw to a private setting where we can discuss the matters that are weighing on yer mind."

He snapped his fingers, and there was a flurry of activity as servants picked up everything on the high table and carried it off. He was already on his feet with his hand out by the time she realized that she'd stepped neatly into his trap.

But it was the challenge on his face that made her place her hand into his. Her chin rose, and she slapped her palm against his before she thought any further.

She was not afraid of the man.

No, only of your response to him...

His fingers curled around hers, and his thumb gently stroked over the delicate skin of her inner wrist while they made their way to his chamber. She ground her teeth with frustration but couldn't deny that excitement was heating her belly. His staff laid out the supper and lit two candles before quitting the room.

The low light struck her as deeply intimate, but the truth was the entire room had that effect on her. She tried to avoid looking at the bed, but that didn't stop her from blushing as she recalled exactly what he'd done to her in it.

What she truly longed for was the way he'd held her after their passion was sated. She'd never felt so cherished, and she suddenly looked at him, searching for hints of the lover she yearned for.

"This chamber is empty without ye in it, Deirdre."

She laughed. It was low but full of appreciation for how well he'd maneuvered her into entering his chamber. She swept into the center of the chamber and offered him a graceful courtesy.

"I concede the victory, Quinton." She straightened up. "At least as far as getting me to enter yer chamber on me own."

He flashed her a devilish grin, and its playfulness made him too handsome by far. That was a side of himself he didn't display at the high table with his Highlanders watching. They expected strength in their laird, and Quinton gave them that.

"Then come here and give me my prize, lass."

She felt a tingle of suspicion cross her thoughts, but the eager look of anticipation on his face was too much temptation to ignore. In his eyes, she could see complete devotion to her and what he wanted from her.

"What is the prize you believe ye have earned?" Her tone was husky and almost sultry.

"A kiss, of course. Isn't that what every lad strains his wits to win from his fair maid?"

Her eyelashes lowered, and her cheeks burned with a blush. She heard his step on the stone floor and looked up to see him closing the distance between them. But the look in his eyes was mesmerizing, so full of desire and pleasure that she remained frozen in place. It made her feel beautiful. No words had ever sent such confidence through her.

"I would have my kiss, sweet Deirdre."

He didn't reach for her but waited for her to make the decision of whether or not to grant his wish.

Choice…

She reached up and slid her hands over the sides of his face.

"Then ye shall have yer reward."

She stretched up, and he leaned down so that their lips might meet. Sweet sensation flowed through her, and everything else ceased to matter… again.

Her belly growled. Quinton laughed, his hands still toying with her hair. Her face was pillowed on his chest as he lay on his back in the bed. Draped over him, Deirdre didn't find her empty belly reason enough to move.

Things were perfect as they were.

But her lover sat up and took her with him.

"We miss too many meals." He tucked her hair behind her ears before standing up. "And ye need a dressing robe since I cannae seem to wait until after we eat to ravish ye."

He pulled the door of the wardrobe open and grunted. She walked toward him and peered around him to see what it was that had gained his approval. A soft laugh passed her lips too.

"Amber does a fine job of tending to me."

Quinton lifted the dressing robe that was hanging neatly beside his shirts and draped it over her shoulders. She shivered as the cool fabric touched her skin.

"It's yer choice, but I think ye should give her the position as yer head of ladies." He raised a finger in front of her nose and pressed it on top of her lips when she opened her mouth to argue.

"Do nae argue with me, Deirdre. No' tonight. Or yer belly is going to remain empty, because I'll kiss ye quiet the next time ye try to tell me why ye are nae staying here with me. Ye need ladies, Cameron women who will keep the gossips from slandering ye."

That much was true. Walking about the castle alone would breed rumors.

The two candles were still burning on the table. Aided by their glow, she could see a longing in his eyes, which sobered her. The chamber was the only place where he might be himself. She understood that well enough, for she'd been the laird's daughter her entire life, and she knew the burden being laird could be when you needed space to be yourself.

Their supper was still on the table, but something else caught her eye. She smiled and reached over to pick up the deck of playing cards that Quinton's personal attendant had left out for his master.

"Well then, I demand that ye offer me the opportunity to claim a prize from ye."

He grinned, wickedness shimmering in his eyes. "The opportunity is yers, but do nae confuse that with the fact that I will make ye fight for it."

She sat down and split the deck before neatly shuffling with an experienced motion that was impossible to fake.

"I would have it no other way, Laird Cameron."

❧

The horizon was barely pink when Deirdre opened her eyes. Quinton placed a soft kiss against her lips as she did so.

"Why are ye dressed so early?" Her voice was gruff with sleep, and she rubbed her eyes to see him better.

He flashed that devilish grin at her in response. "Well now, lass. We cannae bicker if we are nae together."

"I do no' bicker."

He waved a finger at her. "It's a fact that ye are every bit as stubborn as I am. I suppose it's time I recognized that and accepted the fact that I would nae be drawn to ye if I did nae respect ye to stand up to me."

She sat up as he began walking toward the door. "Quinton, we need to talk…"

"If that is how ye feel, Deirdre, I suggest ye resist the urge to run away because ye think I do nae treasure ye. Come sunset, I will be happy to do me best to convince ye that I do. Until then, I must see to me duties, and I'm hoping that ye'll continue in the place I've honored ye with. The Cameron need a mistress like ye; the women need me to give them a woman who understands honor and the way life is here in the Highlands. Ye need to reconsider yer harsh stand on wedding me, for I believe it's a fine idea."

There were several quick glances in her direction as his men clearly heard the word "wedding." She could feel their excitement, even if no one spoke.

"But I need love…"

One of his eyebrows rose. "I could no' love any woman who I cannae trust. So, me men will no longer stop ye at the gate." He winced but stood firm in his decision. "And I do nae care for the doubt that plants in me mind, but ye are very much like me, and I could no' live without freedom, so I will give ye yers."

His words were both a threat and a promise. She nibbled on her lower lip, contemplating the choice he'd just handed her. It was better than any gift, for it was the one thing that she truly craved.

Choice.

She ached to see love in his eyes. That need hadn't left her, but Amber peeked into the chamber, and there was no time to mull over her thoughts. The day had begun, and Deirdre went to face it.

She did pause when she passed the cards that were lying on the tabletop. Some were still in even piles, but a few had fallen onto the floor, where they had been forgotten in a moment of passion the night before. The Earl of Liddell was a complex man, who she realized she did not truly know.

But he'd just challenged her to stay at Drumdeer and learn.

⤴︎

Deirdre lifted her head near sunset and listened to the bells beginning to ring along the walls.

"What is it?"

Amber worried her lower lip and moved to the window to look out. They were working in a study room in one of the east towers. Quinton's mother had attended to all the women's issues in that room, and there seemed to be a steady stream of Cameron women who were happy to have a mistress of Drumdeer to make decisions. Deirdre found herself struggling to maintain her confidence in her advice as they brought to her matters that would have major impact on the families involved.

She didn't feel wise enough or experienced enough to be making such decisions.

"Someone is arriving, Lady Deirdre—a noble person. That's why they are ringing the bells. The only other reason would be siege, but there isn't a stream of people coming in from the village."

Deirdre stood up and walked to the window, but she couldn't see enough. She had to control the urge to climb up onto the battlements, where her sight would not be obstructed.

Women did not belong on the battlements.

Instead, she descended to the ground floor and went out to view the yard. Plenty of other people had come out to see who was arriving. Amber floated near her right shoulder, but Deirdre was becoming accustomed to the girl's presence. Amber did more than serve her: the Cameron girl kept the gossips quiet, because there was now a Cameron witness to what she did every moment of the day.

Amber suddenly gasped. Deirdre turned to see that the girl's face had gone white, and her eyes were wide in shock.

"Who is it?"

"The… um… it is the Countess of Braunfield arriving—Mary Ross."

Icy dread went through her. Deirdre was sure that her heart stopped beating in that moment. She felt suspended between breaths as she watched the columns of retainers ride into the yard. Their kilts were blue and green with gray woven in. The colors of the Sinclair clan. They were the highest of the Highlanders, and their earl a match for Quinton in both titles and holdings.

But the earl was not among the riders. She searched the flags flying from the lead rider's poles twice, and only found Mary Ross's shield on display.

That meant the countess had come to see Quinton alone.

Her heart stopped again, her memory offering up what Quinton had confessed about this woman. He'd loved her. Jealousy rose up inside her until she was sure that steam would come out of her ears.

"I'm sure she's just caught out on the road… and needs shelter."

There was a grunt from Tully. The older woman had come up from the bathhouse. "Say what ye will, but I'll tell ye that seeing that woman here means no good for any of us. She's a blackhearted thing, and I'll no' be sorry I said that either."

Tully looked at Deirdre. "She'll cause trouble; ye'll see."

Quinton appeared at the foot of the eagle tower. His captains stood behind him, presenting a solid wall of Cameron support for their laird.

"Oh, Quinton! It's been forever since I set eyes on yer handsome face."

Mary Ross didn't ride a horse. Instead the woman alighted from a private chair that was suspended between two horses on long poles. The chair was kept private by thick tapestries. Protected inside the draperies, the countess appeared, looking as though she had just descended from the lady's solar. Her hair was dressed perfectly, and her clothing fine. She was by far one of the most beautiful women Deirdre had ever laid eyes upon. Her complexion was flawless and her eyes a lovely blue like a summer sky.

Deirdre felt drab by comparison.

"How may I help ye, Lady Braunfield?"

Mary Ross didn't return Quinton's formal greeting. Instead the woman rushed right up to him and kissed him on both cheeks. She was like a cloud of silk wrapping around him, but what stung Deirdre was the smile on his lips when the woman moved aside enough for her to see it.

That was the blow that sent her walking away. Her stomach threatened to heave, and she knew that she couldn't bear the sight another moment.

"Lady Deirdre… where are ye going?" Amber had to rush to keep pace with her.

"I am… I am going to bathe."

Deirdre turned sharply and headed down the steps to the bath. At least misty eyes wouldn't be noticed there.

But there was nothing she might do for the pain in her heart. It grew as she discovered being out of sight was worse than seeing Mary Ross embracing Quinton. Her mind was happy to concoct ideas of Mary lifting her face for his kiss.

Stop it.

She ordered herself to have the same trust in Quinton that he had for her. But it was not easy to convince herself when she had heard him confess that he had loved Mary Ross once. Jealousy consumed her as she tried to maintain her poise while she bathed.

It was far too difficult.

The bath maids did their job quietly, but there were quick looks cast between them when they thought that Deirdre wasn't watching.

"Now go and take yer place, lady."

Deirdre turned to stare at Tully. The older woman looked her straight in the eye with the length of wet toweling still in her fingers. Deirdre had lingered in her bath, but there was nothing more to keep her in the bathhouse now that her hair had been brushed out and dried in front of the fire.

"I said, go and take yer place, Lady Deirdre, for I find I like ye full well and would no' see that blackhearted woman in the laird's chamber." The older woman was joined by the other maids; they stood behind her with firm expressions on their faces. It was the sort of respect she had hoped to earn, and she felt it deeply.

"Go up there and make him see how noble ye are.

I've faith in me laird. He'll no' have that creature in his chamber, even if he cannae refuse to shelter her." Tully nodded. "Be bold, Lady Deirdre."

Did she dare?

Did she dare not?

Heat flickered inside her, and she suddenly discovered that she would rather spit in the eye of her rival than weep silently in the bed that Quinton had prepared for Mary Ross.

She would never sleep there again.

"Thank ye, Tully. Ye are wise."

There were nods and muttering of agreement, but Deirdre didn't linger to enjoy them. She climbed the stairs and walked through the dark hallways with her hair streaming behind her like a bride.

She was on her way to surrender to her choice of groom. Maybe that was whimsical thinking, but she meant it with every fiber of her being. Amber and the other girls followed, just like her bridesmaids.

But Quinton's chamber was empty.

She stood inside for a long moment, listening to the roar of the river and searching the shadows for him.

"Look, lady… on the table."

Amber pointed, and her finger wiggled with excitement. Deirdre heard her heart beating as she approached the single candle left burning on the table. A letter sat there, folded and sealed with the crest of the Earl of Liddell.

Her name was on the front of it.

Her hand shook as she reached for it, the empty room shattering her confidence. It would be so simple for Quinton to send her away with a letter.

So simple, because she was the one who had insisted on leaving.

> *Deirdre...*
> *The countess brought word that the Earl of Douglas has died. I must attend his funeral and see the proper succession of his son.*
> *I pray that ye shall be waiting upon my return. Please be here, in our chamber. The thought of ye in me bed will keep me warm. I swear it.*
> *Quinton*

"There... all is right."

Amber read the letter over her shoulder and began chattering away in her relief. She sent the other girls to ready the bed, and Deirdre realized they were eager to make sure she slept there.

That was the respect she had wanted to earn from the Cameron women. Now all that remained was to win the heart of their laird.

She lay down in his bed, shifting about because it felt odd not to have been carried there.

She should have been more concerned with praying for Archibald Douglas but instead she discovered her prayers centered around Quinton and how soon he might return to her.

She'd be there. He could trust in that.

❧

"Ye're going to kill yer horse."

Coalan was risking a great deal. Quinton snarled at his captain, but the man refused to relent. He looked at the road ahead and cursed. Still a half day's ride to Restalrig, and then more time as he waited on the earl's family to arrive.

It was his duty to see the passing of the signet ring to the boy's hand, but every fiber of his being rebelled. Suspicion knotted the muscles along his back, but duty had always come before his personal desires.

Mary Ross had been the single deviation from that path. He looked back toward Drumdeer, indecision refusing to allow him to turn his attention to the duty that he should be focused on.

Instead, all he could see was Deirdre's face when he had told her his heart was dead.

He'd been wrong.

❦

"The Countess of Braunfield requires yer presence, Deirdre Chattan."

Amber gasped, and Deirdre looked up from the marriage contract she was reading along with two older Cameron women. They both turned to glare at the personal attendant of the countess. The woman wasn't unimpressed with their displeasure. She lifted her pert nose into the air and sniffed loudly, as though there was a foul scent in the chamber.

"Ye should nae keep the lady waiting."

There was a good measure of disdain in her voice, but Deirdre found herself staring at the woman's attire more. She wore a silk overrobe with silver beads sewn around the square neckline. Her underrobe was simpler, but she had a silver signet circling her head.

"I will attend the lady when I have finished seeing

the Cameron women who have come seeking settle-
ment this day."

The two women in front of her nodded firmly with
approval, but the lady's attendant sniffed again.

"Ye are no' the Countess of Drumdeer, and yer
word should nae carry any authority," she announced.

"The laird said it did," Amber insisted.

Deirdre stood and placed a gentle hand on Amber's
forearm to quiet the girl. Amber closed her mouth,
but she made a low sound beneath her breath that
made it plain she was not happy.

"I am attending to the duties given to me, and my
answer has no' changed. I will attend yer lady when I am
finished with the things that need doing for the clan."

The attendant narrowed her eyes. "Ye had best
make haste. The Countess of Braunfield is yer better
and should nae be kept waiting on the likes of you. It
is yer duty to answer her summons promptly."

Amber sputtered, but the lady's attendant swept
from the chamber with another sniff. The two
Cameron women both shook their heads.

"There's no respect in that one for her elders,
and that's a solid fact," one of them muttered before
turning back to look at Deirdre. "I'm right happy to
see ye are no' impressed with that sort of arrogance."

The compliment was approved by the other
woman, and Amber nodded as well, but Deirdre
couldn't dismiss the feeling of dread that had begun
churning inside her stomach. Mary Ross was a
countess, and many would give her deference without
question. Quinton's words surface from her memory,
and she stood because connection did mean a great

deal among the nobles. Mary had shunned Quinton in favor of wedding a more connected earl.

"Forgive me, but I would no' give that lady cause to speak ill of Laird Cameron because I failed to answer her summons."

Deirdre nodded with respect toward the two older women. They contemplated her for a moment before one of them pointed a finger at her.

"Aye, ye're a clever one, and that's for sure. The earl needs to be thinking of his reputation among all those titled lairds at court. For sure that's why he's placed ye here to oversee Cameron issues."

Deirdre left the chamber with Amber trailing her.

"Ye shouldn't do anything that horrible woman says."

"Yer laird made her welcome. I cannae do any less. Besides, some things are best done quickly so that the thought of them does nae fester."

Amber scoffed at her. "He did nae tell her she might be Drumdeer's mistress. He gave that honor to ye. That woman has been saying the most awful things to everyone. She's no' happy about any service offered to her, and she's taken over the solar like it is her own."

Quinton had prepared it for her…

Deirdre had to force the lump that formed in her throat down. She refused to cower in front of the woman who had hurt Quinton so deeply. Mary Ross was a whore, just like any woman who took coin for her favors on the waterfront. She'd peddled her beauty for a title that she obviously enjoyed very much.

But love was more important. The only thing Deirdre felt was envy, because she yearned to have

Quinton's love. She only felt scorn for the woman who had plunged a dagger into his heart.

Amber went to knock on the door of the solar, but the Sinclair retainers who guarded it refused to allow her close. Amber propped her hands on her hips.

"Yer countess summoned my lady, in spite of the fact that Lady Deirdre has responsibilities to see to."

The retainer nodded and backed up to clear the way to the door. Amber stepped forward to knock. The same attendant opened it a moment later. She sniffed when she identified who was waiting to see Mary Ross.

"Just ye."

"I go everywhere with my lady Deirdre," Amber argued.

The attendant raised one of her manicured eyebrows. "My lady does nae allow her private conversations to be overheard by anyone in whom she does nae have the deepest trust."

Amber scoffed. "Ye mean witnessed by those who will tell the facts plainly without worrying that their pay might be subject to their lady's displeasure."

The attendant drew in a stiff breath. "Why, ye little peasant." She flipped her hand in the air. "Be gone before I have ye removed."

The Sinclair retainer looked at Amber, but Deirdre stepped between him and the Cameron girl. Amber reached out and gripped her wrist.

"Come with me, Lady Deirdre. Ye should no' stay here. The laird would no' like it. Not with such conditions that ye be seen alone."

Deirdre looked at Amber. "There is nothing I

fear from Mary Ross. I'll see what she wants and be down to join ye soon. We couldn't have the Sinclair thinking the Camerons and the Chattan do nae teach their daughters manners."

Amber didn't look appeased. The girl frowned, but Deirdre gently lifted her hand away from her wrist. "Besides, I refuse to think there is anything to fear from being summoned by Lady Braunfield."

Amber smiled. She nodded. "As ye say, Lady Deirdre." She drew out the "lady," and the waiting attendant hissed.

"Peasant," she muttered when Deirdre entered the solar.

Deirdre didn't get to see Amber's response, but the attendant made a snorting sound before she shut the chamber door with a little too much force.

"Alice, have ye taken leave of yer senses?" Mary Ross called from across the solar. "Ye know I do nae care for loud noises."

The attendant turned in a swirl of silk velvet and lowered herself quickly. "Forgive me, my lady. The Cameron girl was insisting on following her mistress in."

"Ye mean Quinton's mistress, for that is all she is. Deirdre Chattan is a shamed woman who has found herself another man to whore for." Mary Ross spoke as though Deirdre were not standing in the room. The Countess of Braunfield eyed her expectantly. Deirdre offered a nod only, refusing the arrogant woman a courtesy.

Mary Ross frowned. "Ye are foolish to tempt my displeasure."

Deirdre moved forward with her chin held high. "I

think ye are presumptuous to demand such currying of yer favor here. This is the Highlands, no' the royal court."

The countess surprised her by smiling. When she did, her face became radiant, until Deirdre looked into her eyes. In spite of the beautiful blue shade, they showed just how calculating Mary was.

It was quite an ugly sight.

"I know where I am, Deirdre Chattan." Mary Ross stood and began walking around the chamber. "I am in the solar Quinton prepared for me." She sounded smug as she stared at all the fine things. At last she came back around to where Deirdre stood watching her.

Mary spread her hands out wide. "Everything in this chamber was bought for me with only one purpose in mind—to please me." She pressed her lips into a small pout. "It was simply too bad Quinton wasn't the most titled man at court that season, but since ye are the daughter of a laird, ye should understand a daughter must catch the best husband possible."

"So ye told Quinton. Personally, I think ye a fool for wedding another."

Mary clicked her tongue. "But I did nae ask ye for yer thoughts on the matter. I would never take any advice from ye. Ye're the foolish one, spreading yer thighs before the wedding. Little wonder ye have naught to show for the two lovers ye've had, except that bastard growing in yer belly."

All the attendants stared at her belly, while Deirdre covered it with her hands. Confusion swept through her as she considered whether she might be carrying a child. She hadn't thought about it, not since the first morning after sharing Quinton's bed. "What are ye talking about?" She tried to resist the urge to feel her abdomen, but she couldn't recall the last time she'd bled either.

Mary went over to the desk and picked up several letters. "I may have married Gower Sinclair because he had more holdings than Quinton, but I assure ye I have always kept myself informed of what Quinton was doing, because he is the man I wanted most of all. It's a desire I have no' abandoned, nor shall I." She looked at the letters. "A very reliable source at Strome reports ye did nae bleed there."

Mary clicked her tongue again and shifted the letter to the bottom of her pile while reading the next one. "Ah… and here I have a report that ye never bled here either. Nae before or since yer return. So…"

Mary laid the letters aside. "Ye are carrying Quinton's bastard." Her tone became menacing. "The first one never shows early on, but yer waistline is thicker, and yer tits are plump. Since ye came in early spring, ye might be as much as four months along now. Do nae be so stupid as to think ye might fool me into believing ye do nae know. Why else would Quinton be suggesting marrying ye?"

Rage coated Mary's words now. Her face flushed as she shot a glance full of hatred toward her. All her attendants lined up behind her, aiming similar looks at Deirdre.

"Quinton needs a son, but I shall be the one to give it to him, not ye."

Deirdre forced her surprise down. It was possible she was with child, and it was slightly embarrassing to admit she had not thought upon the lack of her

monthly cycles. But even the hint of possibility made
her suddenly protective of the life that might be
sleeping inside her belly.

"Ye are wed to another man, Mary Ross, so yer
words are sinful."

Mary suddenly changed her expression. Instantly,
her face became a mask of sadness, but once again
when Deirdre looked into the woman's eyes, she
could see the cold, calculating look that betrayed her.

"It's really very sad, but Gower died last week. Of
course, he was old, and it was to be expected." She
sighed, but her lips lifted into a smile mere moments later.

"So, ye see… I will be wedding Quinton Cameron.
Why else do ye think he has gone so long without
contracting another bride?" Mary laughed, soft and
menacing. "Why, the answer is very clear. He has
been waiting for me."

"I do nae believe that." She refused to accept it.
She laced her fingers over her belly, protecting the
precious life that might be growing there.

Mary scoffed at her. "Believe? Oh aye, ye have
quite a history of men in whom ye believed, but what
did that gain ye?" Mary reached over and shuffled the
letters again before picking one up. "According to a
Sinclair girl who is doing her duty as a nun, ye arrived
in shame, yer lover Melor Douglas having renounced
ye for the whore ye are."

Mary tossed the parchment down. "But I am no'
completely unkind." She picked up another letter. "I
know ye tried to prevent Quinton's seed from taking
root in ye. Men can be such selfish bastards when it
comes to forcing women to bear their babies. Even

ones whom they will no' honor with their names."
She looked up from the letter and smiled with glee.
"Do nae worry. I will help ye get rid of the nuisance."

"It's a babe—"

"It is a bastard," Mary insisted. She snapped her
fingers, and one of her attendants came forward with
a mug with steam rising from the top.

"Drink that, and ye will lose it tonight. Ye cannae
be further than four months along, so it will nae be so
difficult to hide."

"No."

Deirdre spit the single word out and backed away
from the offered mug. Her hands flattened over her
belly, guarding it as she felt the rise of her temper and
an urge to strangle the woman who suggested such evil.

"I may have asked for a brew to prevent a child
from being created, but I will no murder one who
already lives."

"Even if that means birthing a bastard?" Mary
came toward her. "I won't have it beneath my roof,
I promise ye. Once Quinton returns, he'll forget ye
even live. I swear that to ye."

Deirdre lifted her chin, defiance filling her. "Try if
ye will, but I believe ye shall fail."

Mary laughed, as did her attendants. "I will nae fail.
Men are always besotted by my beauty." She opened
her eyes wide. "I assure ye, I know how to apply it
well. Quinton has fallen beneath my spell before, and
now I know so much more about how to keep a
man's attention… it will be simple to regain his favor."

Mary's ladies laughed, narrowing their eyes in a
knowing manner. "Do what I say, and I'll make sure

ye have an escort to where the queen is. But if ye stay here and let yer belly round, I swear I will have revenge against ye and yer brat."

Deirdre scoffed at the woman. "Ye disgust me." And she refused to remain in the room with her another moment. Deirdre turned her back on Mary Ross.

But a splintering pain shot through her head a moment later, and she fell to her knees as her vision went dark.

∽

Deirdre felt urgency pounding through her. She needed to wake up but couldn't remember just why. Still the urge persisted, needling her until she opened her eyes. Her vision was nothing but wavy lines. She blinked and blinked several more times as she tried to restore her sight to normal.

"Alice… get around and tie up her mouth before she wakes up…"

Deirdre tried to sit up, groaning as pain filled her head.

"I told ye to hurry…hit her again so we can get her away from here without her crying out…"

Mary was issuing orders in a hushed tone. Deirdre could hear the attendants' robes swishing as they hurried to obey. Her thoughts cleared in a moment, and she rolled over, hitting Alice's legs as the woman took another swing at her. The long piece of firewood hit the floor, because Deirdre had moved. Alice went headfirst over her and cried out when she tumbled head over heels across the Persian carpet in the middle of the solar.

Deirdre rolled over and struggled against whatever bound her hands behind her back.

"Are ye insane, Mary Ross?"

Deirdre rolled over again and slipped her feet through the bound circle of her hands to bring them up in front of her. A silk veil was knotted around her wrists; although delicate, it held very well.

"I am determined…" Mary hissed. "Ye are an ignorant peasant, and I will split yer skull open before I allow ye to have Quinton's son."

She swung an iron hook that was used to move logs around in the hearth toward Deirdre's head. Deirdre ducked and struggled against the binding on her wrists. The other ladies all circled her, and true fear began to seep past her anger. There were five of them and only one of her. She kept moving while she struggled to free her hands. At least she wore simple clothing, unlike Mary's attendants. They all had to pick up their overrobes to avoid tripping.

There was a muffled cry from outside the chamber door. "Let me in there!"

Mary suddenly looked stricken as Amber's voice floated beneath the door. She snapped her fingers at her attendants.

"Hurry up… ye fools!"

Someone grabbed Deirdre's biceps from behind, and Alice lifted the log above her head to bring it crashing down on Deirdre's skull, but Deirdre bent her knees, and the log hit the attendant holding her with a dull sound.

Deirdre surged to her feet and lunged toward Mary. The lady let out a shriek of surprise and sent a hand swinging at Deirdre's head.

Deirdre grunted when it hit her, but gripped Mary's

hair in a vicious hold, pulling her head up until it was next to her own. The attendants all froze, unwilling to risk hitting their lady.

"The next blow that lands on me will split yer skull too," she hissed into Mary's ear.

The lady opened her mouth and screamed. She screeched loud enough to be heard in the yard below, and the stairwell was full of the sound of men rushing to her assistance. The door was jerked open by the Sinclair retainers, but Amber tumbled into the room first.

Deirdre released Mary with a mutter of disgust, and her maids all clustered about her. But the lady refused to be soothed. She screamed and yelled in spite of the men crowding the solar, her face flushed red with her fit.

"She tried to kill me! She's a lunatic! Lock her in chains before she murders me!"

The Sinclair retainers turned on her with rage shimmering in their eyes. Amber flew between them and Deirdre, covering Deirdre with her own body.

"That is nae true!" Amber shouted. "I heard everything from the storeroom below. Mary Ross tried to murder Lady Deirdre and the child she's carrying— Laird Cameron's child."

The solar became a mass of swearing and yelling. Sinclair plaids faced off with Cameron colors as Deirdre was pushed back against the stone wall of the solar by Amber.

"Stop… everyone… stop…"

No one heard her above the fighting, and she watched in horror as dirks were pulled from boot tops and belts. There was no way to stop the impending bloodbath, no way to be heard above the shouting.

Nine

"Hold!"

Authority edged the tone of the man who shouted that single word. It was something that every man in the solar felt as well as heard. Hands were still clenched around dirk handles, but the men turned their heads to look toward the doorway.

Deirdre whimpered with relief.

Quinton stood there, along with a young man wearing the Sinclair plaid. In the side of his bonnet were three feathers all pointing upward, and the Sinclair retainers lowered their weapons.

"What have ye been about… sweet stepmother?" the Sinclair laird asked. The retainers who had escorted Mary Ross to Drumdeer looked confused, but their laird stepped forward and slapped Mary across the face.

"Ye murdered my father, and I swear ye'll answer for the crime."

Mary trembled visibly. "Ye have no proof, no witness to convict me."

"Do ye think ye are the only one who has spies? I've had ye watched for years, and I assure ye I have a

witness who will swear ye smothered me father while
he lay with ye. If ye had no' taken to the road so
quickly, I'd have run ye down before ye left Sinclair
land. But I have ye now, and ye can be grateful that
I'll at least grant ye a priest before I have ye hanged.
It's more than ye gave me father."

Quinton stepped between the Sinclair laird and
Mary Ross. She smiled at him, her face becoming
radiant. "Quinton, my darling… ye must help me…
Do ye see how it's been for me? Cyric has always
hated me because he was jealous of the love his father
had for me. Ye have to give me protection from him,
keep me here with ye. My father forced me to wed
Gower Sinclair… I wanted ye."

Quinton looked into her eyes, and Deirdre felt
her heart freeze. Mary reached for him, her hands
delicate and trembling. He captured them, only to
push them away.

"I'd rather knot the noose about yer throat
meself. How dare ye come here with a man's blood
on yer hands?"

"Ye love me…" It was a ghost of a whisper, but
Mary's face turned bright red a moment later. "It's
because of her!"

Mary turned on her in a rage. "*Ye Chattan whore! Ye
shall no' have my place!*"

Mary lunged toward her, and the wall behind her
back made it impossible to escape. She pulled a small
dagger from her sleeve, and Deirdre lifted her arms to
protect herself.

Mary never touched her.

There was a soft sound, too delicate for the dire

circumstances, but there was no pain from a dagger entering her flesh. Deirdre looked around her arms and stared into the sky blue eyes of the beautiful woman. Her face was frozen in a mask of disbelief, and the front half of a sword protruded from her chest. It was stained with her blood, and she smiled before her body went limp.

"I could offer ye an apology, Cyric, but it would be a lie." Quinton pulled his sword free and wiped it on the back of Mary's slumped body.

"Ye saved me the trouble of listening to her whimper all the way back to Sinclair land." Cyric Sinclair nodded, but there was no easing of the anger that flickered in his dark eyes. He looked at the Sinclair retainers who had escorted Mary Ross to Drumdeer.

"She murdered my father, and they helped her." He pointed at Mary's attendants.

Every set of eyes turned toward Mary's ladies. They were pressed together, Alice still holding the long piece of firewood she'd hit Deirdre with. Her eyes grew wide, and she suddenly looked down at the log. With a soft shriek, she released it, and it fell to the floor with a dull sound.

"She made me do it... I have no place without her..." Alice muttered. One of the others hissed at her, but Alice continued to babble. "She threatened to turn me out if I—if we did nae help her. I had to... my father will nae have me back!"

"Get them out of here!" Quinton roared.

"No, get me out of this solar!" Deirdre shouted at him before anyone had the chance to move. "I cannae stomach this place another moment."

Deirdre didn't care if her tone lacked respect.

She couldn't breathe and started for the door before Quinton had the chance to respond. She grabbed a handful of her robes so she might run and ducked around the men in the room. Quinton cursed but couldn't follow her, because of his larger size.

She made it down two flights of stairs before she heard him on her heels.

"I need fresh air, Quinton."

He hooked a hand around her arm and jerked her to a halt. "I only demand ye slow down so that bitch does nae gain what she wanted by having ye break yer neck when ye stumble."

She trembled, the look in his eyes setting off ripples of emotion that refused to be controlled. He slid one hand along her cheek, tenderness shining in his eyes.

"I love ye."

Her heart leaped, but Deirdre forced herself to be reasonable.

"Ye do nae have to say that. I'd rather ye be honest with me, Quinton. I'll no' leave ye, for I do love ye, and I cannae turn me back on ye."

He snarled at her and clamped his arms around her, but his body quivered.

"I swear I love ye, and I'm the biggest fool for having to learn it by looking into the eyes of a woman who only used those words to gain what I might give her." His voice was ragged, and she froze as she watched unshed tears turning them glassy. Hope flared up inside her so bright, it was impossible to stop.

"I swear to God it made me want to fall on me knees at yer feet in gratitude for the love ye offer me without a care for anything ye might gain."

"I do love ye, Quinton, but I know it is no' common in men... to love..." Her voice trembled, but she maintained her stance, refusing to lower her eyes. Let him see what she was.

He smoothed his hand over her face. "I love ye." This time, each word was solid and hard. "I swear to God I'm confused by it and frustrated, but there is no denying it's true. Ye are my counterpart, Deirdre, and I finally understand what those damn poets mean by the word 'soul mate.'"

She smiled, too full of joy to do anything else. "I think I'm with child."

His face registered his astonishment, and then rage flickered in his eyes.

"We're getting married."

Arrogant and demanding, his tone was one she knew well. It was the truth that loving him didn't change the fact that she still found the man vexing.

"It's my choice, and that was nae a question, so do nae think I'll be standing for ye telling me what to do, Quinton Cameron."

He rolled his eyes and snarled a phrase in Gaelic that she doubted was polite. "Ye will, hellion. I swear to all that's holy that we will wed before the harvest moon fades."

She propped her hands on her hips, relief surging through her because there was something comforting in arguing with him. But Amber caught up with her, as did several of his men, so she settled for shooting him a firm look that earned her a glint of promise from his eyes.

She was suddenly ridiculously happy. A sense of

rightness settled over her, and she knew without a doubt that it came from the man she was glaring at.

But she didn't smile at him. After all, he was the one who kept calling her hellion.

∽⟡∾

Her belly was growing.

Deirdre lay in bed, her head pillowed on Quinton's arms as he lay beside her and gently stroked their growing child.

"How could ye no' know?"

She made a low sound of frustration and slapped his shoulder. "I've no' been with child before."

He lifted his head so that their eyes met. "I thought women were sick in the first few months."

She laid her hands on her belly and felt the unmistakable bulge of her womb. It was still amazing to realize that she'd been so unaware of the changes in her body.

"I thought it was just the tension of being a prisoner. My belly was unsettled, but I dismissed it."

He frowned at the mention of her time away from him. "We're getting married, Deirdre."

"Ye have still no' asked me to wed ye."

"I'm an earl, madam, and laird of the Cameron…"

She lifted her knee until it was against his erect member. "And I told ye before, Quinton Cameron, and whatever else ye be, I am no' a whore, so do nae expect any of that to sway me thinking."

"True enough. Ye are me lover, and I enjoy that full well. I suppose tomorrow is soon enough for us to argue again, but I plan to win next time."

He contemplated her for a moment but lay down without saying anything else. Suspicion tingled through her, but she was too warm and blissful lying against him to think about things any longer. She fell asleep with the sound of his breathing against her ear.

❧

Cyric Sinclair was waiting for her when she descended to the ground floor the next morning. It was obvious he'd been standing there to meet her because Quinton had left the chamber only moments before she did.

But the Sinclair laird was still waiting at the base of the stairs. Deirdre lowered herself.

"I'm sorry, Laird Sinclair. I did no' know ye were waiting to see me."

"It's barely past dawn, Lady Deirdre. No apology is necessary except the one I'm wanting to give ye. Me men should have stopped Mary Ross from leaving Castle Sinclair. I have never trusted her."

"Ye had no way of knowing she'd do such a horrible thing."

Cyric Sinclair's expression hardened. He had dark eyes but light-colored hair. He'd shaved his beard away, confirming just how quickly he'd been on Mary's trail.

"I suspected she was plotting evil, but my father was laird, and I could nae accuse his wife openly. It brings me no pleasure to be able to prove my position now."

"I understand."

And she wished she might offer more words of

comfort, for it was clear the man was bitterly angry. He nodded before turning to leave, and his men followed their laird.

"He looked furious, Lady Deirdre," Amber muttered when she joined Deirdre.

"Aye, but it's directed at himself."

And little wonder, but Deirdre was too happy to commiserate with the man. She smiled at Amber, and the Cameron girl smiled back.

"When are ye wedding the laird, lady?"

Deirdre frowned. "I am no' marrying him until he asks me."

Amber looked confused, as did the other girls who joined them. Deirdre lifted her chin high.

"But he's the laird…"

"No' my laird. To me, he's me lover, and a lover must ask for what he wants."

Amber frowned, but Deirdre laughed.

He loved her.

She had everything that she desired. She looked at the confusion on her ladies' faces. "Come now, Amber. We've a day to see to, and I will deal with yer laird once the sun sets. Ye would nae want me to bore him with complicity?"

There were knowing laughs and bright smiles in response.

❧

Deirdre was looking out of the window of her study about a week later when two arms wrapped around her. She jumped but laughed when she smelled the scent of Quinton's skin.

He nuzzled her neck while his hands gently settled on top of her belly.

"Daydreaming, are ye? What should I do about that, do ye think?"

Deirdre angled her neck so that he might press a kiss against it. "Encourage me in my whimsical ways. After all, I am yer lover."

"I would have ye be more, Deirdre."

His voice grew deeper and more serious. She laid her hands on top of his.

"Maybe I want to prove my love to ye by refusing yer title."

"Ye've proved it, Deirdre. I realize why I thought my heart was dead; it was because I was always looking into the eyes of women who viewed me as nothing but a fancy possession to get their greedy hands on. It was nae my heart that was dead—it was theirs."

"I love ye, Quinton—just the man."

"And the earl?"

Deirdre clicked her tongue. "I'm learning to have patience with him."

He laughed at her, tossing his head back so the sound echoed off the ceiling.

"I'm relieved to hear ye say that, lass... truly I am."

The bells on the walls began to ring. Quinton maintained his hold on her as she looked toward the gate to see who was arriving.

"Who's here?"

Quinton turned her around and pressed a hard kiss against her lips. His blue eyes were full of love, but there was also the unmistakable hint of victory in his grin.

"Yer father is here... hellion." He smothered her

retort beneath a hard kiss that left no doubt in her mind that he had planned to crush her resistance and was proud of his achievement.

"We're having a wedding, and ye're the bride."

"Oh… ye arrogant beast! Ye had no right to summon me father."

He stepped back, still grinning at her, but one of his dark eyebrows rose. "Admit it, hellion. Ye've been bested. I love many things about ye, and one of them is yer sense of honor. Ye'll wed me by yer father's command, and that's a fact."

Her temper sizzled even as happiness spread through her. She did enjoy pitting her wits against the man's, maybe more than he did.

"That might be so, Laird Cameron, but I'll birth ye a daughter because I decide to, and that is a fact."

He chuckled before offering her a polished bow.

"I can hardly wait… hellion. Wear yer silk finery."

"I will nae! It is nae mine, so I will nae wear it."

He laughed at her but gripped her wrist and pulled her after him. They descended the stairs and went through the stone hallways until they reached the yard. Robert Chattan rode forward with his retainers close at his back. She smiled and felt tears sting her eyes when he looked at her. There was an unmistakable look of happiness in his eyes. He slid from his horse and took the stairs two at a time. She expected him to greet Quinton, but her father came directly to her and wrapped his arms around her.

"Sweet Christ! I've lost half me hair since Kaie wrote me with the news that ye had gone missing from the abbey. Thank God ye're well."

He released her and studied her from the top of her head to her feet before nodding and looking toward Quinton.

"Now what's this I hear about me daughter carrying yer child?"

Quinton rolled his eyes. "Aye, she is, and I'm wanting to wed her—"

Her father sent a hard blow toward Quinton's jaw. It connected because Quinton wasn't expecting it. Deirdre smothered a smile behind her hand as her father winked at her.

Quinton growled and rubbed his jaw.

"Now look here, Cameron. Ye obviously have nae been trying hard enough, and it's a good thing I'm here to sort this mess out. Ye young folks cannae get anything accomplished without help."

Quinton glared at her. "Ye're just like yer father.

"Thank ye," Robert Chattan replied before he looped an arm across Quinton's shoulders. "No' that it has nae caused me a load of worry…"

Deirdre watched them disappear into the tower. She should have been irritated that they were off to discuss her future, but the sight of the Chattan retainers being welcomed by the Cameron ones was too good for her to find anything to quibble about. Merriment filled the faces of those extending their hands in welcome.

It was a fine sight to be sure, made so much better by the feeling of love warming her heart.

❧

Deirdre Chattan married her lover.

She stood in the church inside the walls of Drumdeer Castle wearing the fine silk clothing that Joan Beaufort had given her. Quinton had convinced her that it was her rightful payment for helping the queen escape. Her father smiled behind her, and she felt his respect for her once again.

Fate was kind, indeed, far wiser and kinder than Deirdre had ever asked it to be. In fact, she was grateful for the times that fate had turned a deaf ear to her pleas, for they had brought her to the side of her soul mate.

And knowing Quinton Cameron's love was worth every tear she'd shed along the road that had led her to his side.

He pulled her close as the priest offered the final words of their marriage blessing.

"Are ye ready for the kiss of peace, lass?"

"Ye'd be bored unto death within an hour if I accepted it and became docile as the church expects."

He grinned before claiming her mouth in a kiss that shocked the priest. Deirdre kissed him back with every bit of heat that she felt burning inside her. The assembled witnesses began to cheer, and the priest made the sign of the cross over them with a shaking hand.

But the holy man grinned, for after all, it was a good day when the laird married. A fine day indeed.

❧

"What's keeping ye from supper now, wife?"

Deirdre looked up, startled to hear her husband of a single week inside her study. Quinton wasn't growling at her but raised one of his dark eyebrows. She set the quill down and smiled at him.

"In all the excitement, I never penned a letter to the queen."

Deirdre blew over the ink before folding the paper.

"Do ye regret no' taking a place in her household?"

Deirdre lifted a candle and used its flame to melt sealing wax onto the center of the letter. She pressed the seal of the Countess of Liddell into it before it cooled. Satisfaction filled her as she looked at her seal, the symbol of what she had chosen to be.

"I see ye are seeking compliments tonight..." She stood and went to her husband, leaving the letter on the desk. It was her past and could be sent after she kissed her husband. She reached for him, smoothing her hands along the sides of his face.

"Knowing ye wrote that letter is compliment enough, for it tells me ye are happy here."

He closed his arms around her.

"I am loved here."

"That's right... hellion."

About the Author

Mary Wine is a multipublished author in romantic suspense, fantasy, and Western romance. Now her interest in historical reenactment and costuming has inspired her to turn her pen to historical romance. She lives with her husband and sons in Southern California, where the whole family enjoys participating in historical reenactment.